JEMIMA SMALL Versus THE UNIVERSE

TAMSIN WINTER

USBORNE

First published in the UK in 2019 by Usborne Publishing Ltd., Usborne House,
83-85 Saffron Hill, London EC1N 8RT, England. www.usborne.com

Text copyright © Tamsin Winter, 2019

Author photo © Andrew Winter, 2017

The name Usborne and the devices ♀ ⊕ are Trade Marks of Usborne Publishing Ltd.

A C IP catalogue record f or this book is available from the British L ibrary.

JFMAMJJ SOND/19 04336/3 ISBN 9781474927284

Printed in the UK.

This book is dedicated to everyone who has looked in the mirror and felt like nothing. I hope this story reminds you that you are not nothing.
You are everything.

And to my niece, Lucia,
for always listening to my stories.

1

SPACE

I'm going to tell you the word that ruined my entire life: Big.

Jemima Big.

Jemima Big.

Jemima Big.

Jemima's as big as a whale! Which is completely stupid. Even the smallest species of whale is 2.5 metres long and weighs 181 kilograms. But it's pointless telling anyone that. People at my school don't care about facts. They still say I look like one. They still call me Jemima Big when my name is Jemima Small.

It's typical of my life that I look like the exact opposite of my own name. And you can't change your name when you're twelve because the government doesn't let you. Not without your parents' permission anyway. And considering I haven't seen my mum since I was six, and my dad never lets me do anything good, it's not going to happen. Begging doesn't work with my dad. Neither does emotional blackmail. He's unsympathetic to my problems, mainly because he doesn't believe I have any. Even though she left, I wish I had my mum's surname. Jemima Bouviere sounds a million times better than Small. Adjectives as surnames should not be allowed.

When I was younger, I thought being the biggest girl in my class was the same as being the tallest, or having the longest hair, or being double-jointed like Izzy Newman, who could bend her thumbs all the way back so they touched her wrists. I thought my size was a simple fact of nature, like the freckles on my forearms and Izzy Newman bending her fingers into weird shapes at break time. Then there was this day at the beach when I figured out I was wrong. Like, majorly wrong.

It happened during the summer holidays, a few months before I turned eight. Nana was staying at ours and Dad suggested we all go to the beach. We'd gone to the beach almost every day of the holidays anyway. It's, like, 0.4 miles from our house. So close I can hear the sea from my bedroom. Which might sound good, but it's the reason we never go on a proper holiday abroad. Dad thinks going rock-pooling then putting 2ps in the coin-pusher game at the arcade counts as a summer holiday. It doesn't. It's technically staying closer to my house than going to school.

The first bad thing to happen that day was when I came downstairs in my bikini. The straps were digging in, so I went to show Dad the red marks under my armpits. As I walked into the living room, Dad gave Nana this look I hadn't seen before. It was probably the exact same look the commander of the Apollo 13 space mission had on his face when he found out their oxygen tank had exploded. Like: "Nana, we have a problem."

Dad took me to Dolphin Bay Beachwear, this swimsuit shop on the promenade. Dolphin Bay's the name of the beach. It's kind of false advertising, because you never see any dolphins there. My brother, Jasper, said he saw some through his binoculars once, but he could have been lying. It's the type of thing he does. Dad said dolphins sometimes come here to mate, so actually I'm glad I've never seen any.

The lady in Dolphin Bay Beachwear had pencilled-on eyebrows – I know because one of them was slightly smudged and she raised them as soon as we walked in. She looked down at my tummy and declared, "You're very round!" in a voice that made it sound like a compliment.

But when I looked up at Dad, he was smiling at her apologetically, as though the shape of my tummy was something he should be sorry about. He was standing right next to me with his hand resting on my shoulder, but suddenly I felt like he was galaxies away.

"Puppy fat!" he said eventually, and rubbed his beard, like he always does when he doesn't know the answer to something.

The lady said to me, "Never mind, dear. I have some swimsuits that will help disguise it a little."

My cheeks burned and I felt intensely stupid, like that time in Year Four when Miss Reed discovered I could do long multiplications in my head. She made me stand at the front of the class and asked me to work out 391 x 39. But I got the answer wrong because this boy, Dylan Taylor, was making annoying faces at me and I forgot to add one of the carried-over numbers.

Miss Reed probably felt a bit stupid that day too. She'd got a new poster for our classroom that said: *A diamond is a chunk of coal that did well under pressure!* and I informed her that diamonds aren't even formed from coal. She said, "Motivational posters don't always need a factual basis, Jemima!" Which probably tells you everything you need to know about Miss Reed. Luckily for her, a question about diamond formation didn't come up in our SATs.

But knowing how diamonds are formed and doing long multiplication in my head didn't help me at Dolphin Bay Beachwear. I folded my arms over my stomach and followed the raised-eyebrows lady to a rail of swimsuits, wondering why no one had told me before that I was supposed to disguise my stomach. And feeling utterly brainless that I hadn't figured it out by myself. She held up a black swimsuit, but Dad pretended to faint when he saw the price tag, and told me to choose something from the sale rack. Maybe because he didn't think I'd been humiliated enough already.

When we finally got to the beach, I walked down to the Plank with Jasper. It's this wooden platform that juts out above the sea. No one knows who built it. It's been there for years apparently. My dad remembers it from his childhood, so it could have been there for centuries. It was busy with tourists, so we had to queue up. The wooden steps were wet because of the sea spray, and I walked up slowly so I didn't slip. The proper word for sea spray is spindrift, but if you call it that people look at you weird.

Jasper ran all the way along the Plank and dived in. He always dives in. He says it's seven metres high, but Jasper exaggerates everything. (Mostly his own intelligence.) The sea *below* is about seven metres deep; the Plank's only about four metres above sea level. It still feels like a big jump though. I heard the crash of Jasper hitting the water, then walked carefully to the end of the platform and curled my toes over the edge.

I watched Jasper's head emerge from the waves. He shook the water out of his ears and shouted, "SHARK!"

I ignored him. He says that every single time. The only sharks around here are basking sharks and they don't even attack humans, so he was being doubly stupid. I took a deep breath, pinched my nose and peered down at the water.

Then I heard a voice behind me: "A whale, more like."

Someone sniggered and said, "Yeah, watch out for the tidal wave!"

I wanted to tell them that tidal waves are caused by gravity, not by someone jumping off the Plank, so it was an idiotic thing to say. But they looked a few years older than me and I was worried about my new swimsuit not disguising my stomach properly. Anyway, from the way they were both laughing, I could tell they didn't care about scientific facts. I tugged at the edges of my swimsuit, trying to cover an extra centimetre of flesh.

Then I heard someone else. It was only just louder than a whisper. "She's grotesque."

But it wasn't someone young this time. It was a woman about my dad's age. Her wet hair was swept back and her swimsuit had shapes cut out of the sides, revealing a tummy that looked flat, not round like mine. She glanced at my stomach for a split-second then looked at her husband and shook her head. My brain stopped thinking about gravity and whales and tidal waves then, because I could feel their disapproval surrounding me, like water vapour condensing into tiny droplets and forming a fog. It clung to my skin and suddenly I understood the look Dad had given Nana that morning, and why I needed a swimsuit with brand-new tummy-shaping, silhouette-flattering technology.

I jumped into the sea and swam back to shore without stopping. Jasper called me a few times to come back, but I carried on, even though I was almost out of breath. When Nana asked why I was crying, I told her some boys had called me a whale.

She rubbed a towel over my hair and said, "Oh, sweetheart, it's because whales are strong swimmers!"

But I knew she was lying. She gave me a packet of soft mints and Dad sighed extra loudly then looked at her the same way he had that morning about my bikini, so I didn't say anything else.

Maybe you think people can't weigh you with their eyes, but they can. Maybe you think people who love you don't lie, but they do.

For the rest of that day, I sat on one of Nana's beach mats with a towel wrapped around me watching people walk past. I listened to their feet sinking into the pebbles, and felt the tiny crystals of sea salt on my skin. And this is what I figured out: there are good-shaped bodies, and bad-shaped bodies, and mine was one of the bad ones.

It's called having a moment of realization. Like when Isaac Newton saw an apple fall from a tree and discovered gravity. Well, I discovered I sucked. And once you've figured out something like that, it stays lodged in the frontal lobe of your brain. And each time you look in the mirror, or get changed for PE, or stand up in class, or feel your stomach roll over your school skirt, or notice someone giving you a second look, you get reminded. The frontal lobe is kind of annoying like that.

I didn't move from the beach that whole day. I didn't go swimming or push Nana along the promenade in her chair, or go to the arcade, or get an ice cream. I just sat there trying to figure out a way I could hide my body from everyone. Including myself. But it was impossible. How can you hide from your own body? Especially when you're wearing a neon-yellow swimsuit with a picture of a flamingo on it.

Almost every night after that, before I went to sleep, I wished on the stars to have a body like the other girls in my class. To be the right shape, like them. I wished for my mum to come back too. Because when your dad thinks your body is the equivalent of an outer-space emergency and complete strangers find you grotesque, you kind of need her.

According to my Auntie Luna, when you wish on the stars, it gets beamed out into the universe. She says if you keep wishing, eventually the universe will listen and it will come true. But, when it's the first full moon of the year, Auntie Luna strips totally naked and bathes in the moonlight to capture its cosmic energy. So, she's not exactly a reliable source of information.

Anyway, no matter how much wishing I did, my body stayed the same shape, and my mum didn't reappear either. She was probably like the stars: too far away to hear my wishes. I tried not to think about her, but I could feel this empty space growing in my heart where she was supposed to be. The human heart is only nine centimetres wide, but the empty space inside mine felt bigger than the universe sometimes.

I still wasn't immune to the name-calling, even after my first year at Clifton Academy. I'd been called Jemima Big so many times, my heart should have developed antibodies or something, like my blood cells did after the flu jab.

But it didn't. Which is probably why hearing the stuff whispered about me during the end-of-year Awards Assembly kind of hurt.

Jemima Big knows so much about space because she takes up so much of it.

Jemima Big should do some exercise instead of reading so many books.

Jemima Big can solve maths problems but not her weight problem.

Being clever when you look like me isn't a formula for success. My achievements just meant everyone gawped at me like they'd never seen someone my size holding a certificate before. And instead of feeling proud, I felt disapproval clinging to my skin each time I went up. So when Ada MacAvoy in Year Nine tripped over a chair walking up to the front, I did feel bad for her. But mostly I felt grateful no one was looking at me any more. And she knocked into this annoying boy in my class called Caleb Humphries, which was an added bonus.

I thought Year Eight would be better. I knew I'd still be called Jemima Big, but I thought I'd get used to it. Like Dylan Taylor's voice shouting "sumo" at break times eventually fading into the background. And I had things to look forward to. Like turning thirteen in October, which meant I'd be a teenager and Dad would finally have to raise my pocket money. It would still be way below the minimum wage, but unfortunately my dad thinks household chores don't count as exploitation.

I was still sort of dreading the first day back. I knew people would look to see if I'd had some kind of dramatic transformation over the summer. Well, I hadn't. I was still Jemima Big. And stupidly, I thought that would be the worst thing.

But it's like when you look up at the night sky – what you see isn't the whole picture. And it wasn't long before I started wishing that the entire universe had an escape hatch.

2

ZERO VALUE

It was the first day of Year Eight when it happened. Dad woke me up by shouting my name up the stairs over and over again, and making threats like, "JEMIMA! Get out of bed NOW or I'm taking you to school in your PYJAMAS!" Like I needed another reason for people at school to say stuff about me.

I put my uniform on and looked in the mirror on my bedroom wall. Even wearing my long, black pleated skirt, my calves looked too convex. And my stomach bulged out, even though I spent ages trying to tuck in my shirt to hide it. Nana had told me I'd lose the puppy fat around my face ages ago, but it was still there, creating a semicircle dimple under my chin like a second smile. Maybe it would vanish this year. Or maybe Nana had just lied.

My hair was also a major problem. It was the exact colour of the sludgy sand under the pier. I pulled my phone out of its charger and googled hair dyes. Every colour was named after something amazing-sounding: *honey fire, champagne silk, natural gold*. They didn't sell hair dye in my shade, probably because *sludgy sand* isn't exactly aspirational. I had award certificates and commendations from Clifton Academy up on my pinboard – each one said *Aspire to Achieve* and there was a little gold medal at the top. But brains aren't aspirational either. Brains had precisely zero value at my school. Besides, they're not even visible from the outside.

Dad yelled, "HURRY UP!" even though there was still ages before the bus. I practised facial expressions in the mirror for a while, then took a step back and examined my face again. It definitely looked asymmetrical. I googled *asymmetrical face*. The top result said: *Do you need facial surgery?* I sighed and started putting my books in my rucksack.

My dad would never pay for facial surgery. He told me off in the supermarket last week because I'd put a tea tree cleansing mask in the trolley. It's like he actually wanted me to get spots. There's this other operation called liposuction where they suck all of the fat out of your body. It's good, but you can end up with loads of extra skin, like my nana. She has loose skin that hangs around her neck and the tops of her arms. It feels really soft squishing into you when she gives you a hug. I don't know for sure where all her extra skin came from. I don't think she had liposuction. Maybe it was just natural shrinkage.

"Dad, I need some money, please," I said as soon as I got downstairs. Dad handed me a box of cereal, but said nothing, so I carried on. "For hair dye. It's a human rights issue." I'd read all about human rights ages ago after Dad made me do the washing-up three nights in a row. Just for informing Jasper that naming the magic show he did "spectacular" was a breach of the Trade Descriptions Act. No one in my family has a sense of humour. Or cares about human rights.

"I think ten pounds should cover it," I said, pouring Rice Krispies into a bowl. "I don't want a cheap one because my hair might fall out."

Dad didn't even look up from his *Art + Design* magazine.

"Or I might get an anaphylactic shock."

Dad started humming.

"That's when your face and throat swell up and you can die, by the way," I added.

Dad casually turned a page in his magazine. I could have an anaphylactic shock for real and he probably wouldn't notice.

"Dad, the hair dye. I want to get it this week. I'll accept an advance on my pocket money."

Dad sighed extra loudly. Sighing extra loudly is my dad's thing. That and doing The Look. If he does them both at the same time, then you know it's serious. Last term, this girl in my year, Pippa Williams, was picking teams for rounders. She looked directly at me and said she didn't want a *hippo* on her team. I told her hippos can actually run faster than humans, and that I didn't want to be on a team with someone whose brain resembled a fruit fly's. We both got in trouble with Ms Newton for that. She told us to apologize to each other. I said it wasn't my fault Pippa Williams was excrementitious. Ms Newton looked the word up on her phone, then said she'd be telling my dad about my attitude. Like he didn't know about it already. I got The Look and the extra-loud sighing pretty badly when I got home that day.

"Jemima, hair dye is not a human right," Dad said.

"It is for people with hair the colour of mine." I smiled my best smile, the one I'd been practising in the mirror.

He only looked up for a fraction of a second. Clearly I needed some more smiling practice. "There's nothing wrong with your hair," he said, so I sighed extra loudly. Dad gave me The Look.

"Dad, I inherited this hair colour from you, so I think

it's only right you pay for me to change it to super luminous honey blonde."

Dad gave me The Look again. "You're too young to dye your hair."

"I'm almost thirteen! Anyway, there isn't an age limit on hair dye. If you'd started dyeing my hair years ago then maybe it wouldn't have got this bad."

Dad closed his magazine and took a deep breath. I thought he might finally be listening to reason. He wasn't. "Well, I think it's a nice colour. Same as mine, right?"

"Honestly, Dad? I think yours would look a lot better if it was a light mahogany brown."

Dad laughed and shook his head.

"Anyway, it will probably start turning grey soon so you should let me stock up for you."

"Jemima! I don't need to dye my hair, thank you very much. And neither do you. It looks nice natural!"

I sighed and pushed my Rice Krispies down into my milk with my spoon. "You don't get it, Dad. You have to dye your hair to make it look natural."

"You're not allowed to dye your hair. School rules." The annoying invention called my brother. Jasper thinks he can boss me about even though he's only nineteen months older. "Hurry up, Jemima. I don't want to be late on the first day back." Jasper looked at his reflection in the mirror in the living room and straightened his tie. He had the beginnings of a moustache forming, like, deliberately. "School is a lot more serious for me this year. I'm officially in the Upper School and I'm starting my GCSEs, you know." He licked his two forefingers, smoothed them over his eyebrows and looked at me through the bead curtain. "It's not playtime any more."

"Did you hear that, Jemima?" Dad said. "I hope you'll take a leaf out of Jasper's book."

"No thanks," I muttered. "I'd probably catch something."

"I don't want any phone calls about your attitude this year, Jemima," Dad said.

"Well, that's easy. Just switch your phone off." I beamed a full smile at Dad.

He gave me a super-strength version of The Look. "You know what I mean," he said and collected his paintbrushes from the pot on the drainer.

My dad's an artist, but not the kind that earns lots of money. He paints shop signs and fancy window frames and stuff like that. The best thing he's done was years ago when the council commissioned him to paint the map of Clifton-on-Sea on this huge wooden board on the promenade, to celebrate the pier turning a hundred years old. Dad painted dolphins in the sea, and a basking shark, and people eating candyfloss along the promenade. If you look really closely, you can see me and Jasper playing in the rock pools, with Mum holding our hands and Dad sitting on a rock nearby. We're tiny, just coloured dots really, so you wouldn't know it was us unless my dad told you. I always look at it when we go to the beach, but Dad doesn't. He doesn't like talking about Mum. Or even looking at her painted as a tiny pink-and-turquoise dot.

I promised Dad I'd make "mature decisions" this year then headed upstairs to brush my teeth.

"*Dépêche-toi*, Jemima!" Jasper shouted after me. He always tells me to hurry up in French. It's one of the ways he shows off. Our mum's half-French, so we both spoke it when we were little, apparently, although I can't remember that much. Jasper's won the French Prize every year at Clifton Academy. It's sort of cheating because he's a quarter French so it's an unfair advantage. Also, he over-pronounces the French accent and it's really annoying.

Jasper shouted, "*Dépêche-toi!*" again, so I shouted a French swear word back at him. Not a bad one, but Dad's voice immediately came booming up the stairs, "JEMIMA, DO NOT USE THAT LANGUAGE!"

I leaned over the banister and said, "You mean French?"

The blood vessels in Dad's eyeballs looked like they were about to burst. "You know exactly what I mean!

Don't swear at your brother. In any language. You shouldn't even know those words."

"Tell that to Monsieur Poisson!" I said. "People write them in his textbooks!" Then I got doubly told off for calling Mr Picard that. Like it's my fault his classroom smells of fish.

We arrived at the bus stop just as the bus was pulling in. I hated getting on the bus because people always stared. I held my rucksack in front of my stomach, and let Jasper get on first. I sat on the first empty seat I could find. I hated walking down the bus aisle. There were always a few people who kind of gawped at me. If there wasn't an empty seat, I'd spend the entire journey with my legs squeezed together, trying to shrink myself into the side of the bus, or half-hanging off the seat, worried the person next to me might say I was taking up too much space. I'd always try to be first on the bus on the way home. But we're the third stop in the morning so people have already got the best seats.

I pulled my phone out of my pocket and messaged my friend Miki to say I'd meet him by the front gates. Miki started at Clifton Academy halfway through Year Seven because his parents got divorced so he moved here with his mum. It was about the same time my best friend Alina decided to drop me for Lottie Freeman. We'd been friends since primary school, but I guess there's only so long you can hang around with Jemima Big before you realize your life would be a lot easier if you didn't. Miki didn't know anyone at Clifton Academy, and the only spare seat in our form class was the one next to mine, so I suppose we became best friends by accident. But it was a serendipitous kind of accident, because Miki is the best person I know. Even though he hates maths.

My phone beeped with Miki's reply:

Okay 😴

If I'd known what was going to happen at school that morning, I'd have slammed my hand on the STOP button above my head. But it would have been pointless. Our bus driver ignores it when people do that. It's like my Auntie Luna says, you cannot escape your destiny. Jasper said she stole it from *Star Wars*. I think *Star Wars* stole it from this ancient Greek writer called Sophocles. Anyway, it's true. And unfortunately, that day, my destiny was the equivalent of a giant sinkhole.

3

EARTHQUAKE

Miki was sitting on the wall by the gates as my bus pulled into the school car park. His black hair was flopping into his eyes even though he'd said he'd had it cut and his hoodie was poking out from underneath his blazer. I raised my hand to wave at him, but as I stepped off the bus someone shouted, "Oi! Don't cause an earthquake!" The sun was in my eyes, so I couldn't see his face, but I recognized the voice. Dylan Taylor. He was in a different Year Eight form, and I didn't have any lessons with him, but any time he spotted me around school, he usually shouted something.

Jasper stopped walking and looked back at me. Most of the time my brother is extremely annoying, but sometimes he checks I'm okay. And that's when it's hard not to cry. I didn't care about Dylan and his limited understanding of plate tectonics, but everyone nearby stopped and stared, which made it feel like there *was* an earthquake happening. Inside my heart. And no one could feel it apart from me. (And maybe my left ventricle.)

"Hey," Miki said, scraping his fringe to one side. "Ignore him. That boy's an idiot."

"Yeah, I know," I said, drawing in a deep breath to make sure no tears came out. "No one causes a seismic wave just by getting off a bus."

Miki smiled and we joined the crowd heading towards the hall for assembly.

Mr Nelson, our form tutor, welcomed us back, handed out our new timetables and reminded us to stand in a perfectly straight line. He didn't make us stand in alphabetical order like some teachers, so I walked quickly to the front so I could get a seat at the end of a row. I hated sitting in the middle, because they hook the chairs together so my legs squish over the sides and the metal digs in.

"Mrs Savage's eyes are shooting death rays already," Miki whispered as we walked in to the hall.

Immediately, her eyes fixed on Miki. She must have really good hearing, like a moth. They can hear the highest frequency of sound. Hearing like that helps you evade predators. It's the kind of hearing that would be really useful at my school.

"Good morning!" Mrs Savage said when everyone had settled down. "I hope you're all looking forward to another exciting year at Clifton Academy!" She welcomed the new Year Sevens then reminded us of the school motto, like any of us could forget. It was on the wall of every classroom and even in the toilets. Like she still expected us to "aspire to achieve" on the loo.

"Now," she continued, "I have some very exciting news! Who has heard of the television programme *Brainiacs?*"

My ears pricked up. I'd been watching *Brainiacs* ever since I was little. It was on every Boxing Day. I always knew loads of the answers, which majorly annoyed Jasper. A sea of hands went up, but not mine. It was my favourite show, but when you've got arms the size of mine you don't put them up in assembly.

"For those of you who haven't," Mrs Savage said, "it's a competitive quiz show where the brightest young minds in Britain battle against each other to win the coveted *Brainiacs* trophy and five thousand pounds for your school!"

A ripple of excitement travelled round the hall. Mr Nelson smiled and raised his eyebrows at me. He was probably thinking of all the history books he could buy with five thousand pounds.

"Isn't that the show you like?" Miki whispered and I nodded.

Mrs Savage waved at the IT person and a clip from last year's *Brainiacs* started playing on the screen. The presenter, Dexter Riley, was asking a boy called William to multiply the atomic numbers of gold and zinc.

"Two thousand, three hundred and seventy!" I called out, then clapped my hand over my mouth.

The people in front of me turned round and Miki snorted. I felt completely stupid, even though my answer was correct.

The clip finished with a girl called Tika holding the trophy in the air. She held the record for the highest score in *Brainiacs* history.

Mrs Savage put her hand up for everyone to be quiet. "This year, students from over fifty schools will be competing for the fifteen places on the show and you'll be delighted to learn that Clifton Academy will be one of them!"

Mrs Savage clapped and the whole room joined in. I felt butterflies in my stomach. Or, more accurately, the neurons along my brain-gut axis went berserk. I had the chance to be on *Brainiacs*?

"Isn't that *exciting*?" For once I agreed with Mrs Savage. "The competition is open to people aged ten to thirteen, so Lower School – that means you! The qualifying test will be held right here on Thursday lunchtime next week. You don't *have* to enter of course, but I would like to see lots of our bright sparks trying their luck!" She signalled to the IT person again and the *Brainiacs* website appeared on the screen. "If you would like to put yourself forward, your parents must download the consent form from the website here and email it to the office. I am *certain* Clifton Academy will make for some tough competition!"

Everyone clapped again and Mrs Savage did a fist pump. Teachers should not be allowed to do that.

Miki tugged the sleeve of my blazer and whispered, "Oh my God, Jemima! You can so get on *Brainiacs*!"

Tiny pulses of energy fired through my brain. *Could I really get on Brainiacs?* I looked across at the rows and rows of people sitting in the hall. I wondered if any of them liked *Brainiacs* as much as I did. Just then, someone behind me poked my shoulder and pointed at Jasper sitting a few rows back. He mouthed, *"Brainiacs!"* then gave me a thumbs up. *Jasper thought I could do it?*

I turned back round and my heart suddenly felt kind of warm. I'd been shouting *Brainiacs* answers at the TV every Boxing Day for as long as I could remember. It was practically part of our Christmas tradition, like soggy sprouts and Nana's gingerbread angels and Jasper showing off non-stop. I could barely breathe I felt so excited. I looked down our row again then accidentally locked eyes with Lottie Freeman. She was one of the bright sparks that Mrs Savage had been talking about. Lottie definitely has a brain, but unfortunately she seems to be missing another vital organ. She smirked at me, then filled her cheeks up with air. It was her way of calling me fat without getting into trouble.

I made a face at Lottie like I didn't care what she said. But when she looked away, I folded my arms and squashed in my stomach, surprised I could forget about something so completely enormous even for one second. The group picture of last year's *Brainiacs* contestants was up on the screen. All of them smiling. All of them normal-sized. None of them looked like me. I told myself it didn't matter, and tried to ignore the million doubts gathering in my brain telling me that maybe it did.

Miss Nisha, our drama teacher, stood up to tell everyone about the Lower School Christmas production and Miki practically gave me a dead arm in his excitement about it. Afterwards, Mr Nelson reminded our year about the camping trip that was happening at the end of October. He'd told us about it before we broke up for the summer and now the screen projected a picture of five people almost capsizing on a raft. *Your outdoor adventure begins!* it said underneath. I tried not to groan out loud.

"We'll be camping overnight," Mr Nelson told us, "and you'll be taking part in lots of activities like archery, orienteering, raft-building, nature walks, and you'll even get to forage in the forest for food! Please tell your parents that the equipment list is now up on the website."

I blew out a long sigh. I couldn't think of anything worse than staying somewhere that considered a raft an acceptable form of transport. But Dad had already paid the deposit, so unless an asteroid hit planet Earth wiping out the entire west coast of England (my dad's exact words) I was going. And unfortunately that wasn't likely for at least another 117 years. My dad thinks camping is character-building, but Jasper went on the same trip two years ago, and he was just as annoying when he got back. Possibly even more so.

After assembly, Lottie came up behind me on the way to science. "You thinking of taking the *Brainiacs* test, Jemima? Because no one wants to see your gut on TV."

Miki told her to get lost. I told Miki that I didn't care what Lottie Freeman said, and that no one would be able to see my gastrointestinal system on TV unless they put the camera down my oesophagus. But Miki knew what she said hurt. Best friends have this weird sort of power. They can see what's happening inside your heart. Like an electrocardiogram.

The rest of the way up the stairs, I was conscious of every milligram of my body. I only got a few second glances in the corridor. Like maybe some people had forgotten what I looked like. Or wanted to see if I was any bigger. But then I walked into the science lab. And nothing, not even an electrocardiogram-best-friend, could save me.

4

GRAVITY

I knew something was wrong as soon as I saw Mr Shaw standing at the front of the science lab holding some weighing scales.

"Welcome back, 8N!" he said cheerfully. "It's a special lesson today. You're all going to be measured and weighed!"

And it was like being awake in the middle of a nightmare.

"The principal is collecting the data!" Mr Shaw said, like that was a good reason to humiliate us. He smiled awkwardly as I took my seat at the back. "Every class is doing it. I promise it's nothing to worry about. Just more government data!" He scanned his eyes around the class. "I certainly don't expect anyone to be made to feel uncomfortable."

I stuck my head in my physics book to avoid seeing everyone's eyes on me.

"And…for a bit of fun! May I present: The Bananometer!"

I looked up at the chart Mr Shaw put on the screen and read the conversion formula at the bottom. Suddenly my skin felt like ice. He was going to make us work out how many bananas we weighed, and put it on the board. I had actually liked Mr Shaw until this lesson.

"Let's start with some predictions, shall we?" he said. "How many bananas do you think 8N weighs altogether? There'll be a prize for whoever's closest at the end."

"A lot!" came a voice from the other side of the classroom. Caleb Humphries. He probably had the same number of brain cells as a banana. I put my head down as laughter echoed around me. Every soundwave felt like a punch in the guts.

Then Lottie muttered, "I'm adding an extra five hundred bananas for Jemima."

Mr Shaw called out, "Be sensitive, please!"

I wished a wormhole would magically appear next to my desk so I could be transported through time and space. In theory, it would involve being exposed to high levels of radiation and gravitational waves that could stretch me into human spaghetti, but it still sounded better than being weighed in front of my entire class.

"Don't listen to Rat Face," Miki said, pushing his top lip above his teeth, and wiggling his fingers next to his cheeks so they looked like whiskers. I tried to smile. Miki always called Lottie "Rat Face". Weirdly, she didn't seem to mind. "It will be okay, Jem," he said. "No one cares about how much anyone weighs."

I pointed my pen at Lottie.

"Okay, maybe Rat Face, but who cares what she thinks?"

I glanced back at Lottie. Her face was a bit pointy and her eyes were kind of beady-looking. But she was still pretty, so you wouldn't notice the rattiness unless you looked really closely. Or you got to know her personality.

"So," Mr Shaw said after he'd written up some predictions, "who would like to go first?"

He actually looked surprised when no hands went up. I thought about asking to go to the toilet and staying in there all lesson. But if I put my hand up now, Mr Shaw would think I was volunteering. I could say my stomach was hurting, like I had the norovirus. I watched Mr Shaw checking his clipboard, wondering if science teachers got any medical training.

"All right then," Mr Shaw said. "We'll do it alphabetically."

It's the only time in my life I've been glad my surname's Small. Mr Shaw called Erin to the front. Her cheeks went bright red even though she was one of the thinnest girls in our class. She stood against the measuring stick, then covered her cheeks when she got on the scales. She didn't even look when Mr Shaw typed 193 bananas into the Banan-ometer chart on the board. A few people laughed as though that was a lot of bananas to weigh. But it wasn't. If they'd calculated it, they'd realize 193 bananas was hardly anything.

As more people went up to get measured and weighed, people stopped laughing as much, and the class total on the Banan-ometer chart kept creeping up. Lottie weighed a perfect two hundred bananas. Miki weighed a few more than Lottie; Rohan weighed thirty-two bananas more than Miki; Afzal weighed a few less than that; Alina weighed slightly more than Lottie. I stopped looking at the chart after a while. The whole thing felt like a horrible practical joke. I prayed to God to time-travel me out of this moment. And I don't even believe in God. Or time travel.

When Mr Shaw called out my name, the lab went completely silent. My stool scraped against the floor as I slowly stood up, still trying to think of a way out of it. Caleb whispered that I'd break the scales, and Mr Shaw told everyone he didn't want to hear any comments at all or there'd be detentions. Then it went silent again, which felt worse. I knew people were probably thinking horrible stuff in their heads.

My cheeks burned as I took off my shoes and let Mr Shaw measure my height. Then I felt the heat drain out of my body as I stepped onto the scales. I looked down and swallowed. It took me about two seconds to work out how many bananas I weighed. It was more than anyone else on the board. Just like I knew it would be. I watched Mr Shaw record it on his clipboard. There was no way I wanted my weight on the screen for everyone to see. Being top of that chart was not like coming first. It was coming last.

And that's when I noticed the tray of beakers. The ones we used for chemistry experiments, like what you're supposed to do in science lessons, not stupid weigh-ins. The tray was on the edge of Mr Shaw's desk, right next to where I was standing. I quickly took a step backwards towards the tray and stuck out my arm until I'd pushed it off. I heard glass explode over the floor.

"Jemima Small!" Mr Shaw shouted. Like I didn't know my own name.

"Sorry, sir!" I said quickly. "It was an accident." The beakers had smashed on the floor in clusters, like tiny, transparent galaxies of stars. I could see some inside my shoes.

"An accident!" He shook glass off his feet and tried to find somewhere safe to step. "I saw you tip the tray over with my own eyes!"

"I'm sorry," I said. And I was. But teachers never think you mean it.

Mr Shaw took a deep breath. "Right, Jemima, *very* carefully put your shoes back on then go and wait in the science office, please. And could someone fetch the technicians and tell them what's happened?"

Lottie's hand shot up to volunteer.

In the office, a few minutes later, Mr Shaw said he appreciated that being weighed in front of my class might have been uncomfortable. *Might.* I stopped listening after that. The last thing I needed was a lecture from the inventor of the Banan-ometer. He said I'd have to see Mrs Savage at lunchtime and that I was to work in the science office for the rest of that lesson and break time. It smelled of coffee and my stomach was spinning like it had VFTS-102 in it. That's the fastest revolving star. It spins at a million miles per hour. But even feeling like that was better than seeing my weight up on the screen.

I know that weight is partly gravity. And if I lived on the moon, I'd hardly weigh anything at all. Unfortunately,

I live on Earth. And I have a teacher who thought it was fun to find out I weighed more bananas than anyone else on the planet.

5

INHOSPITABLE PLANET

At lunchtime, Miki waited with me outside Mrs Savage's office. I imagined this was how Anne Boleyn felt in 1536 when she was waiting to be executed. Only she got to wear a special royal robe, not a Clifton Academy blazer with an ink stain on the sleeve. I looked up at the brass sign on the door. Mrs Savage had an adjective for her surname like me. I knew from previous experience that it suited her.

"Jemima." Mrs Savage's face appeared round the door. "Do come in."

Miki whispered, "Good luck," as I pulled down my blazer sleeve to hide the ink stain under my fingers.

Inside her office, Mrs Savage put her elbows on the desk and leaned her fingertips against each other, creating a kind of squashed rhombus shape. Her nails were coral-pink, so she was breaking her own school rule about nail varnish. "Now," she said softly, "I'd like you to tell me what happened in your science lesson this morning."

"It was an accident, miss."

She glared at me.

"I mean, Mrs."

Her glare intensified.

I gulped. "Savage."

She huffed. "An accident?" She turned to her computer screen and clicked the mouse a few times. "That's not quite the way Mr Shaw describes it. 'She deliberately knocked over an entire tray of conical beakers'." Her voice went up at the end like she was asking a question.

"It could have been the angle," I said. "From where he was standing, Mr Shaw's field of vision would have been limited. I'm not saying he's lying just—"

She put her hand up for me to stop talking. It was pretty rude of her, but I didn't point that out. It was what my dad would call a mature decision.

"Jemima, that's not what I mean. This *incident* occurred as you were being weighed, isn't that right?"

I swallowed.

"Because I am sympathetic to the fact that some of our students might be a little" – her eyes travelled down to my stomach then quickly back up again – "*reluctant* to have

43

their weight shared with their class. I do understand." But Mrs Savage didn't understand. Teachers don't get stuff like that. I looked away and she carried on. "If you'd have simply spoken to Mr Shaw at the start of the lesson, you could have—"

"It wasn't that, Mrs Savage," I said. "It was just an accident." I kept my eyes on the desk in case she was good at telling when people were lying. I thought about the most inhospitable planet in the universe. It's called HD 189733 b and it's sixty-three light years away. It has rainstorms of glass, and winds that go five thousand miles per hour. Even living there felt more appealing to me than getting weighed in front of an audience.

"Well," Mrs Savage said, "whatever the reason, I'm sure you appreciate breaking school equipment is rather serious. I'm afraid you'll have to pay for the damage. So, I'll be calling your father this afternoon." A smile spread the entire width of her face. "You may go."

I slowly stood up and headed outside. My dad was going to kill me. If Mrs Savage was an emoji, she'd be the smiling pile of poo.

That afternoon in maths, any time I moved even the slightest bit, Lottie ducked and said, "Look out!" When

Mrs Lee asked me to solve the "problem of the day" on the board about congruent triangles, Lottie whispered, "Uh oh, she's going to smash something again!" So I told Mrs Lee I wasn't sure how to work it out. Lottie was always worse in maths because Miki wasn't in our class. And because Mrs Lee was about two hundred years old and never noticed anything.

At the end of the lesson, Mrs Lee said she hoped we would all be taking the *Brainiacs* test next week.

Lottie turned around and said, "I doubt they'd have a TV camera wide enough to film you."

I wanted to tell her why that was obviously untrue. But the logical part of my brain seemed to disappear whenever Lottie Freeman opened her mouth. I don't know why. Maybe part of me still wanted her to like me.

Dad was on his phone when I got back from school. From the look he gave me, I knew he was speaking to Mrs Savage. He waved an arm at me then pointed at the sofa.

Jasper said, "Unlucky," and pushed past me to go upstairs. "That's what happens when you break the school rules, sis."

Jasper likes rules. I do not like my brother. He ran to the top of the stairs then pretended to fight his way into his room with an imaginary lightsaber.

"I thought you said playtime was over, Jasper!" I called after him, but Dad shushed me and pointed to the sofa again. I dropped my bag by the stairs and plonked myself down.

"Yes," Dad was saying, "I do apologize. She can be a bit difficult sometimes, yes…there were a couple of things last year, but nothing serious. Yes, her attitude really. Oh, the goldfish crowd-funder thing, I'd forgotten about that… and there was a small issue in drama, yes… Jemima reads a lot, you see, Mrs Savage, and she gets these ideas…"

I sighed loudly enough for Dad (and probably Mrs Savage) to hear. The crowd-funder was Auntie Luna's idea. It wouldn't have happened if Clifton Academy had given the goldfish in reception a decent-sized tank. And it wasn't my fault Miss Nisha's dramatization of the French Revolution was unrealistic. As if somebody sentenced to death would do a shimmy roll. Teachers always overreact about everything.

"Yes, it's an awkward age!" Dad said. "Honestly, the amount of times she's threatened to report me to the United Nations for breaching her human rights! Ha ha! Yes…exactly! Hormones!"

My dad was beyond embarrassing. I sank as deep into the sofa as I could without the cushions falling off.

"Thank you for being so understanding, Mrs Savage. I assure you, Jemima will be on her best behaviour for the rest of term." Dad put his phone on the kitchen table and slowly shook his head at me.

He looked like he was about to explode. Conical beakers must be really expensive.

"Right," Dad said. It's how he always starts his lectures. "What on EARTH were you thinking when you decided to smash a WHOLE TRAY of glass beakers in your SCIENCE lesson? Of all the ridiculous things to do, Jemima! On the first day back! It's so…what do you and Jasper say? RANDOM!"

I bit my lip.

"I suppose it was some kind of protest against scientific oppression, was it? Free the sulphuric acid? I mean, come on, Jemima! You actually LIKE science!"

I stared at the painting of the sea above the fireplace. "I don't like science."

Dad sighed at full volume. "Good grief, Jemima. You must have fifty books in your room about science!" His cheeks were turning red and he kept putting his hand to his forehead like he was checking his temperature. He sat on the sofa opposite, leaned forward and rubbed his beard. "Mrs Savage said everyone was being weighed today, is that what got to you?"

I could have told him how it felt. To walk up to the scales in silence with everyone staring at me. And about the stupid Banan-ometer on the screen, and Lottie Freeman, and being called Jemima Big. And wondering whether I should even take the *Brainiacs* test next week because who'd want to see me on TV? But dads don't care about stuff like that. Not my dad anyway. He'd probably tell me getting weighed wasn't a real problem. Besides, talking to Dad about anything to do with my body was totally embarrassing. I still hadn't got over him asking if I needed a "training bra" last year in the middle of Asda. So, I said, "Dad, you could be putting yourself at risk of an early heart attack by being in such a stress about this."

Dad gave me a full-strength Look. "Jemima. I'm. Not. In. A. Stress," he said, then inhaled sharply through his nose.

"Okay, well, your cheeks are red. It could be the first stage of a heart attack. I'll google how to do CPR." I pulled my phone out of my blazer pocket and Dad let out another long sigh. "You look exasperated," I said, "which is probably dangerous at your age."

"Jemima, stop treating this like it's a joke! Those beakers are expensive! You could have been in a lot of trouble! Who exactly did you think would have to pay for them?"

"I didn't do it deliberately."

"Really? Your science teacher told Mrs Savage you deliberately pushed the tray off his desk."

"Well, he's lying."

Dad tilted his head up towards the ceiling like he was praying. Only my dad doesn't pray. He went on about how disappointed he was for approximately a million years. And said the money for the broken beakers would be coming out of my pocket money. Which would take me ages to pay off because he hardly gave me any. But apparently it wasn't a mature decision to point that out.

I watched his reflection in the blank TV screen, wishing he could be like those dads you got in TV shows. The ones who give you hugs and tell you everything's going to be okay. Not the type of dad who jokes with the principal about your hormones and doesn't care about animal rights and gets in a stress about stupid conical beakers and asks about training bras in the middle of Asda. TV dads are way better than real ones. TV everything is better than real life.

"And, young lady," he said, "you can help me clear out the garage next weekend."

"The garage! But it's really dirty."

"It won't be once you've cleaned it!" he said, and smiled at me. It was literally like living with Mrs Savage.

I wish I could have told Dad why I broke the beakers, maybe then he would have given me a hug instead of a lecture. And how, sometimes, it felt like there was a giant crater in my heart, so big nothing could ever fix it. I also wish I'd told him that my education is funded by the government so, technically, I shouldn't have to pay for the beakers. But I didn't tell him that either. Instead, I went up to my room and wrote a stupid apology letter to Mr Shaw like he told me to.

Afterwards, I lay on my bed and looked up at the ceiling. I was genuinely sorry. But not about smashing the beakers like I'd said in the letter. I didn't care about glass. Glass wasn't valuable. It was only made out of sand. There was literally tonnes of it on the beach.

I was sorry I didn't have a family who understood how it felt to be me.

I thought about Tika, the contestant who won *Brainiacs* last year. And about her family in the audience who wore special T-shirts with her face printed on them. Who cheered her on even when she messed up on a question and cried with happiness when she made it through each round. That was what I wanted more than anything: an unconditional love sort of family.

It was the type of love I'd probably feel if Mum was still here. She'd come up to my room and tell me not to worry about what Dad said. She'd say it was gravity's fault the beakers smashed. And the government should pay for them. And who even cares about the stupid Bananometer? Bananas aren't a real unit of measurement. She'd say that Mrs Savage should check Mr Shaw's science qualifications. Then she'd give me a hug. And tell me everything was going to be okay. And she'd probably be wearing a T-shirt with my picture on it.

6

MAGIC TRICK

It wasn't until the end of that first week back at school that I found out what the Banan-ometer was really about. It was like this sleight-of-hand trick my grandad used to do when we were little. He was a famous magician called the Amazing Apollo. Well, famous in Clifton-on-Sea. He used to perform at the palladium opposite the pier. His real name was Harry Small, but the Amazing Harry Small didn't have the same ring to it. He'd show you his empty hands, then pull a coin out from behind your ear, or even your toes if you were wearing flip-flops. I used to believe he'd really found the coin in there. But it was just a stupid trick. He had it hidden in his palm all along.

It was the same thing with everyone at school getting

weighed. It had nothing to do with predictions or formulae or bananas or science. They just pretended it did. And I was stupid to even fall for it.

I walked into form on Friday morning with Miki and Mr Nelson said, "Jemima, a quick word, please." I got this plunging feeling in my stomach, like when you look over the edge of the Plank. Miki and I exchanged glances then I walked over to Mr Nelson's desk.

He lowered his voice. "Mrs Savage would like you to go straight to the sports hall this morning. There's a special meeting she'd like you to attend."

"Meeting?" I asked, scanning my brain for an idea about what it could be.

"It's nothing to worry about. You're not in any trouble," he said. "You'd better hurry." And the way Mr Nelson smiled at me, I figured it was about *Brainiacs*. I thought maybe Mrs Savage wanted to make sure I was taking the test, even though she'd said it was optional. Maybe she'd looked up our SATs results or spoken to Mrs Lee or something.

When I got to the sports hall, about twelve people were sitting on the floor. I recognized Harry and Heidi, the twins in my year from Ms Fraser's class. I'd done the Reading Challenge with them last year. I went over and sat down. Brandon Taylor – Dylan's older brother – was sitting near them. Brandon used to make fun of me at primary school too sometimes, although he'd never said anything to me since I started at Clifton. He looked up and smiled awkwardly. I looked away.

I watched a few more people arrive and suddenly it clicked in my head. I knew why Mrs Savage had sent me here. And it had nothing to do with the stupid *Brainiacs* test next week. It all made perfect sense. Why we'd been measured and weighed on Monday. And why everyone sitting in the sports hall was wearing a blazer about the same size as mine.

I felt stupid and sad and angry all at once. But I didn't say anything. I sat there on the cold floor, probably feeling the same as everyone else who'd also figured it out. In total silence, with my fingers crossed, even though I didn't believe in crossing my fingers. Wishing and wishing and wishing that I was wrong.

Mrs Savage kept a smile plastered on her face, but shifted around on her feet like she was uncomfortable. Maybe she felt bad about what she was going to say. Or she had bunions. "Thank you for coming, everyone. I've brought you here to tell you about a very special programme of lessons that you'll be taking part in this academic year. Think of it as a special club—"

Suddenly, the doors at the back of the sports hall were flung open and a group of boys burst in. They stood staring at us for a moment, as their laughter echoed off the walls.

"Close those doors and get to your form classes!" Mrs Savage's voice reverberated around the sports hall.

"We've got PE in here now, miss," one of them replied.

Mrs Savage sighed and shook her head. "Not yet! The bell for lessons hasn't even rung! I'm using the hall for this special club so please leave!"

There was more laughing as they stumbled out.

Then one of them shouted, "FAT CLUB!" just before the doors slammed shut.

Heidi whispered something to Harry. He nodded, then looked around. Mrs Savage caught my eye for a second, then cleared her throat and moved her mouth into a smile so wide it looked like a Snapchat filter.

The atmosphere felt dense. A bit like the atmosphere on Mars. But that's ninety-five per cent carbon dioxide. This was one hundred per cent humiliation, and I could feel it tightening my chest. I knew for sure now why we'd been weighed. And what Mrs Savage meant by "special club".

This mystery meeting was Clifton Academy's brand-new Fat Club. And it did not feel very special to be a member.

7

BLACK HOLE

I sat on the floor of the sports hall with my legs crossed and my skirt covering them all the way to my shoes. My arms were folded over my belly and tears were forming in the corners of my eyes. I looked down at the floor and tried to blink them away. If I measured how it felt inside my heart right then on the Richter scale, it would be a 9.0: severe destruction.

Mrs Savage picked up a stack of letters from the table behind her. "Now, as I was saying, you are going to be part of a very exciting 'Healthy Lifestyle' programme that will be starting next week right here at Clifton Academy. We've selected you because we believe you will benefit from it the most." A few people shifted around awkwardly. "The classes will be held on Friday lunchtimes and they will be lots of fun. You'll learn all about nutrition, exercise, and I believe you'll even do some cookery!" She paused to smile at each one of us, like we'd won some kind of fat lottery. Except it felt like the opposite: as though every centimetre of my skin had been stamped with a gigantic FAIL. And I felt more self-conscious than ever.

Dear Mr Small, my letter said at the top. Underneath was a graph where the x and y axes represented height and weight. A black line showed the norm for my age and, above it, a red cross represented me. In bold letters it said: *Jemima's result is in the Very Overweight range.*

There were two pages of writing after that, but I didn't read them properly. Tears were stinging my eyes and I had to swallow loads of times to stop them accidentally spilling over on to my cheeks. It wasn't like I didn't already know where I'd be on a graph like that. I'd just assumed it didn't matter to my school. But there it was. Printed on special Clifton Academy paper with the school motto and the oak tree logo at the top. And a giant red cross to show how wrong I was.

As soon as Mrs Savage had finished talking, I stuffed the letter into my blazer pocket and headed outside. I blinked, screwing my eyes shut as tight as I could. There was no way I was going to cry on the way to geography.

From behind me, Heidi called, "Jemima! Are you okay?"

I turned around and nodded. Harry was looking down at his phone. A few more people came through the doors, and a girl I didn't recognize was crying, saying she was going to call her mum. Another girl said the same, and linked arms with her. Brandon stood next to them looking over at me. I turned and headed towards the humanities block. The empty space in my heart felt like it was expanding at the rate of the universe, and the letter in my pocket made me want to disappear into it. I felt so stupid for thinking Mrs Savage wanted me to go on *Brainiacs*! This letter proved that was the last thing she'd want.

I reached the double doors near the geography corridor just as a class was coming out.

"Walk quietly!" a teacher shouted, as a line of green blazers barged past me.

I held the door open and the teacher smiled at me with a perfectly symmetrical face. As the last few people went through the door, someone muttered, "Jemima Big." I didn't look back to see who it was. It didn't matter. They were only saying the truth. I was too big. I saw it every time I looked in the mirror. Or caught a glimpse of my reflection in a window. Or compared my body to someone else's. I even had a letter in my pocket with a special graph proving it. It's what scientists call indisputable evidence.

But right then, standing on the grey concrete, with the

September sun behind me, trying my best to swallow my tears, all I really felt was small.

In geography, Miki asked what the meeting was about, but I didn't say. It's hard to tell even your best friend something like that. Especially when Lottie Freeman is sitting in the chair behind, prodding your shoulder with her pencil and asking the exact same question. I whispered to Miki that I'd tell him at break.

"Tell him what at break, Jemima?" Lottie said, poking her pencil into my back again.

"Nothing, Lottie." I tried to sound casual, but there was a lump in my throat the size of Uluru.

Miki said, "It's nothing to do with you, Lottie."

"I can find out what it was about anyway," she said.

I looked at her over my shoulder. She smirked at me then laughed. There was definitely something rodenty about her. She pulled her phone out of her pocket and started typing. I felt my heart beating faster. If Lottie found out what the meeting was about, my life would be over.

"Lottie!" Mr Kelly called from his desk. "You know the rules. No phones in lessons. Hand it to me, please."

"Oh, but I was just using the calculator, sir." Lottie put

on an angelic voice. She always does it when she speaks to teachers. It's about five notes higher than her normal voice, and five times more annoying.

"Lottie, you don't need a calculator to draw river erosion." Mr Kelly folded his arms over his yellow tank top. "On my desk, please."

Lottie's smile disappeared. "Sorry, sir," she said, but didn't move. "I meant I was checking the time."

Mr Kelly glared at her. "Lottie, it's confiscated. Get over it. Collect it from reception at the end of the day."

Lottie got up and slowly walked towards his desk. "But, sir, I need to phone my grandmother at break time."

Practically everyone in the class rolled their eyes, including Mr Kelly. Lottie scowled as she handed it over. I gave a sigh of relief.

At break time I told Miki I'd meet him in the library, then went down the corridor to the toilets. Someone had written *Smile* :) on the mirror in lipstick. I really did not feel like smiling. I stared at my reflection. Auntie Luna told me ages ago that every girl has an inner goddess. But mine must have been invisible, because all I could see was Jemima Big. She stared back at me with a face that needed facial surgery, hair the colour of sludgy sand, a body in the Very Overweight range, and thousands of voices in my head repeating *Jemima Big, Jemima Big, Jemima Big.*

And the letter in my pocket amplified all of it.

It would have been the perfect moment for my inner goddess to appear, but I couldn't sense her at all. Maybe she was just trying her best not to cry, like I was.

Miki was sitting on one of the yellow stools in the library by the window, playing on his phone.

I sat next to him and pulled the letter out of my pocket. "Hey. I'm officially Jemima Big. This confirms it."

Miki read the first paragraph and screwed up his face. "What? This is what the meeting was about? That's stupid! I thought it was about *Brainiacs.* What did Mrs Savage say?"

I put the letter back in my pocket and made sure no one was listening. "I have to do this stupid class called Healthy Lifestyle. On Friday *lunchtimes*! I've literally been given a weekly detention. For being fat."

Miki shook his head. "Lunchtime? You'd think she'd let you get out of history or something! It sucks, Jem. You okay?"

I nodded and took a book called *Who Wants to Live in Medieval Britain?* from the nearest shelf. I didn't want Miki to see the tears stinging my eyes. But I also did not feel like reading about medieval torture devices. I flicked though the pages as Miki said, "Mrs Savage should give you a letter saying you're...like...the cleverest person in the school or something."

"Well, this letter's the exact opposite of that," I said. "It's like, all the things Lottie and Caleb and people say about me...well, it's like the school thinks them too."

"They don't," Miki said, shaking his fringe out of his eyes. "It was just a dumb weigh-in. Everyone knows Mrs Savage is a dictator."

I smiled. "Exactly. She actually said it would be fun!"

Miki's eyes lit up. "It could be fun!" Then he ducked out of the way like I might hit him over the head with *Who Wants to Live in Medieval Britain?* or something.

"I doubt it!" I said. "She's probably getting the technicians to build one of these right now." I held up the book to show him a picture of a medieval rack. "She'll stretch me out until I'm the right height for my weight. Then she can plot me on her stupid graph again."

"Maybe it will be okay, Jem. At least it's on Fridays. That's when I'll be rehearsing for the Christmas production. Hopefully." He crossed his fingers. "If I pass the audition next week."

"You will." Last term Miss Nisha said Miki had an *enormous amount of talent.* She said I had an attitude problem. Which wasn't technically correct. I had a problem with my character doing shimmy rolls in what was supposed to be eighteenth-century Paris.

"Thanks!" Miki said. "Help me with my lines at lunchtime? I'm auditioning for Bert, the chimney sweep. He's a main part."

"Sure."

"And next week, I'll help you revise for the *Brainiacs* test. You'll smash it."

I smiled as Miki went back to playing on his phone, but inside I felt sick. I looked over at the poster on the pillar by the librarian's desk. *Do you have what it takes to be the next BRAINIACS champion?* I thought about all the times I'd watched *Brainiacs* at home. And Dad saying, "Amazing!" or "Brilliant!" or "How on earth do you know that?" any time I got an answer right.

I closed my hand around the letter in my pocket and looked at my reflection in the window. I'd have loved the chance to go on *Brainiacs*. But over three million people watched the show. Three million! If I got through, they would all see what I was seeing: Jemima Big. And right then, I could not think of anything worse. Apart from the medieval torture technique of putting rats inside your intestines. I looked back at the poster. *Do you have what it takes to be the next BRAINIACS champion?* I didn't even hesitate. No.

8

SATELLITE

On the bus home from school, all I could think about was Dad seeing the letter. It wasn't like the one I got when I qualified for the Clifton-on-Sea Spelling Bee, or the note from the head teacher that came with my SATs results saying, *Outstanding! Congratulations, Jemima!* Or the one Jasper and I got thanking us for taking part in the beach clean-up ages ago. This letter was nothing like those. This letter was bad. Like being in trouble, but worse.

Jasper leaned over the back of my seat and said, "I scored ninety-two per cent in my science test today."

I carried on looking out of the window. "Shame. Better luck next time."

"Shame I'm too old to enter *Brainiacs*, you mean. Because"– he raised his hands and said – "I would crush you like an enemy!" He chopped the back of my seat karate-style. If we didn't both have Dad's sludgy-sand coloured hair, I'd question if we were even related.

"I doubt it," I said. "Unless they do a quick-fire round on how to be a massive nerd."

"Ha! The whole show is about being a massive nerd, Jemima! That's why you'll probably win."

"I doubt it, because I'm not entering."

"What? How come?" Jasper stuck his hand in front of my face to offer me some strawberry Millions.

I pushed it back. They'd probably been in his blazer pocket since last year.

"I thought *Brainiacs* was your favourite show."

"Well, it's not. So, don't mention it to Dad, okay?" I looked out at the grey mist hanging over the sea. I could just see the lighthouse in the distance. It was built in 1882 to replace the previous one that was destroyed by fire. That one was built in 1759 and its tower was dodecagonal. It means it had twelve sides. You learn about stuff like that when you hang out at Clifton Museum all summer instead of the beach.

"Okay. So, what was that meeting about in the sports hall?"

I turned round to face him. "How do you know about that?"

65

"I saw you going in there. My form's opposite." Jasper cracked his knuckles and began shuffling a pack of cards. "If you're in trouble, I am telling Dad."

I sighed. There was no way I was telling Jasper the truth. "Not that it's any of your business, but it's this special class Mrs Savage is setting up. It's for, erm, people with high IQs."

Jasper screwed up his face. "Really? So what was Brandon Taylor doing there?"

I sighed again. It was so typical of Jasper to spy on everyone. "I don't know. Maybe he went in by accident."

Jasper looked at me, trying to figure out if I was lying or not. I turned back round and he started telling me about this new magic trick he was learning. As usual, I didn't listen. Jasper thinks doing magic somehow makes him special. But anyone can do it. You can literally buy boxes of it on the internet. It's nothing special or supernatural or spectacular. It's just buying the right equipment and practising for ages in your bedroom. Eventually he stopped talking and put his headphones on.

I pulled my library book out of my rucksack and shifted on my seat so my back was against the bus window. I opened my book and placed the letter inside so Jasper couldn't see it.

The special programme of lessons on Healthy Living will be delivered by fitness and nutrition specialist Gina Grantley-Bond, and will include a range of learning opportunities including weight management, healthy eating, teamwork and mental well-being.

I kept reading. The class didn't sound that bad in a way. It would be easier than saving up for facial surgery and probably less painful than getting all my fat sucked out. Miki would probably be rehearsing for the production on Fridays anyway. I liked learning new stuff, and Heidi and Harry would be there.

"Hey, look at Big taking up two seats."

I looked up. It was a boy sitting on the back seat. I closed my book and turned back to face the front.

I thought about the boys who shouted "FAT CLUB!" earlier. How long would it be until it was all around school? What if this Gina person made us run laps of the field at lunchtime? In our PE kit? It would be even more humiliating than getting weighed in science. I had to convince Dad not to sign the form. Maybe I could say Mrs Savage was a dictator. Although, I didn't know how Dad felt about dictators. He probably liked them.

When I got home, a strange smell was emanating from the kitchen. I peered through the bead curtain. Dad had his head in a recipe book, turning the page back and forth and tutting. He did that a lot when he was cooking. I pushed the beads to one side and leaned against the worktop.

"Hey! How was school?"

"Okay," I lied. "What are you making?"

"Kale soup," he said, wiping his hands on the tea towel over his shoulder.

"Kale soup?" It was definitely weird. My dad never made anything healthy-sounding. Maybe it was Auntie Luna's idea. If there were any strange occurrences in our house, they usually came from Luna.

"There was a load of kale on offer at the supermarket!" Dad said.

Or they could be explained by a special offer at Asda.

"Dad, I need to talk to you about something," I said, feeling like my intestines were filled with medieval rodents.

Dad looked up from the saucepan. He was about to say something when Jasper strolled in to boast about his science test result.

"That's great, Jasper, well done! Now, have you got some homework or something to do upstairs? Your sister wants to talk to me."

"Sure," Jasper said. "No problem, Dad. I'll get right

on it." He raised his eyebrows at me like I should somehow be impressed with his sucking-up skills.

Dad turned down the cooker then pulled out two chairs from the table. I waited until I heard Jasper's bedroom door close, then sat down and pushed the letter across the table. Dad didn't say anything for ages.

"It's an abomination, really," I said to break the silence. "Mrs Savage runs the school like a dictatorship."

Dad kept his eyes on the letter. His face looked serious. Worse than when he found out about the science beakers.

"Oh, Jemima!"

I didn't know what that was supposed to mean, but it wasn't good.

He rubbed his hand across his beard and let out a long sigh. "I-I don't know what to say." He looked at me and smiled, but something in his eyes made me want to cry. "Listen, I don't want you to worry about this, okay?"

"I'm not worried about it," I said, half-lying. Maybe fully lying.

"I mean, obviously, there's a...problem," he said. And it felt like being smacked in the face with a football. I don't know what I was expecting him to say, but it wasn't that I was a "problem". I could feel tears starting in my eyes again. "It's just...you've always been...chubby, you know? Ever since you were a baby."

"Great. I was a fat baby."

Dad laughed, then his face went serious again. "I'm sorry, Jemima. I mean, you've always been…how you are. Oh, I don't know. Maybe we should have done something sooner. The way they've said it here…I feel responsible." He picked up the letter and put it straight back down again. Probably because he'd already read it ten times. "Oh jeez, with things like this I really wish your mum had stuck around." He sighed. "I'm sorry. This isn't your fault. It will be okay. I don't know what else to say."

"You could say I don't have to do the class."

"Oh, Jem, you've got to do the class. In fact, this Gina Grantley-Bond sounds—"

"Deranged?"

"No!" Dad laughed. "She sounds great. It says here she's got lots of experience with…"

I stared at him.

"*Young* people. And look, she's even worked with the British Paralympic team!"

"That could be a lie."

Dad sighed. "I don't think Mrs Savage would lie."

"Well, you don't know her. Anyway, I'm not doing the class because…" I thought of those boys again, and the words "Fat Club" echoing around the sports hall. "It's illegal."

He tutted. "Don't be ridiculous! Of course it's not illegal. The class Is designed to help you."

"Well, I don't need that kind of illegal help. I can lose weight on my own in my bedroom."

Dad looked sadly at me across the table. Probably remembering that time before I started at Clifton Academy, when I tried doing a high intensity workout from YouTube. Dad came running up the stairs saying it sounded like I was entertaining a herd of buffalo. Obviously, I didn't try that again.

"Jemima, honestly, I think this is the best way. Get you some proper support...from, you know, a professional." He signed the form at the bottom of the letter.

I looked at him like he was signing my death sentence.

"Don't look at me like that! I'm sure you'll enjoy it! It will be fun." He was outright lying now. "You'll make some new friends who, you know...understand what it's like. You love learning facts and things, don't you? You'll just be learning about healthy things and not...quantum particles. Great timing with this kale soup, hey?"

Dad got up and stirred the bubbling pan of soup that apparently I'd be eating for dinner, probably for the rest of my life. "You know what? We should start playing basketball again! We've barely used that hoop since I put it up." He patted his stomach. "I could do with getting back in shape myself! We'll do it together." He took out a teaspoon and tasted the soup. "Hmm, not too bad!"

I found out later that that was a lie too.

"Jemima, I know just having me isn't the same as having a mum around. But…I am here…if you ever want to…you know. And you've got Luna!"

We both looked out of the steamed-up windows at Auntie Luna's wooden cabin in the back garden. Dad built it ages ago after Uncle Alfie left her. Luna's heart broke so badly she had to go to hospital. She's okay now, but she has to live with us so Dad can make sure she doesn't get poorly again. Also, Uncle Alfie emptied their bank account, so she didn't have much choice. Luna says money's not important. It can be replaced. But nothing can fix a broken heart because hearts are irreparable. I think she has the same empty feeling in her heart like I have about Mum. Only hers is Uncle-Alfie shaped.

"You should talk to Luna about this, Jem. I appreciate her advice can be a little…out of this world. To say the least. But, anyway, the point is, we can all go on this health kick together. Me, you and Jasper." Dad squinted at the recipe book. "*Pink Himalayan* salt?" He tutted. "What's so special about the Himalayas?"

"Well," I said, "the Himalayan range is almost fifteen hundred miles long, it's spread across five countries, and contains the highest peaks in the world, including Mount Everest. It has one of the largest deposits of snow and ice on the whole planet, after the Arctic and the Antarctic, obviously. In fact, the name Himalaya means 'the abode of snow'." I thought for a moment. "I guess the salt's pink because of the mineral content."

Dad stared at me. "I don't know where you get it from."

I shrugged. "Probably Waitrose?"

Dad walked over and rubbed my head. "I meant you and your encyclopaedic knowledge! How did you get to be such a genius, hey?"

"I don't know," I said. "Must come from Mum's side of the family."

"Ha! Probably!"

Without thinking, I said, "Hey, guess what? Our school is—" Then I stopped. I looked down at Dad's signature on the letter – confirmation of how totally unsuitable I was for *Brainiacs*. It was best not to even tell him about it. "Erm, doing *Mary Poppins* for the Christmas production. Miki's auditioning."

"Good for him! You'll have to get us some tickets. Now, herbs!" he said. "Back in a minute." He opened the back door and went over to the little herb garden Auntie Luna planted a few summers ago.

I stared out of the window for ages, feeling like a satellite orbiting a planet. Totally alone. Realizing that the only thing that was ever going to matter about me was my size. It was only Friday night, but already I was dreading school on Monday. Everyone at school had probably already shared stuff about Fat Club. I wished I could stop time. Stay sitting at the kitchen table for ever. Just ideally not with the smell of kale soup in the background.

9

AUNTIE LUNA

At dinner, Jasper was telling us about how brilliant he was at everything. I corrected him, so he said, "Jemima, you don't know it all! I bet you can't even tell me three facts about" – he held up his soup spoon – "kale!"

So I told him that, *one*, it's green because its cells contain chlorophyll; *two*, it was used as a medicine in Ancient Greece; and *three*, he had some down his T-shirt.

Afterwards, I went up to my room and watched the sky. It was full of grey cumulonimbus clouds. They're the really massive ones. It's the cloud type that most resembles my brother's head. Orange street lamps were dotted along the promenade, and I could see the green neon glow of the Sphere on the Pier, this fairground ride that spins round really fast. The floor drops away and you stay there, stuck to the wall. Jasper calls it the Vomit Comet. The sign says *Experience zero gravity!* which is false advertising. What you're actually experiencing is centrifugal force. But, believe me, the people who work on the ride do not care about that.

I could hear Dad laughing loudly at the TV, followed closely by Jasper. I pulled on my jumper, walked downstairs, and out the back door to where Auntie Luna's cabin glowed in the moonlight.

The wooden steps creaked as I walked up to her door. The sign said: *You say I'm a witch like it's a bad thing.*

Jasper says she should change it to BEWARE OF THE WITCH. But he never says it when Luna's around. Jasper always says stuff like that when no one's listening. Sometimes he calls me fat even though he's not allowed. If I tell Dad, Jasper just says I'm lying, and Dad always believes him. No one believes you if you're the youngest.

Auntie Luna isn't a witch, by the way, she's a psychic. She tells fortunes using tarot cards. And reads auras. An aura is this special kind of energy that surrounds your body. Only psychic people can see it. There are loads of different colours your aura can be, depending on your personality. I only half-believe in auras because there's no scientific evidence. And because Luna said mine's yellow and I wanted a purple one like Emma Watson.

Hermione meowed as I knocked on Luna's door. She's supposed to be my cat, but Luna sort of adopted her. I don't mind that much. She used to pounce on me in the middle of the night and any time she left a dead mouse outside the back door, Dad always made me put it in the dustbin, even though I told him I could catch the hantavirus.

I opened the door and went in, sneezing from the dust. Luna says there's no such thing as dust, only particles of Mother Earth. Each one of them is sacred and she needs them to channel her psychic energy. That excuse for not cleaning your room does not work on my dad.

Luna was sitting on a cushion in the lotus position with her eyes closed. Her hair was pinned up in big curls around her face. It was the colour of cinnamon and it reminded me I wanted to dye my hair as soon as possible. I looked at the books piled next to her bed. One was called *Astral Projection: How to leave your body and travel the universe*. I picked it up and turned it over. *A step-by-step guide to leaving your body.* It sounded like the exact book I needed. I checked Luna's eyes were closed, then shoved the book up my jumper.

Luna slowly opened her eyes. They glowed silvery-blue like a wolf's, and her gold eyeliner glittered in the fairy lights. She was wearing a T-shirt that said GOOD VIBES.

It's the name of her friend Jupiter's crystal shop.

"Tonight is the full moon," she said. "It's time to bathe in her light and harness her feminine energy." Luna stood up, took my hand and we headed outside.

"Jemima," she said, after we'd wrapped up in blankets, "I can feel something blocking your energy."

I swallowed and tried to reposition my body so she couldn't see the outline of the astral projection book up my jumper.

"Tell me what's on your mind."

I looked up at the grey clouds partially covering the full moon. I thought about telling Luna about the letter, but the last time I told Luna about being called Jemima Big at school, she told me to rub lavender oil into my skin for inner peace. The next day, Caleb Humphries told everyone I smelled like a granny. I changed the subject.

"I wish I had psychic powers," I said, even though I didn't fully believe in psychic powers. "Then I could work at psychic fairs with you and I wouldn't have to go to school."

Luna tilted her face towards the moonlight. "You never know, Jemstone. Sometimes psychic powers get awakened later on in life. Some people get them in their thirties or forties."

I sighed. It was so annoying. What was the point of

getting psychic powers when you were too old to even use them?

"I'm sorry, Jemstone," Luna said, squeezing my hand. "I wish I could make things better for you at school. But, you know, everything you'll ever need is already inside you."

Sometimes I forgot how weird Luna could be.

I lay there for a while, looking out into the expanding universe, as Luna told me our skin was absorbing the full moon's powerful feminine energy, just like it absorbed sunlight. Although how moonlight got through all the layers and blankets we were wearing, I don't know.

I didn't feel very powerful by the time I went back inside. But I had figured out what I wanted: to be a completely different girl from Jemima Small. And I knew it would take something much stronger than moonlight to do that.

10

INFINITY

That night, I stayed up late reading *Astral Projection: How to leave your body and travel the universe*, the book I'd borrowed from Luna. I could not put it down. Astral projection was the best thing ever. You lie down, close your eyes, concentrate really hard, then your soul leaves your body and soars through the universe. It's not dying or consuming someone's soul like a Dementor or anything. It's this special thing which meant I could escape from my body. Even if it was only for a moment, I'd know how it felt to not be Jemima Big. Like magic, only real.

I waited until Dad had gone to bed, then I lay really still under my duvet, trying not to fidget. I looked up at my bedroom ceiling. It was still covered in bits of

Blu Tack from when I put posters up ages ago. They all fell down because gravity is a lot stronger than Blu Tack.

I closed my eyes and imagined the night sky above me, mapping out the constellations in my mind with their billions of stars, trillions of miles away, expanding into infinity. I took a deep breath and tried as hard as I could to push my soul out of my body. Only I wasn't sure where to start pushing.

I needed to find out where the human soul was located exactly, so I could push it out. I didn't want to push out the wrong body part. I didn't want my intestines floating about in space for ever. I wondered if my soul was inside my brain somewhere, but what if it was inside my heart? Astral projection was kind of confusing actually.

I put my hands in the mudra position that Auntie Luna had shown me ages ago, with my middle fingers touching my thumbs. It was supposed to stimulate energy flow, so I hoped it would stimulate my soul to hurry up and get going. But after about ten minutes nothing had happened.

I opened my eyes. I could just make out a blob of Blu Tack on the ceiling that still had part of Hermione Granger's face stuck to it. I wished I could astrally project my soul into Hermione. But I was pretty sure souls can't go into made-up characters.

I closed my eyes again and pictured my soul travelling through space, hoping it had some kind of built-in satnav. I imagined having to tell Dad that my soul had gone missing somewhere between my bedroom and outer space. He would kill me. It was bad enough when I lost my phone at the beach that time.

I don't know what happened next. But somehow, the strong urge to push out my soul must have been replaced by the strong urge to sleep. Because the next time I opened my eyes, my bedroom was filled with light. I was lying on the same bed, in the same body, and I had to be Jemima Small all over again.

11

DUST

On Sunday it wasn't raining, which meant I had to help Dad clear out the garage with its fifteen years of accumulated junk. My punishment for smashing a few stupid beakers. I explained to Dad that most of the stuff in there came from before I was even born, so technically it wasn't my responsibility. But he said that was irrelevant and handed me some overalls.

"It's gargantuan!" I said as Dad swung open the double doors. "There's no way I can clear all of this out in one day!"

"There's always next weekend as well," Dad said, actually laughing.

I surveyed the never-ending stacks of boxes, old toys, planks of wood, tools, and approximately ten billion

83

cobwebs. "This is so unfair," I said, stepping into the overalls and rolling up the sleeves. "Smashing the beakers was an *accident*. I'm being punished for an *accident*."

"Mrs Savage didn't seem to think it was an accident."

"She wasn't there, so how would she even know?"

Dad sighed. "I'm not getting into this again. You're helping clear this out and that's that. A bit of physical labour isn't going to do you any harm, is it?"

I glared at him.

"Sorry, I didn't mean…"

I blew out my breath and tied my hair back. "Fine. Let's get on with it. But, if I find any disease-carrying insects or rodents then I'm going back inside."

Dad laughed. "Deal. I'm sure they'll all be hibernating at this time of year anyway."

"I doubt it," I said as Hermione padded in. She rubbed against an old box, then caught a spider in her claws and started chewing on it. "Gross."

"See?" Dad said with a grin. "You've even got your own spider catcher. What more could you want?"

"Basic human rights?"

Dad chuckled and handed me a broom. "I'll bring you an apple juice."

After a couple of hours, my arms felt like they'd moved a thousand boxes, but the garage was only half clear.

"Wow! Well done!" Dad said. "Give me a hand getting this lot into the van then you can have a break while I go to the tip."

We filled up the van and Dad shouted to Jasper that he was going. He still thought Jasper needed to look after me, even though I'd be thirteen in a matter of days. Thirty-five to be precise.

"Give the floor a sweep while I'm gone, hey?"

"I thought you said I could have a break!"

Dad got into the van and gave me The Look through the window. "It will take you two minutes!"

I watched Dad drive off, then sat on an old armchair at the back of the garage, watching sunlight stream through the gaps in the wooden door. Dust particles floated in the air, glittering like tiny stars. And this moment I will probably remember for ever. Because there, right in front of me, was a box covered in a thick layer of dust, with one word written on it in black pen: JOANIE.

The whole garage could have collapsed around me and I wouldn't have noticed. There's this story in Greek mythology called Pandora's box. It's about a box with all this evil stuff inside. Only Pandora doesn't know what's inside. She only knows she isn't supposed to open it. Sitting there with that box in front of me with my mum's name on it, that's sort of how I felt. Like opening it might tell me something I didn't want to know. Maybe why she left. I was too scared to open it and too scared not to.

I looked at it for a minute, surrounded by dust and cobwebs and rusty toys and Jasper's old scooter. Then I stood up, wiped the dust off the box with my sleeve, and opened it.

Something gold caught the light. It was a jewellery box with a broken clasp at the front. Inside were some silver bangles that had tarnished and turned almost black. They felt cold and smelled kind of rusty. Normally, when I thought about Mum, I got that horrible empty feeling. But looking through her old stuff, I didn't. It felt like goosebumps, only warm. Like for once she didn't feel so far away.

There were a few boring-looking documents, some old postcards, a framed certificate from an accountancy course dated a few years after I was born, some old gloves and a CD. I pulled out a brown envelope and some photos dropped out.

I picked them up and there we were. In our back garden. In the summer. I was sitting on Mum's lap looking at a piece of chalk or something in my hand, maybe three years old. Dad had his arm around her and Jasper was standing next to him pulling a funny face. Above Mum's head were little circles of lens flare, those coloured spots you get in photos when the light's too bright. She was leaning against Dad with her arm wrapped around my tummy. There she was. My mum. Smiling into too-bright sunlight. And I was sitting on her lap like it was no big deal. As if she would be there for ever.

I looked closely at Mum's face, searching for clues about why she left us. But I couldn't find any. I guess people don't wear clues on their faces when they decide to disappear from your life. Although, the photo was taken a few years before she left, so maybe she just hadn't decided yet.

Before Dad got back from the tip, I went and hid Mum's box under my bed. Dad never even wanted to talk about her, so I doubted he'd want to see her things. Besides, I was worried he might want to take it to the tip. I shifted a few boxes out of the way so I could start sweeping. And that's when I saw the paintings. There must have been twenty of them. Some of sea creatures. Some of the pier. Some of me and Jasper. And loads of Mum. In one she had bright orange hair flowing out like flames. One was just of her eyes filled with tiny stars, as though the whole universe was inside them.

I was sat down looking at them as Dad's van pulled up.

"What have you got there?" he called as he walked in.

I quickly stood up. "They fell down as I was sweeping."

Dad picked up a painting, then slowly looked through the rest. "Gosh, I painted some of these fifteen, twenty years ago! Forgot I kept them." He gazed at the painting of Mum with her hair like flames and shook his head. "Feels like I did them in a former life."

I stood next to him and looked at the thick swirls of orange paint around Mum's face. "You must have loved her a lot. To paint her like that."

Dad smiled, his eyes still fixed on the painting. "Like what?"

"Like she's a goddess or something."

"Yeah, I loved your mum, Jemima. I loved her a lot, but…" Dad sighed and put the painting down. "I should probably just take them to the charity shop." He picked up a painting of me and Jasper. Huge yellow clouds floated above our heads and the sea was pink in the background. "Maybe I'll keep this one."

I took a deep breath. "Don't you…ever wonder where she is?"

Dad put his arm round me, the painting of me and Jasper still in his other hand. "I'm usually too busy worrying about what you're up to."

We walked out of the garage towards the house, followed closely by Hermione. Dad leaned down to stroke her black fur.

"Luna not got up to feed you yet, hey? Come on, let's get some lunch." Dad opened the front door. "Now, who do you think should wake Luna up, you or me?"

"Hmm," I said. Last time Dad made me wake Luna up, I had to participate in her sun-worshipping ritual. It involved drinking nettle tea. And chanting. "Definitely Jasper."

12

ORBIT

I spent the next couple of days worrying if anyone in my class knew about Fat Club, and trying not to think about the *Brainiacs* test on Thursday. Which wasn't easy. Because it was all anyone was talking about. But I hadn't signed up. I could work out simultaneous equations and recite the entire periodic table; I knew facts about every planet in the solar system and could tell you virtually every constellation in the sky. But none of that solved the problem of my size. And it made everything else about me dissolve into nothing.

It was Wednesday morning, and I was in geography, when I noticed Lottie hiding something under her desk. She nudged Alina and laughed extra loudly. Alina didn't laugh, but she looked over at me then whispered something. Usually I'd ignore them, but today I couldn't. It was a gut feeling or intuition or something. Maybe my psychic powers were awakening. Or maybe it was Lottie's ratty sneer that told me whatever she was hiding under her desk had something to do with me.

"Is there something you'd like to share with the class, Lottie? Alina?" Mr Kelly said. "What's so amusing?"

"Nothing, Mr Kelly," Lottie said. "We're just enjoying learning about coastal erosion." Lottie was better at sucking up than my brother.

"Okay," Mr Kelly said suspiciously and went back to writing on the board.

Lottie slipped whatever it was into her bag. It looked like a newspaper. She looked over at me and smiled. Something weird was going on.

"My audition's at lunch," Miki whispered, squeezing my arm.

"Miki, is there something *you'd* like to share with the class?" Mr Kelly said, putting his hands on his hips.

Miki sang, "Only that I'm going to slay the *Mary Poppins* audition today!" He jumped out of his seat and took a bow.

Even Mr Kelly smiled at that. I tried to smile, but the neurons in my brain were too busy trying to figure out why Lottie would hide a newspaper under her desk.

At lunchtime, I walked to the drama studio with Miki, and told him to break a leg. As if he needed any luck.

He twirled his way through the door, singing "Chim chim cher-ee".

I still had Miki's song in my head when it happened. The words "FAT CLUB!" came hurling at me across the playground, like someone had kicked a football at me. It's not just the pain of it. The pain you get used to. It's the embarrassment. And not having anywhere to hide. It's everyone staring because they all heard it too. Like you're the most grotesque thing ever. Or like they feel sorry for you. Or they're waiting for you to say something back. Well, I didn't want to shout anything back because the only thing in my head were lines from Mary Poppins. So, I smiled. Well, I pretended to smile. You can't smile for real when you feel so embarrassed you want to cry.

I caught eyes with Jaz from my maths class, who was standing nearby with her friends.

"Hey, don't worry about it," she said. "My dad always says, 'today's newspapers will be tomorrow's chip papers'!"

I literally had no idea what she was talking about. "Okay, thanks," I said and walked towards the library. I don't know why I didn't figure it out right then. My brain must have been having an off day.

I was sitting at a table in the corner of the library reading my book, when I heard, "Ah, Jemima!" I looked up to see Mr Nelson walking towards me. "I thought you might be in here." He perched on the edge of the table with his foot up on a chair, which you're not allowed to do. Stormtroopers stared up at me from his socks. "I've just taken a look at the list of students signed up for the *Brainiacs* test tomorrow, and your name wasn't on there."

I avoided eye contact, with Mr Nelson and the Stormtroopers.

"Jemima, you are planning on taking the test, aren't you?"

I bit my lip. How could I explain that I wanted to go on *Brainiacs* more than anything, but I didn't want people to see me on TV? And that anyway, Lottie was right – no one else wanted to see me on TV either. But I couldn't tell Mr Nelson that. He wouldn't think it was a genuine problem. He thought a genuine problem was being invaded by the Barbarians. Plus, he wore the same socks as my brother.

"I can't sit the test, sir," I said. "My dad doesn't agree with TV."

"What?"

"Yeah." I nodded. "He's really old-fashioned. He'd prefer me to enter a, erm…" I glanced at the nearest book I could see. *Sewing for Beginners*. "A…sewing competition or something."

"Really?"

"Yeah, my dad's quite, erm, sexist."

Mr Nelson raised his eyebrows. "Oh! Well, I have to say, that is a shock, Jemima. Your father certainly seemed very pleasant when I met him at parents' evening last year. And proud of all your achievements. But we do need his permission." Mr Nelson reached over and picked up *Sewing for Beginners* from the display stand, then looked at me knowingly before putting it back. I sank into my chair. "Well, it's a shame. I mean, I have no idea how good you are at *sewing*, Jemima, but *Brainiacs*? I think you're made for that show. In fact, I'd say you're Clifton Academy's best hope."

And when he said that, a tiny part of me glowed, like a star when it's just beginning to form. I didn't think about my stomach shrinking or my legs undergoing major surgery, or my arms getting infected with a flesh-eating disease. I didn't think about any of that stuff. I looked down at the page of the book I'd been reading about animals' craziest camouflage. And I remembered, for the first time in ages, just for a moment, what it felt like to not want to hide away.

My heart thumped in my chest as I looked up at Mr Nelson. "Is it too late to sign up?"

13

NEURONS

When I got to English that afternoon, Miki was standing in the corridor.

"Hey, you didn't message me," I said. "How did your audition go?" I tried to walk into the classroom but Miki stood in front of the door.

"Sorry, what?" he said, not looking me in the eye properly.

"Your audition! Literally the only thing you've been talking about all week, Miki! How did it go?"

"Oh, yeah. It was good." He fiddled with his fringe.

"*Good?* That's it? Are you feeling okay?"

"Miss Nisha said it was fabulous," he said quickly. "She's putting the list up next week."

"That's awesome!" I said. "So why don't you look

pleased?" I tried to open the classroom door, but he blocked me again. "Miki, what's going on? Why won't you let me go in?"

"I just thought we could wait for Mr Jackson out here instead."

Miki is good at acting. But he's bad at lying. I stood on my tiptoes and peered over his head into the classroom. Caleb was at the front reading a newspaper. It was the *Clifton Echo*. I could hear Lottie's exaggerated laughter. My heart rate rapidly increased. Miki looked down at his feet and mumbled something. Then I heard the unmistakable tapping of shoes down the corridor.

"Jemima Small," Mrs Savage called. Her face was fixed in a smile, like she'd hairsprayed it. She was carrying a newspaper under her arm. "Come with me, dear. Mikio Hurami, go into your classroom, please!" Miki rolled his eyes at me. He hated being called Mikio. He tapped his blazer pocket where he kept his phone, meaning for me to message him, and pushed the classroom door.

Suddenly, Mrs Savage took a gigantic step forward and shouted through the open door, "SIT DOWN, ALL OF YOU!" at approximately two hundred decibels. Miki was standing right next to her, so he got the main blast of it. You should never stand too close to Mrs Savage. It's the same with lions. Dad took me and Jasper to Bristol Zoo once, and the lion's cage had this notice saying *BEWARE, I SPRAY!* Jasper ignored it. He kept banging on the bars, trying to wake the lion up. I didn't because I believe in animal rights. And because I pay attention to signs like that.

Jasper jumped up and shouted, "ROAR!" for about the millionth time. Then, suddenly, the lion stood up and sprayed a huge jet of liquid straight at Jasper. It went all over his clothes and even in his mouth. Dad cleaned him up with paper towels, and Jasper laughed like he was proud of getting drenched by a lion. But only because he hadn't figured out what the liquid jet was. So, I informed him: it was urine. Jasper didn't say a word the whole way home. It was one of the best days of my life.

I followed Mrs Savage as she knocked on the next classroom to get Harry and Heidi out of their lesson, then she led us across the school to an empty room in the history block. Some other people I recognized from the Fat Club meeting in the sports hall last week were sitting down. We all watched Mrs Savage with the newspaper in her hands, waiting for her to speak. Everyone looked kind of embarrassed, even Mrs Savage.

"Now," she said, "you are probably wondering why I've taken you out of lessons. But I want to speak to you now to clear up any confusion. This article has only just been brought to my attention." She unfolded the *Clifton Echo* and held it up.

A girl from our school was on the front page. The one who'd been crying after the meeting. She was standing next to her mum who was holding up a letter.

The headline read:

MOTHER APPALLED AT DAUGHTER RECEIVING "FAT LETTER"

"I don't want any of you to worry about this," Mrs Savage said.

"That's Freya," Heidi whispered behind me. "Her mum rang the paper."

Harry leaned over. "She's refusing to let her do the class."

Mrs Savage smiled directly at Harry. But it was the kind of smile that resembled a loaded gun. "You certainly should not feel in any way ashamed by the letters you received last week. That absolutely was not my intention…"

I looked up at the photo of Freya's mum, and the headline saying she was appalled. She did look extremely appalled. She must have practised loads in the mirror to get it that good. I wish I had an appalled parent. Some people are just born lucky.

"So, if you get any negative comments about the letter, or the Healthy Lifestyle class, or anything related to it, you must report it to me directly at once."

Harry put up his hand. "Miss, some girls in my class were saying stuff to me and Heidi at lunchtime."

"NOT NOW, HARRY!" Mrs Savage bellowed. "I'm in the middle of talking!" She smoothed her hair down at the front. "As I said, this is a serious matter. But, please, don't worry about this article. I will be putting in a complaint to the *Clifton Echo* myself."

Okay, I thought, *stay calm*. So there was an article in the *Clifton Echo* about us. Lottie and Caleb knew about it, and they'd obviously told my whole class. But it wasn't like everyone in the school knew. The *Clifton Echo* wasn't national news. It was only a local newspaper that old people like my nana read.

"And, of course," Mrs Savage carried on, "I will be getting every form teacher to speak to their classes about this first thing tomorrow."

I must have temporarily forgotten that Mrs Savage is evil.

When I went back to English, Lottie kept blowing her cheeks out at me behind her *Pride and Prejudice* book.

Caleb whispered, "What did *your* mum think about the letter, Jemima?" and, "What's it like being famous for being fat?"

Miki told him to shut up, and Mr Jackson warned them about talking during private reading. I sat there staring at the same page of my book, wondering how long it would take for the *Clifton Echo* to be recycled into chip paper.

Maybe you think I could have told Mrs Savage, and Caleb and Lottie would have stopped. But our school doesn't really work like that. Nothing works the way teachers say. Like later in the lesson when Mr Jackson said that humans only use ten per cent of our brains. But that's not true. Virtually all of the human brain is active all the time. Although in Caleb's case I'd have to make an exception.

On the way to the bus after school, a group of Year Elevens went past me. One of them closed his eyes and put his arms out in front of him.

"I can't see!" he shouted. "It's a solar eclipse! Oh no, wait! Fat Club girl's blocking out the sun."

And they were all staring at me so I pretended to laugh.

"You're not funny," Miki shouted over to them, then said quietly, "You okay? I'll beat them up for you if you want." Which made me laugh for real.

"It's okay," I said, swallowing the lump in my throat. "I'm not going to listen to anyone who doesn't know there won't even be a total solar eclipse until 2090."

Miki grinned, and walked towards his bus. I quickly walked to mine, hoping there'd be an empty double seat, and that the tears starting to roll down my cheeks would evaporate before I reached the doors.

All the way home, I thought about the *Brainiacs* test tomorrow and wished with every one of the hundred billion neurons in my brain that I hadn't promised Mr Nelson I'd sign up.

14

EVERYTHING TO DO WITH EVERYTHING

As soon as I got back from school, I knew Dad had seen the *Clifton Echo* article because he had this look in his eyes like he felt sorry for me.

"Nana called," he said, sitting on the sofa. "Sorry, Jem. I can't believe that girl's mum called the paper!"

"Yeah, it's a shame," I said, pulling my library book out of my bag and sitting down. "I was looking forward to doing Gina's class as well."

Dad looked confused. "Jemima, you're still doing the class."

I should have known even the media couldn't change my dad's mind. I did an extra-long sigh. "Dad, why can't you just be appalled about it like Freya's mum?"

Dad rolled his eyes. "I think Freya's mum is appalled

enough for all of us. She's started a Facebook group apparently. Hey, where's Jasper?"

"Mechanics Club," I said. "So, have you joined the Facebook group?"

"Don't be silly. A load of outraged mums? No thanks."

I sighed extra loudly again.

Dad stood up and wandered into the kitchen. "You should do a club like Jasper this year, Jemima. Challenge that brain of yours!"

"I'm already going to Fat Club!" I called back. "Isn't that enough for you?"

Dad poked his head through the bead curtain. "Don't call it that."

"Why not? That's what everyone calls it," I mumbled.

"I mean, like Science Club or something! They do loads at your school. I'm amazed you don't take more of an interest."

"I tried Science Club last year, remember. No one had even heard of an endothermic reaction!"

Dad sighed. "Anyway, I suppose you might have something else to occupy you soon. I got a phone call from Mr Nelson earlier."

I heard the printer going, then Dad poked his head back through the beads. "He asked if there was any reason you hadn't signed up for the *Brainiacs* test tomorrow."

My heart stopped. I still hadn't told Dad about the test. And I'd made Jasper swear on his life not to tell him. Because I knew Dad would force me to enter, the same as Mr Nelson. For a tiny moment I'd thought I could, but the newspaper article had proved I was right the first time. I was already officially too fat for school; I didn't need *Brainiacs* pointing it out to the entire nation. There was no way I could do it.

Dad came into the living room holding whatever it was he'd just printed. It was probably the *Clifton Echo* article. Maybe he was going to stick it on the fridge next to the camping trip letter and all the other things ruining my life.

"I can't believe you didn't tell me!" Dad said. "I mean, *Brainiacs*! We watch it every year! You're so good at it! And now you've got a shot at being on the show."

I shrugged.

"Jemima, you can't have forgotten!"

I fiddled with the plastic cover on my book. "I'm not taking the test, Dad," I said quietly. "I don't want to be on *Brainiacs*."

"Jemima! The amount of times we've all sat on this sofa at Christmas with you answering those impossible questions—"

"It's not that, Dad. I don't want to go on TV. Not... the way I am."

Dad looked at me, confused and disappointed, like I'd given the wrong answer. He sat on the sofa opposite me and rubbed his beard. "I can't believe you feel like this," he said gently. Like I hadn't been telling him for ages.

I rolled my eyes, then put my hands over them in case I started crying.

"You never used to let it bother you. Remember the spelling bee you won! That was in the palladium in front of loads of people!"

"Dad, that was in primary school. And it wasn't on national TV. Anyway, Miss Reed emotionally blackmailed me into doing it."

"I'm just saying, it would be a shame not to enter *Brainiacs* simply because of your weight. Your weight doesn't have anything to do with the competition!"

But Dad was wrong. My weight had everything to do with it. It had everything to do with everything. It was the reason people would probably laugh if I even showed up in the hall to take the test tomorrow. Competitions aren't meant for people like me. Especially not televised ones.

"I don't want to do it, Dad," I said, which was almost a full lie. I would have entered *Brainiacs* in a heartbeat if I wasn't Jemima Big. "Seriously, who'd want to see someone like me on TV?"

Dad took a deep breath and let it out through his nose. "Okay, it's up to you. I can't force you, I suppose." He glanced down at the piece of paper he'd printed out. "Probably for the best. I mean, those kids are seriously smart! You'd need to know things like it was Monet who painted *The Persistence of Memory*; and that Pompeii was destroyed when Mount Etna erupted; and that the cheetah's the fastest creature on the planet; which metal is represented by Xe on the periodic table; and the answer to twenty-five squared divided by four. I mean, who on earth knows any of that stuff, right?"

"Oh my God, Dad," I said, putting my hand on my forehead. "*Salvador Dali* painted *The Persistence of Memory*. Monet wasn't even a surrealist! You should really know that, Dad, considering you went to art college. Pompeii wasn't actually *destroyed*; it was covered in volcanic ash when Mount *Vesuvius* erupted. Mount Etna is on the island of Sicily! And everyone thinks the cheetah is the fastest creature in the world, but it's only the fastest *land animal*. The peregrine falcon can go, like, three times faster. Xe is the symbol for xenon and it's a noble gas, by the way, not a metal." I rolled my eyes. "And twenty-five squared is…625. Then divided by four is…" I closed my eyes and worked it out. "156.25? I think." I pulled out my phone and tapped the sum out on the calculator. "Yep," I said and looked up.

Dad stood up, smiling ridiculously at me.

"What?"

He held up the piece of paper in his hand. It said: *Could you be the next BRAINIACS champion?*

"I printed this off their website. That's where those questions are from. It says if you know the answers, then you should take the test." He looked at me intently, like Luna did whenever she told my fortune. "Who'd want to see someone like you on TV? I would."

My dad could actually be okay sometimes.

15

FIRE

When I got to the hall at lunchtime the next day, there was a line of people standing by the entrance. Two women were sitting behind a desk wearing bright yellow T-shirts that said *Brainiacs!* in a spiky bubble like a comic book explosion. I joined the queue and watched them ticking off names on a clipboard, but I kept noticing my shadow on the wooden floor. I crossed my arms across my stomach and tried to angle my body so it didn't look so big compared to the others.

"What's your name, sweetheart?" one of the women behind the desk asked when it was my turn.

"Jemima Small." I scanned the upside-down list and watched her tick off my name, trying to ignore the bubble of embarrassment that burst in my brain every time I had to say my surname.

"Don't be nervous, Jemima," she said, handing me a lightning-bolt key chain and *Brainiacs* pen. "It doesn't do your brain functioning any good!" She smiled and moved on to the person behind me.

I chose a desk at the back of the hall. It was one of the tiny single ones they used for exams and I couldn't tuck myself in very comfortably. I watched people walking in. Every single one of them was smaller than me. My skin felt hot, like it was going through some kind of thermochemical reaction. I tried to think about what Dad had said about my weight not mattering. But sitting in the hall, watching all the normal-sized people take their seats, I couldn't help feeling like I shouldn't be here.

And that's when the woman in the blue jumpsuit walked in. Her hair was shaved at both sides and she had thick black braids twisted into a plait that sat high on her head. She strode past the desks, jogged up the steps to the stage, flashed a smile at Mrs Savage and then stood up straight. Right at the front. Like she didn't mind about people looking at her. Even though she was big like me.

Mrs Savage handed her a microphone and she didn't put her arm across her stomach, or care that sunlight was streaming through the windows, illuminating her body. It was like she didn't think about it. Didn't notice. Didn't want to hide. She reminded me of the High Priestess from Luna's tarot cards. Massively powerful. Massively proud. And kind of the exact person I needed to see right now.

The High Priestess card means you should trust your gut instincts. I looked down at the paper in front of me. *Brainiacs Qualifying Test: Brain Busters.* My stomach lurched, but a tiny voice inside my gut seemed to say: *Jemima Small, if there's one thing in the entire universe you can do, it's brain busters.*

"Good afternoon, everyone!" the lady in the blue jumpsuit said. "I'm Yolanda, one of the producers of *Brainiacs,* and I'm very happy to see so many of you here today! Everyone applying this year is taking the qualifying test today. The questions are quite tricky, so don't worry if you can't answer all of them. Just do your best. Those of you with the highest scores will be invited to our Selection Day in London in just over five weeks' time." Yolanda nodded at Mrs Savage, who clicked a button. A timer appeared on the screen behind them. "You have thirty minutes to answer fifty questions." The women at the desk stood up and closed the hall doors. Yolanda smiled. "May your brains be with you!"

The timer began counting down. The hall filled with the sound of people opening their test papers, but all I could hear was every second ticking away. Fifty questions.

My hands were shaking as I turned the page and read the first question. A quadratic sequence.

Maybe it was because I loved quadratic sequences. Or maybe it was the sunlight pouring through the windows onto my skin. But suddenly, I felt like I had a fireball in my stomach. Fifty brain busters in thirty minutes. I looked up at the timer. Twenty-nine minutes and fourteen seconds, to be exact. I took a deep breath and picked up my pen.

After the maths questions, there were puzzles made up of crosses and circles and triangles. There were anagrams; 3D shapes you had to match up; questions where you had to pick the right spelling out of a list; periodic table calculations. The last section took me the longest. Not because the questions were hard. Because of the way they were worded: *What's one fifth of one tenth of one half of 600?* The kind of questions that Miki would say give you brain ache.

Once I'd double-checked all my answers, I put my pen down and looked up. Most people were still writing. There were four minutes left on the clock. The time had gone so quickly. For those minutes I was answering the questions, it was like being in the Very Overweight range didn't matter. As though that red cross on the graph representing me was completely irrelevant. Like it didn't even exist.

Mrs Savage caught my eye and smiled. She nudged Yolanda, pointed to something on her clipboard and said something I couldn't make out. Then they both smiled at me. Mrs Savage's smile looked less sinister than usual. I didn't have psychic powers, but somehow I knew what Mrs Savage was thinking. She thought I had a chance of getting through.

As I closed my test paper and wrote my name on the front, I felt happy and terrified at exactly the same time. A bit like when I was younger, when I used to go on the rollercoaster by the pier. You'd hear the slow clack-clack-clack of the cars on the tracks as it took you to the highest point. Well, sitting in the hall after completing the *Brainiacs* test was like sitting in that rollercoaster car. Knowing I'd answered every single question. Almost certain I'd answered them correctly. Feeling like I was on the precipice of being hurtled into the unknown and there was no way of getting off. And it wasn't such a bad feeling, actually.

16

FORTUNE

Luna texted me on the way home from school asking me to see her urgently. She wanted to tell my fortune. I knew because she'd used the crystal ball emoji. I'd just taken the *Brainiacs* test and it was the first Fat Club tomorrow, so maybe Luna telling my fortune was exactly what I needed. A break from reality.

The curtains were closed, and Luna's whole cabin glowed with fairy lights.

"Jemima," she said as I went in. Swirls of gold eyeliner framed her eyes, and coloured jewels were stuck along the tops of her eyebrows. It was like a kind of fortune-teller's uniform. "I can feel a change coming. A feminine energy! I've had a premonition."

Luna had premonitions occasionally. It meant she

could see the future. Not like when meteorologists predict the weather, or seismologists predict earthquakes. Those are based on actual science. Luna's predictions were based on her communicating with Earth goddesses. Which is why I only half-believed them.

A pack of emerald-green tarot cards seemed to appear from nowhere, and Luna began shuffling them. She spread them out in a semicircle on the table and told me to pick five.

I knew the cards couldn't predict my future, or see inside my head or my heart. But that's the thing about Auntie Luna. Sometimes she makes you forget the stuff you've learned in science lessons. I chose my cards and Luna slowly placed them face down in a criss-cross shape, then picked up the card on my left.

"This card is how you see yourself," Luna said, turning it over. "The Ten of Wands."

It had a picture of a woman trapped underneath a stack of wooden sticks, and a dead sheep on the grass next to her.

"Great," I said.

Luna smiled. "This *is* a great card!"

"Luna, it's got a dead sheep on it."

"I mean, it's great that we're seeing it *now*. This card tells me you've got a lot of worries, you're feeling burdened, and it's hard to see a way forward." She tutted a few times. "It also tells me now is not a good time to do the healing ritual I'd planned for you this weekend."

I shook my head. "Shame."

Luna smiled and turned over the next card. "This represents your potential. The Tower."

Maybe the Tower sounds like good potential to you, but this tower had a bolt of lightning striking it, a huge crown falling out of the top window and the whole thing was engulfed in flames.

Luna's steely-blue eyes flashed. "So, this card means your life is—"

"A total disaster?"

"No!" Luna laughed. "This card may look a little... frightening, but it signifies a sudden change – see this bolt of lightning here as a flash of inspiration. The foundations of the tower give way to a new truth. A new knowledge..."

"Right," I said, and stopped listening.

Whichever card you picked, Luna always made it sound good. It's probably why she was so popular at the psychic fairs she went to. I sat up and looked over at my reflection in Luna's dressing-table mirror. No wonder my fortune was a burning tower of disaster and a dead sheep. I looked at Luna's sparkling bracelets and crystals, and little pots of glittery make-up. I wished I could look like her. But if I ever said anything to Luna about feeling ugly or fat, she'd force me to listen to her chime music for hours and put healing stones in my pockets.

She was saying something about order and harmony, when I noticed her gold eyeliner pencil on the floor. It was exactly what I needed. Even if it made me look one per cent better for Fat Club tomorrow, it would be a start. I checked Luna wasn't looking, then slowly reached down and put the eyeliner into my pocket, wondering if Dad would notice if I wore make-up to school. And that's when Luna turned over the next card.

It was a woman sitting in a forest, wearing a long white dress with a crown of gold stars on her head. Her hair was super luminous honey blonde.

"What does it mean?" I asked, but I already knew it was good. An empress with a crown of stars and super luminous honey blonde hair could not, in any way, be bad.

"The Empress." Luna smiled at me. Being smiled at by Luna was a bit like seeing a rainbow. You know it's just a normal thing, but it still feels magical. "The daughter of heaven and earth!" Luna cried, raising her arms and almost knocking over a giant crystal. "The symbol of feminine power!"

I thought, *This has to be good news for eyeliner!*

Luna held my hands tightly in hers. "This card is a

116

good omen, Jemstone. A message from Mother Earth!"

I hoped this didn't mean I'd have to rub scented oils into my skin again. Luna gazed intensely at me, like she could see into my soul. As though she knew how worried I was about starting Gina's class tomorrow, and like she could see the Mum-shaped hole in my heart. As though she understood how badly I wanted to get on *Brainiacs*, and how much I wanted to look like someone else entirely. It was like she could see every brainwave, feel every heartbeat.

"Jemima," she said, keeping her eyes on mine. "A powerful goddess lives within you."

But Luna always said that. I looked down at the Empress card, then back at my reflection in the mirror. *If that's true*, I thought, *then she sure is good at hiding.*

17

LIGHT YEARS

The next morning, it was exactly seventy-three days until NASA would be sending its latest spacecraft through the Martian atmosphere; forty-five days until the "hypothermia is fun!" camping trip; thirty days before I turned thirteen, and zero days until my first Fat Club.

As I got dressed, I pictured crowds of people gathering outside the sports hall at lunchtime, hurling rotten vegetables at us, like they did to criminals in medieval times. Mrs Savage had said Gina's class wasn't a punishment, but getting ready for school that day, it definitely felt like one. And I had to leave the house without Dad seeing my face.

"You feeling okay this morning, Jem?" Dad asked.

"Yep," I said, putting my head as far inside my rucksack as it would go.

"It'll be fine," Dad said, leaning against the banister and slurping his coffee. "Don't worry."

"Thanks, Dad." I closed my bag and noticed a list of equipment I'd need for the school camping trip in Dad's handwriting on the cabinet. I looked closer. I'd be sleeping in a muddy field in the freezing cold in close proximity to Lottie Freeman needing…an *emergency survival whistle*? My life could not get any worse right now. I kept my back to Dad as I pulled on my blazer.

"Jemima's wearing eyeliner," Jasper announced as he walked downstairs.

"Thanks, Jasper," I said and accidentally knocked my rucksack into him as I put it on my shoulder.

"Jemima!" Dad said. "You know the school rules about make-up. You'd better go and wash it off. Quickly."

I had no intention of washing it off. Everyone would be talking about Fat Club today. Everyone would be looking at me. I had to look a tiny bit better than normal. Or one per cent less grotesque. "Dad, everyone at school wears make-up."

"I don't," Jasper said, and Dad raised his eyebrows at me like he'd proved me wrong.

"Jemima, you're only twelve. You don't need to wear make-up. And certainly not to school."

"*Only twelve?* I'm almost thirteen. Which is old enough

to make decisions about my own face. Anyway, eyeliner is cheaper than facial surgery."

Dad sighed. "Jemima, you don't need facial surgery and you're absolutely not wearing make-up to school. That's the end of it. You look perfectly all right as you are."

Parents are supposed to think their children are beautiful. My dad thought I looked "all right". I examined my face in my phone camera and sighed until I didn't have any air left in my lungs.

Jasper boasted about his latest magic trick as he did his shoes up. "It's so cool, Dad. I can turn water into ice in front of your very eyes!" Jasper did his weird magic hand movement thing and Dad said, "Wow!" He made it so obvious Jasper was his favourite.

"Turning water into ice isn't magic, Jasper," I said. "It's physics."

"Right," Jasper snorted. "And can physics transform water into ice in a matter of seconds?"

"Yes, if you use frozen carbon dioxide."

Jasper rolled his eyes. "Well, can physics do this?"

Suddenly, my phone vanished out of my hand and reappeared in one of Dad's trainers. It's a magician thing. Or maybe it's just a Jasper thing.

"Gross, Jasper," I said, grabbing a tissue from the front pocket of my rucksack and wiping my phone.

Tissues were an essential item around my brother. And antibacterial hand gel.

"If you've quite finished, you can wash that make-up off, please," Dad said.

"Make-up is a form of self-expression, Dad. If you don't let me fully express myself, you could do permanent damage to my identity."

Dad took a deep breath. "I haven't got time for this, Jemima. I'm starting a big job at that new hotel this morning. Just go and wash it off. Now."

I thought about everyone at school laughing at me and my heart started pounding like it was about to crack my ribcage open. "Fine. Forget about me ever fitting in with normal society, Dad," I said. "I'll be a freak show like they had in the 1800s. *Take a Look! The Freak of Clifton-on-Sea! The girl not allowed to wear a TINY bit of eyeliner even though she's practically an adult!*"

Jasper laughed and said, "Drama queen." Like performing your own magic shows isn't dramatic.

Then Dad laughed as well. "Don't knock those freak shows, Jemima!" he said. "Some of our ancestors made a lot of money at those shows. The Small family were known far and wide for Auntie Lilian's talking beard."

Jasper snorted again.

"This family is so weird," I said.

"I'm serious!" Dad said. "It could tell your fortune! In fact, I bet there's a photo in that old tin I found in the garage. Now, where did I put it?" Dad opened the cabinet drawer.

"Great. So thanks to your genetics, Dad, I'll probably grow a beard."

Dad looked at Jasper and they exchanged this smile, like they had a special conspiracy about how ugly I was or something. That's why I said it. Because I felt like the odd one out. And because tears were starting to sting my eyes.

"I wish Mum was here. She'd let me wear eyeliner. She wouldn't make me live in this oppressive regime."

Dad screwed up his lips.

I braced myself for *SMALL FAMILY ARMAGEDDON: DAD'S STRESS LEVELS GO NUCLEAR!*

But he said, "Actually, your mum never really wore make-up."

I should have stopped talking then. But my heart was beating really fast and my cheeks were hot, and I felt like any minute my tears might escape. My mouth just kept going. Like that fortune-telling robot on the pier called Zenor, whose mouth keeps moving after your money's run out. "Maybe Mum didn't wear make-up when she was married to you, but she probably does now. You wouldn't know because you don't even know where she is!

No wonder she decided to…*escape* this family." I regretted it as soon as I said it. I wished I could pick the words up and put them back in my mouth. But it was too late.

"Right, that's enough, Jemima!" Dad shouted, slamming the cabinet door closed so the glasses in the cupboard clinked together. "You've gone too far now. Go upstairs and come back down when you've learned some manners and respect!"

Jasper muttered, "She'll be up there a long time." Dad glared at him and he added, "Sorry."

"Fine!" I said, sniffing my tears back. "I get to miss school then." I swished round extra dramatically, only one of the straps from my rucksack got caught on the bottom of the banister and it took about ten seconds to get it free.

"For goodness' sake, Jemima!" Dad said, and I ran upstairs. When I reached the top he shouted, "You've got three minutes!"

I shouted down, "No one can learn manners and respect in three minutes!" I quickly went into the bathroom and locked the door as hot tears spilled onto my cheeks. I splashed my face with cold water and rubbed my eyes, leaving gold-brown glittery streaks on a cream-coloured towel that Dad would probably tell me off about later.

I wanted to go downstairs and say sorry, but that feeling I'd had when I sat the *Brainiacs* test yesterday, when I had that fireball in my stomach, had been extinguished. I couldn't feel even the tiniest ember.

Out of the window, the clouds looked distorted through the patterned glass. I knew the stars were beyond them. But no matter how many times I wished for my first Fat Club to be okay, I also knew that they were just burning spheres of gas, completely indifferent to my wishes. Sometimes, knowing stuff about space could be intensely annoying.

18

FAT CLUB

"**J**emima!" Lottie whispered for the millionth time in our French lesson. "Are you free at lunchtime? Oh no, sorry, I forgot, you've got Fat Club!" Which she accompanied with a fake sad face. "Don't feel bad. I'm sure when the teacher sees you she'll...make you captain!"

I sighed. Sitting within two metres of Lottie Freeman should be considered a breach of your human rights.

"Leave her alone, Lottie," Miki said. "You should go to Zero Personality Club."

"Oh, don't say that Miki!" Lottie said. "Not when we're starring in the production together!" She smirked at him.

"What?" Miki said.

"Didn't you go to the drama studio at break? Miss Nisha's put the list up. You got Bert!"

"I GOT BERT?" Miki shouted. "Oh my God!"

"Quieten down, Miki!" Mr Picard said. "And if you have to speak, at least try to do it in French."

"Brilliant!" I whispered.

Mr Picard stared at me so I put on a French accent and said, "I mean, *Brilliant!*"

He rolled his eyes. Like it was my fault the word "brilliant" is the same in French. He turned around and went back to helping Caleb, who was deliberately just speaking English words with a French accent.

"By the way, I got Mary Poppins!" Lottie whispered sweetly over the desk, deliberately making eye contact with me. "So, Bert, I guess we're best friends!"

Miki looked at me, then back at Lottie. "Only in the production, Lottie." He whispered in my ear, "Lucky I'm good at acting."

Lottie narrowed her eyes. "Shame you can't be in the production as well, Jemima. But, I guess you've got other priorities."

I couldn't think of anything to say back to her, so I turned the page of my textbook and started copying out some verb phrases. What could I say? Lottie was technically speaking the truth. Anyway, Dad had already banned me from swearing in foreign languages.

Miki drew a rat in the corner of my page. "Hey," he

whispered. "Don't listen to Lottie. Everyone knows she's ninety-nine per cent rodent."

When I got to the sports hall at lunchtime, nerves flooded my body as though they were attached to my blood cells. There were some boys kicking a football against the outside wall, and a group of Year Tens were standing around a bench opposite, looking at their phones. A few people watched as I walked up the path to the entrance. I flinched, expecting someone to shout something, but one of the PE teachers appeared and started doing keep-ups with the boys' football. I put my hand on the sports hall door, took a deep breath, and pushed it open.

The first thing I saw was a flash of super luminous honey blonde hair. It was swept back with a black headband covered in white stars. The Empress card I'd picked from Luna's tarot pack last night came into my mind. I closed the door behind me and she turned around. It was Gina Grantley-Bond. Her black sports leggings were covered in little lightning bolts, exactly like the ones on the Tower card. I started to feel a bit weird. Luna's premonitions were usually wildly inaccurate.

"Welcome!" Gina said with an extraordinarily wide smile. "Jemima?"

I nodded and her smile went even wider, until it covered approximately seventy per cent of her face. If she smiled any harder she'd probably get a facial injury. I didn't understand why she was so pleased about running Fat Club. Maybe she liked humiliating people.

"I'm Gina! Come in!"

Heidi, Harry and Brandon were putting out chairs in a circle. I recognized two others from the meeting we'd had about the newspaper article. They looked like they were in Year Ten or Eleven.

"You're the last one," Gina said. "Sit down!"

"The last one?" I said. "But there's only six of us."

Gina's smile dropped by about thirty per cent. "I'm afraid this is it." She looked around awkwardly as Brandon stacked some of the chairs back up. "Some of the parents read the article in the newspaper, you see, and they started a group. They made it seem like my class was…well, most people didn't agree to their children taking part." Gina suddenly clapped her hands like she was breaking a spell. "Anyway! The main thing is that you're all here! And I am so excited to start my healthy lifestyle programme with you!" She clapped again and smiled the biggest smile I'd ever seen. It radiated from her, as though her skin was made of pure smile, nothing else. Like a real live goddess was beaming right at me.

It was annoying. Because it made it really hard not to like her.

Gina explained how we weren't there as a punishment. Which was sort of a lie, because it was lunchtime so it was technically a detention. But I made a mature decision not to say anything. Mainly because that morning before I'd left the house, Dad had confiscated the eyeliner and given me strict instructions not to mention any of the following during Gina's class, or I'd be cleaning his van tomorrow:

1. Punishments (including medieval torture techniques).
2. My human rights.
3. Exaggerations or lies.
4. Anything Luna had ever told me.

It didn't exactly leave much to talk about. Apart from my dad being a tyrant dictator.

Gina said we mustn't feel like we'd done anything wrong. But that was exactly what the class felt like, so I only half-believed her. "Now, let's start by playing a little game to get to know each other!"

I'm not psychic, but I'd had a feeling she would do something like this. I sank into my chair.

"Tell us your name and something totally *awe*some

129

about yourself! I'll start. I'm Gina and I used to be a Paralympic coach!"

I wondered what had gone wrong in her life that she used to be a Paralympic coach and now she had to teach at Clifton Academy.

She looked down at her clipboard. "Where's Nathaniel Jackson? As you're in Year Eleven, let's start with you."

The boy sitting opposite Gina lifted his hand. "Hi, it's Nate."

"Okay! Tell us something totally *awe*some about yourself, Nate!"

I looked at the row of pin badges on the lapel of Nate's blazer. There was an Eco Council badge, a Prefect pin, a photography club pin, a tiny flag of Nigeria, and one at the bottom just saying *Legend*. He had loads of things to choose from.

"Well," Nate said, "I met Jesse Lingard over the summer."

"Wow!" Gina said at exactly the same time as everyone else.

I made a mental note to find out who Jesse Lingard was after the class. By the time Gina got to me, I'd learned that the girl in Year Ten, Maya, had just passed her Grade Four flute, Harry had read ten books over the summer holidays, Heidi had started writing a book called *The*

Souls of the Forest, and was already on chapter nine. And Brandon Taylor was Year Ten's unofficial arm-wrestling champion.

So when Gina said my name, I couldn't think of anything.

"Oh, come on, Jemima!" Gina said. "I'm sure there are lots of *awe*some things about you!"

"I don't know," I said. The only thing coming into my mind was the spelling bee I'd won in Year Five, which sounded stupid.

Gina's face dropped, like she was actually upset I wasn't joining in.

Don't feel sorry for Gina, I told myself. *She's the reason this stupid class was invented.*

"Didn't you win the Science Award last year, Jemima?" Heidi said. "And the Maths Prize?"

"Yeah, and the Reading Challenge!" Harry added. "She beat me by two books!"

Gina beamed at them. "Thank you, Heidi and Harry. Wow, Jemima! That sounds pretty *awe*some to me!"

I felt my cheeks glow pink. "Oh yeah." It's weird how people can list your achievements and you still feel like an idiot.

"Fantastic! Thank you, everyone!" Gina said, clapping herself. "What a totally *awe*some game!" She should probably check the definition of the word "awesome". And "game". "I'm so excited to start working with you all!" Everything Gina said ended in an exclamation mark. My English teacher, Mr Jackson, was always telling us you shouldn't do that. "So, my programme is designed to help you live your healthiest life…"

Gina started going on about all the things she would be teaching us this term. I stopped listening, and looked down at the lines marking out the basketball courts. They reminded me of last year. When I would stare at them while everyone else got picked before me. As if the whole team would lose if it had me on it. That's what people assume when your PE kit says XL on the label.

They don't care that you begged your dad for new trainers with a special grip pattern on the soles because you wanted to make an extra effort in PE at secondary school. They don't care you've had a basketball hoop up in your drive since for ever and that you're actually pretty accurate at shooting. They don't know it's the only sport you enjoy. All they see is you stepping backwards, and telling Ms Newton you don't feel well, so you don't have to see their disappointed faces when you end up on their team. Then you sit on the bench with your hoodie up and try not to watch the game. Try not to care. Because why try to win for a team that didn't want you in the first place?

"So!" Gina was saying. "I thought it would be nice for us to have a little picnic and get to know each other in this first class!"

We looked at Gina in silence as she stood up and dragged a cool box into the middle of the circle. She handed out paper plates and forks then started taking out little containers.

"Come on, everyone! Tuck in!"

But no one moved. It was a weird feeling, a bit like whenever Jasper was nice to me. I could never be sure if he was secretly planning something bad.

Like this time ages ago when he said he'd got me a present. He made me close my eyes and hold out my hands. Only when I opened them his pet tarantula, Tornado, was about to crawl up my arm. I froze. It was the first time I'd ever held a tarantula. Jasper told me later that it was a good thing I did freeze, because he'd found out that tarantulas can die from being dropped. Luckily for Tornado, I already knew that. They have a really fragile exoskeleton. So, Jasper's stupid trick to scare me backfired. I froze because I also knew that tarantulas are a nervous species. And when they're nervous, they flick their bum hairs at you.

I looked around the circle. No one was eating.

"Okay," Gina said. "Let me show you what I've got,

and maybe you can all just try a little bit." She picked up a box and said proudly, "This is quinoa! I don't suppose you've heard of it, but it's—"

"Edible seeds from a herbaceous plant," I said, kind of by accident. "The ancient civilizations of South America used to eat it and…" I stopped because everyone in the circle was staring at me. "My auntie's a vegan," I explained. "You have to eat stuff like that when you're a vegan." I didn't tell them about the UN declaring 2013 the International Year of Quinoa, or that quinoa has been into outer space because astronauts take it on long voyages because it keeps for ages. I'd already learned from my "show and tell" presentation last year that people are not interested in the history of quinoa.

"That's brilliant, Jemima!" Gina beamed. "And quinoa is very low in fat and high in essential minerals like iron, potassium, calcium and magnesium, so it's—"

"Like eating the periodic table," Nate said.

"Sort of!" Gina laughed. "But it's delicious!" She went round the circle scooping some onto our plates.

Harry raised it to his nose and sniffed. Gina brought out more boxes of food and piled more onto our plates until we had lentil salad, vegetables, black beans, super grain spirals, spinach mini muffins and crisps made out of beetroot. It was like having lunch with Willy Wonka. If Willy Wonka had a vegetable patch instead of a chocolate factory.

While Gina told us about the class, and promised we wouldn't be running laps around the field, I swallowed a forkful of lentils. They actually tasted okay, like the type of stuff Luna cooked. Jasper called it fart food. I made sure I didn't eat too much. The last thing I needed on the first day of Fat Club was flatulence.

"As it's such a small group," Gina said, "maybe you'd like to share how you felt about being selected for my class."

"Selected?" Maya said. "*Selected* makes it sound good. People get selected for sports teams. Being selected for a class because you're fat isn't good."

Gina looked at Maya sympathetically, but she didn't say anything. Probably because there wasn't anything she could say. Maya was right. Being selected for Gina's class was so bad it made front page news.

"My mum's gone mad about it," Maya carried on. "She said I have to lose weight in this class or we might not go on holiday next year." Maya's mum sounded worse than my dad. I didn't think that was even possible.

"We wanted to be in the Christmas production," Harry said. "But our mum said this was more important."

"Yeah," Heidi said, putting her empty plate on the floor. "She doesn't want us to end up like her. She's got… bad knees."

Gina's eyes looked sad and her smile had completely disappeared.

Brandon shrugged. "My mum says there's more of me to love!"

I hated Brandon, but I couldn't help smiling. It was probably the type of thing my mum would say if she'd stuck around. Like the exact opposite of anything my dad said.

"Jemima?" Gina said. "What did your mum say?"

And I wanted to bury my head in the tub of quinoa. Brandon looked at me. He was probably the only one who knew about my mum. He was still friends with Jasper when she left.

"Jemima lives with her dad," Brandon said. He smiled at me, which was extremely weird considering the number of times he'd called me "Cowpat" at primary school.

"I'm sorry, Jemima!" Gina said.

I shook my head like it didn't matter.

"So, what did your dad say?"

I put my fork down and thought for a minute. But whenever someone mentioned my mum unexpectedly, that empty bit in my heart hurt. And it was hard to think properly. So I said, "My dad is basically a dictator, so he grounded me and confiscated some of my belongings."

"What?" Gina said, her eyes widening. "Because of this class?"

"Yeah, I had to clean out his garage and everything. He said the physical labour would do me good." It wasn't completely untrue.

"Oh my goodness!" Gina said. Everyone stared at me like I'd won first prize for Fat Club's Worst Parent.

I shrugged. "It's just what my dad's like."

Brandon gave me a weird look, but what did he know? He hadn't seen my dad for years. He could easily have turned into a dictator since then.

"I'm sorry to hear that, Jemima," Gina said. "I'm sorry to hear what you've all said. Those letters weren't supposed to get you into trouble. Quite the opposite. The aim of the class is to empower you, all of you, to make good decisions about your life and your body. I truly believe the key to doing that is appreciating how *amazing* you are. I've worked with all kinds of people, with all kinds of different bodies, from world-class athletes to primary-school children. And I've never failed once. Never. Maybe, right now, you're feeling like you've failed. But, I promise, after a few weeks, you'll be feeling stronger and healthier and happier than ever before." Then she clapped her hands. "That's the GGB effect!" She stood up and pointed to the back of her T-shirt. "See?" It had a picture of the British flag and the Olympic logo on it. Underneath it said *Team GGB* in black letters.

"It's spelled wrong, Gina," I said. "It's supposed to be GB for Great Britain."

"Ha!" she said. "No, it's GGB! Gina Grantley-Bond! You're on my team now!" She smiled another gigantic smile.

And no matter how hard I tried, it was literally impossible not to smile too. It was like she'd cast a magic spell over us, making it seem normal to have your own initials printed on the back of your T-shirt.

"Oh! I almost forgot!" She picked up a metal flask and poured a dark-green liquid into paper cups. "I'll also be teaching you about different types of nutritious drinks, including plant milks."

Brandon scratched his head. "Plant milks? How do you milk a plant?"

Gina stared at him and blinked a few times. "Why don't you have a look on YouTube later, Brandon? Now, this small cup of wheatgrass juice will do wonders for your body and mind! And, not only that, it tastes delicious!"

I held mine up to the light. It looked like pond water. If Gina's drink gave me dysentery, I would definitely sue the school. Gina tipped her head back and gulped it down in one.

"Delicious! Wheatgrass is one of the most nutritional

liquids on the planet. It will give you an immediate sense of well-being."

I watched Maya and Heidi eyeing their cups suspiciously. I peered into mine. Could a cup of wheatgrass really make me feel better about myself? I took a deep breath and poured the whole cup down my throat.

Immediately, a memory popped into my mind – when Dad took me and Jasper to this city farm ages ago and Brandon and Alina came with us. We all had a go at milking this gigantic cow with huge, swollen udders. It was terrifying. And unhygienic. Brandon kept pushing me until I was squashed up right next to it. Suddenly, the cow stepped sideways and there was this loud, squelching noise. The next thing I knew, my legs were covered in cowpat. I could feel its disgusting warmth absorbing into my socks. I cried for the rest of the day and made Dad clean my wellies off with a hose. Brandon called me "Cowpat" almost every day at primary school after that. I remembered the cow's hot grassy breath, the saliva dripping from its mouth, and the stench of fresh manure on my feet.

That was exactly what Gina's wheatgrass drink tasted like. Like being breathed and pooed on simultaneously by a cow.

Brandon held his cup to his lips. "What's it taste like, Jemima?"

I looked at him for a moment, then smiled my best smile. I tried to get it to exactly seventy per cent of my face. Just like Gina's. Then I said, "Delicious!"

19

GREAT-GREAT-
AUNTIE LILIAN

Obviously, I went home that day and lied to Dad about what happened in Gina's class. There was no point in being forced to do Fat Club if I couldn't get some sympathy about it.

"She made you do laps of the hockey pitch?" Dad asked, wide-eyed. "How many?"

"Thirty!" I said. I knew it sounded like a lot. The perimeter of the school hockey pitch must be about three hundred metres. Which meant I'd just told my dad that Gina made us run over five and a half miles. I looked at Dad's face. I was pretty sure he had no idea. Anyway, he'd never feel sorry for me unless the class was extremely bad.

"Thirty! My God!" He shook his head in horror.

It was going so well, I thought maybe if I carried on, he'd stop me doing Gina's class altogether. Then I could watch Miki's rehearsals on Friday lunchtimes like a normal person.

"And she made us lift weights!" I said. "And do press-ups."

"All in one lunchtime?" Dad tutted. "I'm amazed you're still standing!" The tiniest hint of a smile flickered in the corner of his mouth. I needed to make it sound a lot worse.

"My legs are kind of aching." I rubbed my calf muscles. "It was like a boot camp. She didn't let us have a break, or any water."

Dad's mouth dropped open. "No."

"I told you the class was illegal, Dad. You should have listened to me."

"Yeah, maybe I should have. The class definitely breached your human rights, I'd say."

"I know!" I smiled. My dad actually agreed with me about human rights for once! Or maybe he was just being extra nice because he'd shouted at me this morning. "It's a miracle I'm not in hospital with dehydration." I took off my rucksack and collapsed onto the sofa, trying to look as dehydrated as possible. "I did warn you about Gina, Dad. But it's okay. You can just send Mrs Savage an email saying you don't want me to do the class any more and we can both just forget about it."

Dad smiled. "It sounds—"

"Torturous!" I said, putting my feet up. "Just like I knew it would be."

"*Torturous*, exactly!" Dad said, leaning forward. "In fact, even a prisoner wouldn't be subjected to that sort of treatment. And, what with you being grounded because of the class, and forced to clear out the garage, and your belongings confiscated, that must make it even worse." Dad leaned back and folded his arms.

My heart sank. I should have known his sympathy wasn't genuine. He raised his eyebrows like he was expecting an explanation. But I didn't say anything. It's called the right to remain silent.

"That's right, Jemima. You see, Gina phoned me after the class."

"What?" I sighed extra loudly. "School will literally be FaceTiming you soon."

"And what was it Gina said to me? Oh yes, she was concerned about you being in so much trouble over the class."

I screwed up my face. "I seriously don't know where she got that from."

Dad took a deep breath. "She got it from you telling

her, Jemima. She said you made me out to be some sort of tyrant!"

"Well, she's lying."

He sighed full volume. "Right, an ex-coach of the Paralympic team of Great Britain is lying."

I thought for a moment. "She could also be lying about that."

"Jemima!" Dad shook his head about a million times, then his shoulders started shaking with laughter. He walked over and rubbed my head. "Oh, what am I going to do with you, hey?" He was in an extremely good mood. Which was extremely weird. "Anyway, I had a good chat with Gina! She seems great! She said you did really well today!" I eyed him suspiciously. "Listen, I'm sorry about shouting this morning. I should have known you were just worried about the class. Oh, and the eyeliner thing." Dad held out his hand and Luna's gold eyeliner dropped onto my lap. "If you want to wear a bit of make-up now and again – not to school, and not that I think you need to – then that's okay by me." He must have had a lobotomy at work or something.

"Thanks, Dad!" I said, picking up the eyeliner pencil. "Guess I'd better ask Luna if I can borrow it then."

Dad rolled his eyes. "Jemima! Yes, you'd better!"

"How come you changed your mind?"

"Let's just say that Gina Grantley-Bond might share some of your thoughts on self-expression. And that reminds me…" Dad pulled an old photograph out of his pocket and handed it to me. "That was taken in 1908."

And there she was. My Great-Great-Auntie Lilian, the famous fortune-teller. She was wearing a huge dress with flowers around the collar, like an old-fashioned nightie. She was staring into the camera with stone-cold eyes, dark hair piled high on her head, and a full beard.

I peered closer. "That's stuck on!"

"Not according to your nana. Anyway, we're seeing her tomorrow so you can ask her about it."

"Great, so I inherited Mum's brains and Great-Great-Auntie Lilian's body type." I felt my chin. "Maybe I should start shaving."

Dad laughed and headed into the kitchen. "You know, Jemima, your Auntie Lilian was widely celebrated in her lifetime. She was an astute businesswoman and toured the country with that fortune-telling beard. I think she had something like twenty proposals of marriage!" He stuck his head through the bead curtain. "She was a smart, strong woman, and you could do a lot worse than having her blood running through your veins."

"Not her blood, Dad," I called. "That's not how genetics work!" I studied the photo of Auntie Lilian.

Her dark eyes seemed to pierce right into my soul. "But," I said to myself, "maybe I got some of her DNA."

The next day we went to visit Nana Small. She lives in this special village for old people about ten miles outside Clifton-on-Sea. It's called Pacific Heights. It's approximately eight thousand miles away from the Pacific Ocean, but Dad said the developers probably thought the English Channel Heights didn't have the same ring to it. Everyone who lives there has grey hair apart from my nana. Hers is platinum blonde. It sits in a huge bun right on the top of her head. She always wears sunglasses, even in winter, has a tattoo on her wrist of a hand with an eye in the centre, and some of her back teeth are made out of gold.

When we arrived, Nana said she wanted some fresh air, so I helped her into her wheelchair and tucked a blanket around her. Dad pushed her through the courtyard and over the little bridge by the lake. We stopped at her favourite spot, next to the weeping willow trees. Nana said the leaves were turning brown, which signified a time for reflection and calm. I said it signified their chlorophyll breaking down, but Dad gave me The Look so I stopped talking.

Jasper circled the lake with this tiny putt-putt boat

he'd made from an old Coke can. He'd called me Auntie Lilian approximately fifty times that morning, and said he could see stubble growing on my chin. I watched him light the candle on the boat and carefully place it on the water. I secretly hoped it would sink. I sat on the bench next to Nana's chair and took out the old tin of photos from my bag.

"Goodness me!" Nana said. "Wherever did you find these?"

"Dad forced me to clear out the garage because of an accident."

Nana tutted. "He's worse than your grandfather."

I opened the tin and placed it on her lap. She picked up a photo of her mum, my great-grandmother. She had the biggest hair I'd ever seen, like she'd walked head first into a beehive.

Nana looked at it for a minute, then held it to her heart. "Oh dear, old age sends you daft!" she said, wiping her eyes with a hankie. "Now, your dad said you took a special exam for a TV show!"

"Yeah, *Brainiacs*. I'll find out if I've qualified for the Selection Day soon. We watched it last Christmas, remember?"

Nana thought for a moment. "Is that the one with the nice lady who picks the letters?"

I smiled. "No, Nana. That's *Countdown*."

"Oh, maybe I was resting my eyes when *Brainiacs* was on," she said.

Actually, I did kind of remember her snoring through the maths round.

We looked at the old photos as Jasper watched his boat sail across the lake and Dad stood on the bridge half watching, half looking at his phone.

"Now, will you look at her!" Nana said, picking up a photo.

I looked closely. It was my Great-Great-Auntie Lilian, minus the beard. I recognized the stony eyes. "See, Dad! Auntie Lilian's beard was stuck on!"

"Oh, no, love," Nana said. "That's not Lilian. That's her twin sister, Mabel."

I looked at Nana.

"I'm telling the truth, young lady!"

I forgot Nana was a professional mind-reader. "So, Auntie Mabel didn't have a fortune-telling beard as well then?" I asked.

"Oh no," Nana said, popping a soft mint in her mouth. "Mabel was a bare-knuckle fighter."

Dad stood on the bridge, typing on his phone, while Nana told tales of my great-great-aunts that were stranger than anything I'd read in a fiction book.

"Oh, look at this, Orion! One from your birthday! You look just like Jasper. Thank goodness you both grew into your ears!"

And Jasper looked so annoyed, I had to try really hard not to laugh.

"Thanks!" Dad walked over and peered at the photo in Nana's hand. "Looks like you cut my hair that year too. God, look at the size of that cake!" He tutted and dropped the photo back in the tin. "It's almost time to start thinking about your birthday, Jemima! I expect you can tell us precisely how many days it is until you become… a stroppy teenager!"

"Very funny," I said. "Twenty-nine."

Dad sat down and squeezed my shoulders. "Exciting times, hey? Turning thirteen, this brilliant new class with Gina—"

I folded my arms. "Not the adjective I'd use."

"And I'm sure you'll get through to the next round of *Brainiacs*."

"Yeah, well, maybe it wouldn't be so bad if I didn't."

"Why ever do you say that, love?" Nana asked, leaning over the photos to look directly into my eyes. It was a mind-reading thing. Like your eyeballs had to be practically touching hers before she'd believe a word you said.

I shrugged. It was impossible to lie to my nana, but it

was impossible to tell her the truth sometimes too.

Jasper shouted from the far edge of the lake, "She thinks she's too fat for TV!"

"Jasper!" Dad shouted back. "What were we talking about just this morning?"

So, now I knew they'd been secretly talking about me.

"I wasn't *calling* her fat."

"Oh, sweetheart," Nana said, squeezing my arm. "Have a soft mint."

That day, I thought being in a family where no one understood how you felt was the worst thing that could happen to you. But it's not. Some things hurt even worse than that.

20

WEIGHTLESS

On Monday in form, Mr Nelson reminded us about the camping trip, and read out a list of people who still needed to bring their permission slips back, even though it was still six weeks away. I put my hand up and asked how it was legal for us to sleep outside in tents in late October. He told me I was welcome to come back at lunchtime and read the school's 250-page health and safety policy document that explained the answer. Miki giggled as I shook my head.

Then Mr Nelson showed us pictures of the camping site. It looked like the set from a horror film. Afzal made a joke about werewolves, and Lottie asked innocently about Bigfoot. Mr Nelson told her it was American folklore, then Lottie looked directly at me and slowly mouthed, "Bigfoot."

Maybe it was getting compared to a mythical ape-like creature that inhabits the forests of North America, but I spent the rest of the day hoping I'd break my leg over half-term so I wouldn't have to camp with Lottie Freeman.

For the rest of the week, if people weren't talking about Camp Go Wild! and how funny it would be to capsize into freezing water, like they'd never heard of hypothermia, they were talking about *Brainiacs*. People who took the test had attached the lightning-bolt key chains to their pencil cases or bags and used their special yellow pens in class. I kept mine in my pencil case. Miki distracted me by singing *Mary Poppins* songs, and every lunchtime we went through his lines. By the end of the week, I knew his part so well I could probably have auditioned to be his understudy.

On Friday morning, Erin sat next to me in maths, talking about how hard the *Brainiacs* questions were, and playing clips of last year's show on her phone before Mrs Lee arrived.

"It would be so cool to be on it!" Erin said. "Apparently, Mrs Savage is going to announce who's got through in assembly on Monday! I can't wait! I've got no chance. I couldn't even answer half the questions. But everyone's saying you'll get through, Jem. You get full marks in everything!"

But I felt sick thinking about it. I dreaded the idea of standing up in Lower School assembly, so how could I stand up in front of hundreds of brainy strangers at the Selection Day? Or millions on national TV? I wished they recorded *Brainiacs* on the radio instead.

As I walked into the sports hall that lunchtime, Gina was dragging a mat from a pile in the corner. She greeted me with a gargantuan smile.

"I hope you're ready for a relaxing class!"

"We're doing a meditation," Brandon said as I put my bag down.

I'd heard of meditation from Auntie Luna. It helps clear your mind and restore your energy levels. And sometimes it makes you fall asleep. Last time I meditated with Luna, I was so bored I practised my twenty-six times tables. It wasn't really meditation, more like homework.

I helped Gina pull a green mat into a space near Heidi's and lay down with my arms by my sides.

"First, I would like you to breathe," Gina said.

I rolled my eyes. Like I wasn't already doing that.

"Take a really deep breath in, and out. Put your hands on your tummy and fill it up as big as it will go!"

I wanted to tell Gina it's your diaphragm that fills up with air, not your tummy, but you're not allowed to talk during meditation. I could hear Heidi slowly breathing in and out. She had her eyes closed and her belly was going up and down. I looked the other way and saw Brandon's feet twitching. One of his toes was poking out of a hole in his sock. The only good thing about Gina's class was being about the same size as everyone else. For once, I didn't worry about how far my belly stuck out, or how much space I took up.

"Just relax, Jemima," Gina said. "Close your eyes."

I took a deep breath and covered my eyes with my hands. "Imagine you are lying on a soft cloud…"

I tried to ignore Gina's voice and do my fifty-three times tables, but it was impossible. Gina's got this soothing kind of voice. I wished humans had a way of closing our ears, like crocodiles.

"You are floating on a cloud…"

I imagined a cumulus cloud. They'd probably be the comfiest. I took a deep breath and let my hands fall down by my sides.

"You can feel a warm and gentle breeze, and sunlight on your face. Let every part of your body completely relax into the cloud. You feel at peace. You feel at ease. You feel comfortable in your body…"

I don't know what happened next exactly. Gina must have the psychic gift like Luna and my nana. Because I was lying on a mat in the sports hall, in a body that usually felt heavier than Jupiter. But it felt like I was floating. Past the clouds, right up to the edge of Earth's atmosphere, to the Karman line, where space begins. I felt like I was bathing in sunlight. And every single cell in my body felt peaceful, like it was supposed to be there. Like it was okay.

Gina counted us back down to Earth, and I sat up. I rubbed my eyes to keep them open. She said meditation restored your energy, but it made me want to nap.

"Now," Gina said. "I have some homework for you."

Brandon groaned, then apologized as soon as Gina looked at him.

"Firstly, I'd like you to take a thirty-minute walk. Get some fresh air! Go with a friend or family member if you like, maybe along the seafront. Everyone think they can do that?"

I nodded and pulled my homework planner out of my rucksack.

"And secondly" – Gina handed each of us a small, red notebook – "over the next week, any negative thoughts you have about your body, I want you to write them down in here."

"Like a list?" Maya asked, writing her name in big

swirly letters on the front of her notebook.

"Yes, a list or a diary. It's up to you. If you hear any negative comments about your body, I want you to write those down too."

I flicked through the blank pages of my notebook, wondering if there'd be enough space.

"But won't that just make us feel worse?" Nate asked. "Writing down all the bad stuff you think?"

"I hope it's going to make you feel better." Gina smiled. "Trust me."

Maya stood up. "Well, I'll start with all the stuff my mum says!" She was laughing, but that way you laugh when you really want to cry.

"Like what, Maya?" Gina asked.

Maya sat down again and her bag dropped to the floor. "She's put us both on this diet. We're only allowed to eat green leaves and raw vegetables. And when I say I'm hungry she makes me this special drink and tells me to concentrate on what I want to look like."

Gina's eyes widened. "Right, maybe she misunderstood when I spoke to her last week. I'll give her a call this afternoon, okay? Now listen, I want to make this very clear: nobody here should be on a diet. Diets go against everything I believe in. And besides, who wants to eat only green leaves and raw vegetables?"

"A tortoise?" I said.

"Exactly!" Gina's smile stretched back to the usual seventy per cent of her face. "You must be absolutely starving." She went over to a table by the wall. "Look, everyone, this class is about having a *healthy* lifestyle. There is nothing healthy about cutting out vital food groups! Here." She picked up a big tub and pulled off the lid to reveal chocolate brownies. "Help yourselves! A little treat from GGB for being such an *awe*some group!"

"Thanks, Gina!" Brandon said, taking a brownie in each hand. He bit into one and said, "Mmm mmm!" then stuffed the rest into his mouth.

I took a bite from mine. It was okay, but it didn't taste that chocolatey. There was something a bit grainy about it too. Maybe Gina didn't mix the ingredients up very well. I could feel bits of it getting stuck in my teeth.

"We all deserve a treat once in a while!" Gina said, taking a brownie for herself. "I mean, who doesn't like sweet potato?"

21

THE LIGHTHOUSE

That weekend, Miki was staying at his dad's in London, so on Sunday I put the notebook from Gina and my *Brainiacs* pen in my coat pocket, started my phone timer, and headed towards the sea.

I stepped out onto the promenade and walked uphill towards the lighthouse. I went past the brightly coloured beach huts, the harbour where the steamboat pulled in to pick up tourists, a little row of shops, then up the concrete steps that were always covered in pebbles. I pulled my phone out of my pocket and pressed stop on the timer. Thirty-eight minutes. I wiped the seat of the bench behind me and sat down. If I took the same time walking back, I'd have done 153 per cent more walking than Gina told us to do. Dad couldn't say I wasn't making an effort now. I was probably her best student.

It wasn't like I didn't already have loads of homework. I was doing an extension project on light refraction and dispersion for Mr Shaw, and Mrs Lee had given me some A level algebra questions to try as well as the regular ones. Gina's homework was only writing thoughts and things down. And she'd given us a whole week. It should have been easy. But it felt harder than everything else. I stared down at the empty page, feeling like anything I wrote would sound stupid.

I pulled out my phone and messaged Heidi:

Hey, started your notebook hw yet for GGB?

Heidi replied:

Yeah 🙁 started it when I got home on Friday.

A few minutes later my phone beeped and a photo popped up. It was Heidi's list. Although it looked more like an essay. As I started reading, this horrible feeling spread from my stomach to my heart.

1. A Year Nine boy said "Shut up, fatty" to me on the bus and I wasn't even talking to him.

2. Harry's friend said "Woah, don't squash me!" when the bus went round a corner. I don't know if it counts because he said it to Harry, but it still made me feel bad. His friends always say stuff to him and it feels like they

mean it about me too, even though Harry says they don't.

3. It was my cousin's birthday party last weekend and when it was time for the cake, my uncle looked at my mum as though he didn't think I should have any. It was really awkward so I said I wasn't hungry. I felt left out and embarrassed and wished I could go home.

4. As we were leaving my uncle said, "Next time we see you two, I hope we don't recognize you!" That just made me want to cry.

5. My gran texted saying she was proud of me for not having cake at the party and she'll give me a pound for every pound of weight I lose. My mum said she was just trying to encourage me, but I feel like she thinks there's something badly wrong with me and that she's not proud of me the way I am.

I blinked a few times, and the breeze blew one of my tears across my face. Words out loud are just sound vibrations that travel through the air. Bits of energy that eventually run out. Like someone shouting, "Earthquake!" at you across a car park. Words written down are permanent. You can't just act like you didn't hear or pretend they don't exist. And the worst thing about reading Heidi's list was: I knew exactly how much it hurt.

I wiped another tear from my eye, and put my pen to

the paper. It wasn't difficult knowing what to write. It was knowing where to start.

When I got home, I could hear hammering coming from the garage, so Dad must have been in there. I went straight upstairs to my room, pulled my cardigan off and closed the door. I don't know how long I stayed like that. Sitting against the door with my cardigan at my feet. But I think it was a long time. I heard Jasper practising his magic show about a hundred times. Writing that list up by the lighthouse was a stupid idea. I'd walked all the way home with my head down, so no one would see the tears that kept falling down my cheeks.

I heard Dad come in, and Jasper running downstairs. I dried my eyes on my sleeve and looked at my phone. A message from Heidi was on the screen.

Hey, my cousin just sent me this. It's a JK Rowling quote:
Is fat really the worst thing a human being can be?
Is fat worse than vindictive, jealous, shallow, vain, boring or cruel?
☺

They were only words on a screen. But they felt like magic. Maybe because JK Rowling said them. Or because

Jasper's magic show music was still playing in the background. Or maybe it was having a friend like Heidi who understood what the stuff in my notebook felt like. Luna had told me ages ago about this feeling she gets sometimes while she's telling someone's fortune. She says it makes her soul smile. Well, I still hadn't exactly located my soul, but wherever it was, I could feel it smiling.

My phone flashed Heidi's name again and there was the *Brainiacs* lightning bolt logo.

Fingers crossed for you tomorrow xHx

My eyes went kind of blurry again as I looked down at my legs squashed against the carpet. I thought about school tomorrow. Mrs Savage would be announcing who'd made it through to the Selection Day in assembly. What would happen if she did call my name? I'd have to stand up at the front. People would gawp at me. Or maybe laugh. They'd probably wonder how somebody like me could be clever enough for *Brainiacs*, or why I'd even put myself forward.

But still, there was a tiny part of me – maybe only one of the 37.2 trillion cells in my body – hoping she would call my name. And that if she did, maybe I wouldn't feel like the worst thing a human being could be.

22

A THOUSAND THOUGHTS

The next morning, Mrs Savage was standing at the front of the assembly hall with her finger over her lips, waiting for complete silence. I was sitting in the middle of a row, with my feet on tiptoes and my thighs pressed together so my legs didn't squash into Miki or Erin too much. I knew Miki wouldn't care, and Erin had never said anything bad to me. I guess it had just become a habit. Trying to take up less space.

"Good morning, Lower School!" Mrs Savage's voice echoed around the hall. "I have a very special announcement this morning! It's the news you have all been waiting for! Has anyone from Clifton Academy qualified for the next stage of the *Brainiacs* competition?"

A murmur went round the hall and Miki squeezed my arm. "You got this."

My heart was beating so fast it felt like it was about to explode through my chest. Which in assembly would be totally embarrassing.

"Places at the *Brainiacs* Selection Day are reserved for people who scored the very highest percentage on the qualifying test." A smile stretched across Mrs Savage's face. "So, without further ado, I am very excited to announce that *three* of our brilliant Clifton Academy students are on the list!"

Everyone broke into applause and Mrs Savage had to wait for ages for it to go quiet again. I took deep breaths and rubbed my sweating palms on my skirt.

"Our three students will join over two hundred others from all over the country to take part in a special day of mental challenges in London, in just four weeks' time. Only one student from each school can get through to the show, so, not only will our three students be competing against other schools, they will also be competing against each other! We shall, of course, be rooting for all of them! So, who are they?"

The hall buzzed with excitement and Miki squeezed my arm even harder. My heart pounded against my ribs. I wanted to hear my name, but my cheeks were already burning at the thought of standing up in front of everybody.

"If I call your name, come to the front so we can give you a special Clifton Academy cheer!" Mrs Savage waved at the IT person. "We'll need a photograph for the school website!"

My palms were still sweaty even though I'd wiped them loads of times. If Mrs Savage called my name, I knew someone would whisper "Big". I knew I'd see people's eyes going from my head down to my feet, like when I collected my certificates and prizes at the end of last year. As though they were judging every kilogram. They say you can never know people's thoughts, but you can. You just look at their faces, and you can hear them. A thousand voices all saying the same thing: *Jemima Big*.

"Jemima Small!"

People started clapping and everything seemed to slow down, like I'd fallen into a space-time vortex. My stomach dropped and my head was spinning and Miki had to practically push me out of my seat. I carefully made my way to the end of the narrow row, trying my best not to tread on people's feet or bump into their legs, which was impossible. I could feel my cheeks burning bright red, and my heart thundered with fear, and my hands were shaking, but somewhere, deep down, there was the tiniest fizz of excitement.

But, a few minutes later, as I stood onstage next to the other two people who had qualified, I didn't feel happy or excited or proud like Mrs Savage was saying I should. I barely listened to her talking about the extra studying we'd be doing after school, or telling me to stand up straight for the photograph. I didn't even care what people in the audience were thinking.

Because standing right next to me, grinning like she'd just won the Nobel prize, was Lottie Rat Face Freeman.

When I got home, Dad was waxing a surfboard on the kitchen table.

"Hey," I said, and he practically jumped out of his skin.

"Jemima!" he said, putting his hand to his chest. "I didn't hear you come in! Is that the time already?"

"What are you doing?"

"Thought I might go for a surf at the weekend!" he said. "Haven't been in years! What with our health kick and considering the weather's still pretty mild, I thought we could go to Dolphin Bay. See if I've still got the moves, you know?" He bent his knees and pretended to do what I assume was supposed to be surfing. "Where's Jasper?"

"He got a different bus. Said he needed something for his magic show from that Hocus Pocus shop on the pier.

He said he'd messaged you. Is surfing a good idea at your age?"

Dad stopped waxing, picked up his phone, then looked at me. "What do you mean 'at my age'? I'm only forty-six! It's hardly ancient."

"Oh my God, Dad, FORTY-SIX? You're practically geriatric. It's probably why you're in a stress all the time."

"Jemima, I am not geriatric. Your nana's geriatric. And I'm not in a stress all the time either, thank you very much! Which is a miracle, considering." He leaned the surfboard against the wall, washed his hands then took a watermelon that was the size of a beach ball out of the fridge. "Gina suggested trying some different fruit and veg this week, so…"

"Gina?" I said. "You spoke to her again?" I put the cloth back on the table and placed the newly filled fruit bowl in the centre.

Dad's cheeks turned pink. "I just wanted some advice, you know."

I stared at him. "*You* phoned *her*?"

"She said to phone if I had any questions!" Dad smiled awkwardly. "I just want to get this right."

"Okay, well first of all stop phoning my teachers." He handed me a plate with two tiny slices of watermelon on it. "And second, don't starve me to death."

"Ha! Right, no, of course. Sorry. Here." He sliced another tiny piece of watermelon and handed it to me.

"Thanks," I said, sitting down. "Watermelon is ninety-two per cent water, you know."

"Who's starving to death?" Jasper appeared through the bead curtain. His uniform still looked as immaculate as it had this morning. He must secretly iron his clothes at school or something.

"Dad's trying to starve me to death," I said, pointing to my plate.

"Jemima, that's the last thing I'm trying to do." Dad handed Jasper a plate with two tiny slices of watermelon on it. Maybe watermelon was just really expensive.

"It'll take a long time," Jasper whispered, then whistled as he spotted the surfboard. "Hey, you got your board out!"

"Dad, did you hear that? Jasper called me fat."

"I didn't."

Dad sighed. "Jasper, we've had this conversation so many times. Leave your sister alone. She's at a sensitive age."

"*You're* at a sensitive age," I mumbled.

Dad gave me a tight-lipped smile. Like he was covering up how much of a stress he was in because he'd only just claimed he never got in a stress. "Yeah, I thought we could

168

go to the beach at the weekend." He lowered his voice. "Just go easy on your sister, okay?"

"Sure, Dad," Jasper said, in full suck-up mode. He sat down opposite me, reached his hand out to mine and patted it. "I'm sorry, sister."

"Good!" Dad said. "Now, can we all just sit nicely and eat this watermelon together like a normal family?"

"I got one hundred per cent in my French test today, Dad," Jasper said, raising his eyebrows at me. "Mr Picard thinks I could take my GCSE at the end of this year if I want."

"Wow, Jasper! Very good! Or should I say *très bien*?"

Jasper laughed really loudly and for ages. I waited for him to blurt out about me qualifying for *Brainiacs* and make a sarcastic remark, but he carried on talking about his major French achievements as though passing a test on conjugated verbs made him Napoleon or something. Then I realized. Mrs Savage must have only made the announcement about *Brainiacs* in Lower School assembly. Jasper had no idea I'd qualified.

When he'd finally finished talking I said, "Well done, brother. That is a remarkable achievement," and reached across the table and patted his hand. "By the way, I just got through to the Selection Day of the popular TV show, *Brainiacs*."

Dad almost choked on his watermelon. "Jemima! That's fantastic!" He jumped up, gave me a massive hug, then shouted to Luna to come inside. He grabbed his iPad and moved his chair right next to mine as he looked up the *Brainiacs* website to see what the Selection Day would be like. He booked train tickets for us, saying how brilliantly I'd done and how I didn't have to do any chores while I revised for it, and said how proud he was exactly sixteen times.

Jasper stared at me over his plate of half-eaten watermelon. Like he was suddenly figuring out he wasn't the smartest person in our family. Even though I'd been telling him that for ages.

23

A BILLION YEARS AGO

The next day at school, I couldn't stop yawning. I'd stayed up late timing myself doing equations. Getting through to the *Brainiacs* Selection Day was amazing, but also like getting loads of extra homework.

Miki and I had been working on a presentation for the last few lessons in geography. I loved researching stuff, but I hated presenting in class. When you look like me it's not just your presentation slides people stare at. Everyone had chosen a "geographically interesting" place to present. It could be anywhere in the world, provided it was on the list of geographically interesting places Mr Kelly had put on the board. We picked Lake Superior. It's this really old lake that stretches across Canada and North America where over six thousand ships have sunk. I thought it sounded interesting, which was good because Mr Kelly didn't let us pick until last and it was the only place left.

I researched on the iPad while Miki drew a perfect bird's eye view of the lake for our poster. He added rocks, fishing boats, salmon, birds of prey, a lighthouse, and even a shipwreck at the bottom. Mr Kelly made him rub out the mermaids.

"I'm so excited you're going to be on *Brainiacs*!" Miki said, gluing triangles of blue paper to the picture so they looked like shark fins.

"It's only the Selection Day," I said. "I probably won't get through to the actual show."

"Probably won't get through *the door* you mean," Lottie whispered, snatching the glue from our table and scurrying back to her desk.

"Oh my God, you *have* to beat Rat Face," Miki said. He stopped drawing and his eyes lit up. "But, just in case you don't…I've had an idea."

"What?" He grinned at me. "Miki, don't do anything to get in trouble. Not because of Lottie."

"I won't! Now, were you serious about me drawing a sea serpent, because Mr Kelly did *not* like my mermaids."

I nodded. "According to legend, or in this case Wikipedia, an ancient spirit animal called Mishipeshu lives in Lake Superior. Like the Loch Ness Monster, basically. Only scarier. Look." I turned the iPad round to show Miki a dark-blue serpent with the face of a lynx. It had pointed teeth, huge red spikes on its back and long, twisted, copper horns.

"Mishi-whaaat?" Miki said, wide-eyed. "It's Lottie on a good day." He picked up a blue pencil. "If Mr Kelly doesn't think our presentation is amazing, then there's something wrong with him."

We practised the presentation during lunchtimes that week, and I spent every evening studying difficult-to-spell words, scientific discoveries, philosophers, poets. I even found out that three per cent of the ice in Antarctica glaciers is actually frozen penguin urine. I didn't think that question would come up on the *Brainiacs* Selection Day, but that's what happens when you click on a link Jasper sends you.

On the day of our presentation, Miki was even more excited than usual, but my palms were sweating before the bell even rang. The only good thing was our poster ended up so massive, I could almost hide behind it. When Mr Kelly called us up, Miki whispered, "Channel the spirit of Mishipoop." And weirdly, trying not to laugh was a good way of calming my nerves.

My hands were shaking a little bit at the beginning, but once I started talking about how the lake began forming over a billion years ago, it seemed like my class was actually interested in the size of Lake Superior, not me. Apart from Lottie, who sat there blowing her cheeks out.

"Excellent presentation!" Mr Kelly said as we took a bow at the end (Miki's idea). "One of the best so far! Can I just ask, what's that?" He pointed to the fold-out piece of paper attached to the poster.

"Oh, I forgot," I said, opening it up. "This is what Lake Superior looks like from space."

Mr Kelly smiled. "Of course, thank you, Jemima. Now, Alina's away today so, Lottie, do you want to wait until next lesson?"

Lottie immediately sprang out of her seat. "No. I can do it by myself."

I pulled my chair out to sit down just as Lottie was trying to walk past.

She waited and whispered, "Biggest lake in the world by the biggest girl in the world."

My chest felt tight as I sat down. Mostly because it was stupid. Lake Superior is only the biggest *freshwater* lake. The Caspian Sea is almost five times bigger. Lottie didn't know what she was talking about.

I whispered to Miki, "I really hope she loses at the Selection Day."

Miki smiled. "Don't worry. She'll lose way before then!"

Lottie waited until everyone was quiet then she took her hand out of her blazer pocket, did a twirl and tossed gold glitter into the air.

A few people said, "Wow!"

Mr Kelly said, "You'll have to clean that up at the end."

"My presentation is about the Cave of the Crystals in Mexico," Lottie said. "Or should I say, *La Cueva de los Cristales!*"

I had to try so hard not to roll my eyes.

Lottie explained the different chambers inside the cave, and how some of the crystals were eleven metres long. It actually did sound pretty interesting. Auntie Luna would definitely like it. And her friend Jupiter. He could get some new crystals for his shop. Lottie started talking about the largest crystal ever discovered, when suddenly there was this noise. Like a really loud fart. Lottie's cheeks went bright red and everyone started laughing.

Caleb called out, "She's fired a stink rocket!"

Mr Kelly told him to be quiet and Lottie carried on talking. Then, about thirty seconds later, she farted again. And again.

Caleb shouted, "Lottie FARTman!" and the whole class erupted into hysterics.

Mr Kelly stood up and warned us to quieten down or

he'd set a whole class detention. I couldn't help laughing a bit, but I still felt sorry for Lottie. It can't be easy to describe the metamorphic process of crystals when you have chronic wind.

She rushed through the rest of her lines, then farted again as she did a curtsy at the end. "It's not me!" she shouted over everyone's laughter. "SHUT UP, everyone!"

"Best not be in my tent when we go camping!" Caleb shouted. "Lottie FARTman!"

"That's your last warning!" Mr Kelly said and everyone went silent. "Now, Lottie, do you need to go to the toilet?"

And everyone laughed again even harder.

At the end of the lesson, Miki said he'd dropped something when we were doing our presentation, so I waited for him outside.

"Hurry up, Miki!" I called into the classroom. "We'll be late for French!"

"Got it!" he said and ran over to me. In his hand was a small, rectangular box, and some kind of remote control with red buttons. He checked no one was listening, then a gigantic smile spread across his face as he said, "Fart machine."

24

EVOLUTION

It was Friday lunchtime, a week since Gina had asked us to write our lists, and she was sticking a huge piece of paper to the sports hall wall. Her white trainers had glittery ticks on them and she was smiling as usual. I held my notebook on my lap and tried to ignore the fluttering in my stomach.

"So," Gina said, "who managed their thirty-minute walk?"

Everyone raised their hands.

"Well done! And keep your hand up if you enjoyed it!"

I was the only person who put my hand down, so I sighed and put it back up again.

Nate said he'd played five-a-side football after school

on Tuesday, and Maya said she'd done a yoga DVD with her mum.

Gina cried, "Fantastic!" and practically exploded with excitement about it. "So, we'll do the same homework for next week. Thirty minutes of light exercise. A walk again, or something else you enjoy. Now, before we start looking at your notebooks, I want to remind you that what we say in here is completely confidential. I'm sure we can all trust each other, right?" Gina beamed out a smile equivalent to the energy magnitude of the sun. "Would anyone like to go first?" She looked hopefully around the semicircle of faces. "Anyone?"

The last thing I wanted to do was share my list of humiliations with Gina. Every atom in my body was telling me not to put up my hand. But she looked kind of disappointed. And so far she didn't seem *completely* deranged. I raised my hand.

"Jemima! Thank you!" Gina clapped, and signalled for the others to join in. Gina held her pen against the paper on the wall and said, "Ready when you are." Her eyes sparkled, like they contained the entire Andromeda Galaxy.

I took a deep breath. "Fat, obviously," I said, feeling stupid I'd even written that one down. "Whale. Grotesque. Jemima Big." I looked up at Gina writing them on the sheet of paper. "People saying, go on a diet. Saying I've got diabetes, that I'll cause an earthquake. I'm blocking out the sun. I'm gross. I'm the biggest girl in the world." I carried on reading until I got to the last thing on my list. "And...not wanting to do the *Brainiacs* Selection Day because there's going to be two hundred and fifty people there. Plus everyone's parents, and they'll probably be thinking all the things that I've just said." I closed my notebook. "That's it."

Gina's eyes had tears at the edges. I didn't look at anybody else. Because so did mine.

"That's awful, Jemima. I'm so sorry you heard all of this. Well done for sharing."

Brandon put his hand up. "I'll go next. People don't say that much to me at school."

Nate snorted. We all know Brandon was a bigger bully than anyone who said anything to us.

"But I wrote down 'people staring at me' and my grandad's nickname for me is 'chunk'. I know it's not as bad."

"If it makes you feel bad, Brandon," Gina said, "then it's bad."

"And this kid in my class who told me to take off the fat suit," Brandon said. "That's why I got suspended."

Gina's eyes widened. "He said that and *you* got suspended?"

Brandon smiled. "I reacted badly."

After Brandon, it was Nate's turn, then Maya, then Heidi and Harry, and by the time we'd all read out our lists, the piece of paper was so full Gina had to squeeze the last words down the side. It was hard to even look at it.

"Okay," Gina said, clearing her throat. "You've all been incredibly brave sharing all of this. I found it hard to listen to, and it wasn't even being said about me. Look at these words. Take a good look. None of this is true."

"You think we're lying?" Brandon said.

"No, Brandon. I know you're not lying. But the words written on this paper do not in any way represent the truth about you. About any of you. None of these words describe the kind, determined, fun, clever, brave, *awe*some individuals I see sitting here. The last thing you should do with these words is believe them."

Gina told us to visualize the words disappearing into the sky. And said to let go of the shame attached to them too. She said if you imagine people's negative words vanishing, it helps the pain disappear too. But it wasn't that easy. I could memorize a whole pack of fifty-two cards and the entire periodic table. Those words inside my notebook were permanently stuck in the medial temporal lobe of my brain, like they'd been superglued. And no amount of imagining would get rid of them.

"So, from now on, any time you hear anything like this," Gina said, "I want you to say something good about yourself out loud, like: I was kind to someone in class, or I listened to my friend, or I worked hard today or I'm *awe*some! Imagine their insult is an arrow and the positive thought is your shield. Each time you have a positive thought about yourself, that shield gets bigger and stronger. Now," she said, pulling the piece of paper off the wall, "let's tear up these words!"

We all watched as she tore the paper up and handed us each a piece.

"That's right! Tear them up! And your notebooks."

Brandon laughed and ripped his bit of paper in half, then tore the cover off his notebook.

Heidi whispered, "Is she for real?"

"I hope so." I ripped the pages out of my notebook and tore them into pieces.

By the time we'd finished, the floor was covered in little bits of paper, like insult confetti.

"Ordinarily, I would set fire to these," Gina said, sweeping the pieces into the bin. "However, Mrs Savage wouldn't agree to that. The sports hall has a highly sensitive fire alarm system, apparently. So this bin will have to do! Let's imagine they have been burned up, replaced with all the good things you know about yourself."

And as we threw the last pieces in the bin, Gina recited all the "*awe*some" stuff we'd told her about ourselves in that first class. She must have a really good memory.

It was nice listening to everyone's good stuff again. But if anyone believed those negative words had vanished because they were in the bin, they were wrong. Even if Gina had burned them, they'd have turned into carbon particles and water vapour, so they'd still technically exist. Stuff can change into something else, but it can't disappear completely.

I put my rucksack on my shoulders and pushed open the double doors, squinting in the bright sunlight. I knew those words hadn't vanished, but my rucksack felt kind of lighter without them. I just wished that all my good qualities weren't on the inside. If only it was the opposite way round. It would be so much better to have kind arms, or intelligent legs, or a loyal torso, or hair with a good sense of humour. Why did our good qualities have to be so invisible to everybody? Human evolution had a major design flaw.

25

COPPER ALLOY

In science that afternoon, Mr Shaw was demonstrating photosynthesis using a torch, a pot plant and a mini watering can when the school receptionist knocked on the door.

"Do you have Lottie Freeman and Jemima Small in here?" She held out two bright-yellow A4 envelopes. "A special delivery from *Brainiacs*! I thought you might want them for the weekend. I expect you've got some revising to do!"

"Yes, yes!" Mr Shaw said. "Wonderful! Come up here, girls!"

Immediately my heart sank. Standing at the front of the class was bad enough, but standing next to Lottie, who weighs approximately five thousand per cent less than me, was mortifying. I slid off my stool and stood as close to Mr Shaw's desk as I could, feeling it digging into my side.

"Congratulations!" Mr Shaw said, indicating to everyone to give us a round of applause.

Miki whooped and cheered from behind his textbook.

"May I wish you every success! You've still got a few weeks to revise, I take it."

"Yes, Mr Shaw. May I wish you every success too, Jemima!" Lottie said loudly, then whispered as we went to sit down, "Hopefully you won't embarrass the school by getting through."

I tried to do what Gina said, and think of something positive about myself to shield Lottie's insult arrow. But all I could think of was that I already understood photosynthesis. And that made kind of a weak shield.

At the end of the lesson, as everyone was tidying equipment away, Miki whispered, "Hey, my mum just sent me this. Look, you're on the school website." He handed me his phone.

It was the picture they took in assembly on Monday. I was standing in between Lottie and Noah Chamberlain, the boy from Year Seven who'd got through. Mrs Savage was smiling proudly behind us. I felt sick looking at it. I zoomed in on Lottie's body, then on her hair wrapped into a perfect bun. If Mrs Savage could pick someone to represent our school on *Brainiacs*, she'd choose Lottie. No offence to Noah Chamberlain, but he wasn't even smiling. Not that I was any better. What people said about me was so bad it had to be thrown in the bin.

"Hey, *read* it!" Miki said, nudging me.

I zoomed out of Lottie's image and scrolled down.

Former Clifton County Spelling Bee Champion and current holder of the Clifton Academy Lower School Science Award and Maths Prize, our Year Eight student Jemima Small (Form 8N) will certainly make for some tough competition! Mr Nelson, Head of History, believes Jemima will be "difficult to defeat".

I took a deep breath because my eyes had gone blurry with tears and I did not want to make a scene in a science lesson again this term.

I gave Miki his phone back and said, "Thanks." From the outside, I was tidying the equipment away like everyone else. But on the inside, my heart felt as though it was being given a healthy dose of water and sunlight.

I thought back to what Mr Nelson had said to me that day in the library. How he'd phoned my dad to make sure

I took the *Brainiacs* test. Mr Nelson believed I could make it onto the show. But more than that – it was like he actually *wanted* me to. As I collected the textbooks from our bench, I noticed Lottie sitting down while Alina and the rest of her group tidied away. And I thought that, unless Mr Nelson was completely deranged (which was actually possible considering the Yoda impression he'd done in form that morning), he didn't think I'd be an embarrassment to the school at all.

That weekend, I was in my bedroom trying to memorize sixty cards in a row, when Heidi messaged me:

Take a break from studying! You heard of her?

I tapped the link and YouTube opened. A woman with bright orange hair and tattoos all the way down her arms appeared on the screen. Her body was big, much bigger than mine. And Heidi's and Maya's. She was called Tabitha Hendrix and she used the words *fat* and *big* as if they weren't bad. Like they were just the same as *strong*, *tall*, *loud*, *pretty*. Her flame-coloured bikini matched her hair and she showed off her body to the camera, pointing out bumps and dimples and rolls like she was proud of them. Like she didn't care about me seeing. I scrolled down. *490K views!* Like she didn't care about *anyone* seeing.

And I could see why. She didn't look too big. Or like she'd cause an earthquake. Or like she'd block out the sun. Her skin glittered, as though it was made out of sun particles. She looked like Eos, the Goddess of the Dawn. Like someone who could be on the cover of a magazine. Or a TV show.

I looked in the mirror and scooped my hair to one side. I didn't look like Tabitha Hendrix. Definitely not in grey leggings and the periodic table hoodie Jasper got me for my birthday last year. It uses the symbols for nitrogen, erbium, and dysprosium to spell out *NErDy*. I wore it to school on non-uniform day last year. Which was the day I figured out it's not a good idea to wear clothes with science jokes on them to school. I spent the entire day explaining what it meant. And how you can't spell the word *fat* using chemical symbols. Alina stopped hanging around with me after that. But I still like the hoodie. It's the best thing Jasper has ever got me. Last Christmas he got me a phone case shaped like a giant cockroach. Taking that to school didn't exactly boost my popularity either.

I didn't look like a YouTuber. And I definitely didn't want half a million people seeing me in my swimsuit. But when I looked in the mirror that night, something felt different. Because for the first time in the entire history of the universe, I didn't see just the bad stuff.

I took Luna's eyeliner from my desk drawer and started writing straight onto my mirror. Mr Nelson told us ages ago about a Roman army that had used copper alloy to strengthen their shields before they went into battle. It has a high resistance to corrosion.

Well, when I looked at myself in the mirror next to the quote from Mr Nelson, it felt like I'd just made my first piece of copper alloy.

Jemima Small: difficult to defeat

26

DESTINY

It was the first week in October and I stayed behind after school for some extra maths practice with Mrs Lee, because the *Brainiacs* Selection Day was only three weeks away. It would have been okay, if Lottie hadn't been there too. Any time Mrs Lee was explaining something, she filled one of her cheeks with air, and moved it from one side of her mouth to the other, like a lopsided guinea pig. It made it really hard not to smile when she messed up easy questions like 189 x 48.

It wasn't cold, but it started raining on the way home and I didn't have my coat, so I was soaked by the time I got to my house. When I walked in, I shook the rain off my blazer and noticed Jasper standing in the living room wearing a cape.

"Doesn't he look fantastic?" Luna beamed. "It's Grandad's old cape!" She snipped a thread from the hem and stood back to take a look. "There. Good as new."

Luna is amazing at making clothes. She doesn't like shopping on the internet and the only clothes that shops in Clifton-on-Sea sell are old-lady clothes. Even my nana doesn't want to dress like an old lady and she is one.

"Thanks, Luna!" Jasper said, admiring himself in the mirror. He balanced on one foot, practising his levitating trick, and almost knocked Dad over as he came in.

Luna spotted me trying not to laugh. "Jasper's following in the long line of magicians and psychics in our family. Your brother is bravely following his destiny."

I will always feel grateful it wasn't my destiny to wear our dead grandad's cape.

Luna looked like she had read my mind.

"It looks great, Jasper, very…mystical," I said quickly and sat on the sofa. Luna sat next to me and linked her arm through mine.

"Okay, I'm ready." Jasper tapped his phone and his magic music blasted out of the speakers. "Dad!"

"Right!" Dad cupped his hands around his mouth so his words amplified around the living room. "May I welcome to the stage, the UNBELIEVABLE—"

"Incredible!" Jasper whispered.

"Right, sorry. The INCREDIBLE illusionist, Jaspeeeeeer Smaaaaaall!"

"Diamond!"

"What?" Dad's hands fell away. "Diamond?"

I felt Luna squirm. Her surname's Diamond. It's Uncle Alfie's name. She didn't want to change it back to Small even though Alfie left her broken-hearted and emptied her bank account. That's how bad our surname is.

"Sorry, Luna," Jasper said. "Jasper Diamond just sounds better. I'll change it if you want."

"No, don't be silly! It's fine." Luna caught Dad's eye. For a second they looked like they were communicating telepathically. "It's *fine*. Jasper Diamond sounds... incredible! Let's see some magic, shall we?" She patted the sofa and Dad sat down.

Jasper spun round and the purple cape flew out behind him. He wasn't the Amazing Apollo, but it did look kind of incredible. He slowly pulled a gold handkerchief out of his pocket. I leaned back in my seat. I'd seen this trick a million times. Jasper wove the handkerchief between his fingers and threw it up into the air. I waited for it to disappear. But suddenly, it transformed into a ball of flames. I couldn't believe my eyes. Jasper's trick was actually good. He must have been doing a lot of practising.

"JASPER!" Dad shouted, springing from the sofa.

He started wafting out the flames with his bare hands, but they had already disappeared. Then the smoke alarm went off. "What on EARTH were you thinking?" Dad shouted, opening the living room windows and waving a tea towel under the smoke alarm.

Jasper stopped the music and laughed. "It's magic, Dad! See? It turns into this." He held out a shiny gold ball.

"Burning the house down is not magic, Jasper!"

I pressed my lips together to stop laughing. Jasper tried to explain to Dad that the giant ball of flames we'd all just witnessed was not a fire hazard. It did not go well.

"Right. Show's over!" Dad said.

Jasper pulled off Grandad's cape and started putting away his equipment.

"And if you've got that blasted tarantula down here, take it upstairs! Now!"

"Oh, lighten up, Rion!" Luna said. "There's no harm done. That trick was genius! Jasper needs some encouragement." She fixed her steely eyes on Dad. "If he wants his own show one day, then he has to practise!"

"Thanks, Luna," Jasper said, putting a large axe into a box.

I suddenly felt relieved he'd started with the ball of flames.

"He doesn't want his own magic show!" Dad turned

to Jasper. "Do you? In the palladium? Like your grandad?"

"No, Dad." Jasper said. "I want my own YouTube channel."

Luna squealed and kissed Jasper's face, leaving a glittery kiss mark. "That is a brilliant idea."

Dad stood on a chair and checked the ceiling for singe marks. "Great! So it will all be under my roof. Wonderful. I suppose I'd better invest in a fire extinguisher." He got down and noticed the axe poking out of Jasper's box. "And a more comprehensive first-aid kit."

"Next time, maybe do your show in the garden," Luna said, patting Dad's shoulder. "To keep your dad's stress levels under control."

Dad let out a long breath. "Okay, well, we won't need to wrap up warm, what with Jasper setting fire to us!"

Jasper laughed really loudly. Clearly on a code-red level suck-up after getting told off.

Luna tapped an app on her phone. "Oh, perfect! Look, it's a full moon next Sunday. Your birthday, Jemima! Jasper could do his show."

"Okay," Jasper said. "I've got loads of tricks even more impressive than that."

"Great," Dad said. "I'll notify the ambulance crews."

"We could go to that pizza place by the lighthouse," Luna said. "Your treat, right, Rion?"

193

Dad sighed. "Fine. You only get to be thirteen once, I suppose."

"Thanks, Dad!" I grabbed my phone. "Okay if Miki comes?"

"Yes, why not? It can also be a celebration of you being super brainy. It's only a week after that we'll be in London!" He ruffled my hair, then Jasper's. "If Jasper doesn't incinerate us."

"I'll make you a new dress for your birthday, if you like?" Luna took my hand, pulled me through the bead curtain into the kitchen and picked up Dad's iPad. "Show me the kind of thing you like and I'll make one to fit you perfectly."

And that's why having a psychic auntie who lives in your garden could sometimes be one hundred per cent amazing.

27

ADRENALINE

The next day at school, Miki brought his *Mary Poppins* script to the canteen at lunchtime so I could help him learn his lines. I didn't like going to the canteen when it was busy. People looked at my tray to see what I'd chosen to eat, even some of the dinner ladies. Some people looked at me like I shouldn't be eating at all. The whole canteen smelled of chips anyway. I probably gained calories just breathing the air.

"Miss Nisha's getting a screen for the back of the stage!" Miki said as we joined the queue. "She's going to add some animated bits, like—"

Suddenly, Dylan Taylor shouted, "Guard your food!" from a nearby table. "She's hungry!" He laughed and made pig noises until one of his friends told him to shut up.

Miki held onto my arm because he could sense I was

about to walk out. "Ignore them. Everyone has to eat." He gave me a serious look. "And I have to eat doughnuts."

We got our food and sat on a bench facing the windows. Miki took out his script and I started reading it with him in between forkfuls of pasta. But it was impossible. Not because of the pasta. Miki kept bursting into song or getting up to show me the dance steps.

"Oh no," I said, looking over his shoulder.

"What? Did I say that bit wrong?" Miki asked.

I shook my head and nodded to Lottie and Alina walking towards us.

"Hi, Miki!" Lottie said.

Alina smiled awkwardly at me.

"Oh no," Miki said. "I mean, hi, Lottie."

"Learning your lines?" she asked. "You're so brilliant as Bert!" Lottie sang a perfect "*Supercalifragilisticexpialidocious!*" It was only slightly rat-like.

Miki looked at me cross-eyed. I tried not to laugh. Miki had been begging me to bring Jasper's tarantula into school so he could scare Lottie in rehearsals. But I'd never do that. Not to an innocent tarantula.

Lottie turned to me. "I'm playing Mary Poppins. It's the star part."

"I know, Lottie," I said. "You've told everyone a thousand times."

She gritted her teeth. "Anyway, some girls in Year Nine auditioned. But Miss Nisha chose me." She elbowed Alina.

"Lottie's got the biggest part in the whole play," Alina mumbled, as though she was reciting a line she'd had to learn. It didn't take a genius to work out who was directing.

Lottie laughed. "It's going to be a really BIG production. The BIGGEST ever!"

Miki sighed and picked up his bag. "You're not funny, Lottie. Come on, Jemima. Let's go and practise in the form room."

I tried to think of something to say back. But Lottie was standing there with her honey blonde hair, and perfect weight, and the star role in the Christmas production, and qualifying score for the selection round of *Brainiacs*, linking arms with my old best friend, and I couldn't think of anything. Because there wasn't anything to say. She was just like Mary Poppins: practically perfect in every way.

I picked up my bag, dumped my plate on the trolley and started walking towards the door. Then I stopped. There *was* something wrong with her. I told Miki to wait and went back to where Lottie was standing.

"You're right, Lottie," I said. "You have got the biggest part in the play. But Mary Poppins is famous for being kind. So I hope you are REALLY good at acting." I smiled. "Good luck revising for *Brainiacs* with all those lines to learn. And the extra ones you're writing for Alina."

My hands were kind of trembling. But it was only my brain releasing adrenaline into my bloodstream. That's probably why I didn't care about asking people by the drinks machine to move, or having to squeeze past the pillars near the back tables, or that a couple of Year Sevens were gawping at me. I stood by the doorway and glanced back at Lottie. She was making Afzal and his friends move tables so she could sit by the window.

"You know what, Miki?" I said. "I am going to *obliterate* Lottie Freeman at *Brainiacs*."

"I don't know what obliterate means," Miki said, "but I totally agree." And he high-fived me on the way out.

As we headed to our form room, I thought about all the words Lottie had said to me, and how their sound waves had run out of energy by now. I thought about all the things I'd recorded in my notebook, the pages I'd torn up and thrown in the bin. And I realized, walking in the fresh October sunshine with the first autumn leaves at my feet, those words were already beginning to decompose.

28

DISAPPEARING
TRICKS

After breakfast on Saturday, I went out in the garden. Luna was on her sun deck staring at her laptop.

"Good morning, my beautiful niece!" she said, sunlight reflecting off her bracelets. "Everything okay?"

"Yeah," I said. "You're up early."

"Yes, I wonder what woke me!" she said, just as Dad's power drill started up again.

"Can I do some yoga with you today? Gina said we have to exercise again for homework."

"Of course! We can do it now if you like." Luna put her laptop on the table and tied her hair into a bun. "What a blissful idea! Although, let's go in the house. Escape this racket. Oh, hang on – I got you something." She disappeared inside her cabin and came out with a copy of *Sweet* magazine. "You can't spend all weekend studying."

"Thanks!" The only magazines I usually read were *Go Science!* or *Amazing History*. Maybe it would be good to read a magazine that wasn't in the school library. "Are you working on your website?" I asked, pointing to her laptop.

"No, your dad found a box of my stuff in the garage. There were some photos on a memory stick; I was just having a look. There are some old ones of me and Uncle Alfie." She moved the screen round so I could see. Alfie had his arm around Luna and the lights of Clifton Pier glowed in the background. "That was a few weeks before he left."

"He looks really happy."

Luna took a deep breath. "Yeah, well, a picture doesn't tell the whole story." She stared at the screen. "Alfie's a Pisces. They love being close to the water."

"He should have stayed here then," I said. "You can't get closer to water than living in Clifton-on-Sea."

Luna smiled then turned to look at me. Her eyes glittered like a silvery-blue kaleidoscope. "I love you very much, Jemima," she said, squeezing my hand so much it was kind of painful. "I'd never do anything to hurt you. You know that, don't you?"

I nodded. But, for some strange reason, I felt like I should only half-believe her.

After contorting my body into strange positions called things like downward facing dog, mountain pose, side plank and the tree, I collapsed into what Luna told me was "corpse pose". It felt kind of appropriate. My legs were burning and I could feel sweat soaking into the back of my T-shirt.

"My muscles hurt," I said, stretching my arms. "All of them."

Luna rubbed something smelling of oranges into my temples. "Well, please don't sue me."

"Sorry. It was good, thank you." I examined my thighs. "It hasn't made me look any thinner though."

Luna pulled me onto my feet and wrapped a pink, glittery blanket around my shoulders. "Jemima, yoga isn't about looking a particular way. It's about feeling content, feeling happy in your own skin."

But it was okay for Luna. Her legs were long and thin, and probably not even aching. I wondered how many yoga sessions I'd need to do to have legs like hers.

"Luna, how long have you been doing yoga?"

She thought for a moment. "About ten years now."

Ten years! If I got through to *Brainiacs* I'd be getting filmed next month! Maybe there was an extreme version I could do instead.

When I went back upstairs, I could tell Jasper had been in my room. Some of the books on my desk had been moved.

"Jasper!" I shouted. "Don't touch my stuff!"

"I was just helping you with your French homework!" he shouted back.

I picked up my French book. We had to write two paragraphs describing our dream holiday for homework. Jasper had written a list of French words on a sticky note for me.

"Oh, okay thanks!" I said. "Although obviously my dream holiday wouldn't include dodgeball!"

It wasn't until later when I noticed what else Jasper had done. Next to where I'd put *Jemima Small: difficult to defeat* on my mirror, he'd drawn a fat person wearing sunglasses, and a speech bubble saying good luck in French. Even when Jasper was being nice, he was still really annoying.

That afternoon, I went over to Miki's house. His mum was making vegetable dumplings and sticky rice and the house smelled amazing. We watched the old *Mary Poppins* film as we ate and Miki made me join in with all the songs. Afterwards, he showed me some Japanese letters his mum had been teaching him and then tested me on them. He gave me a score using his own *Mary-Poppins-style* system which equated to: *practically perfect in every way*.

"*Arigatou gozaimasu*, Niko," I said to Miki's mum, as I climbed into her car.

It wasn't that far to my house, but she always gave me a lift home, and I always said thank you to her in Japanese. It was about the only thing Miki had taught me to say. Apart from "a weasel's last fart" which wasn't exactly useful. He told me it was a famous saying in Japan, but I wasn't sure if he was serious and I definitely wasn't going to try it out on his mum. Even though he'd dared me about a million times.

"You're welcome, Jemima! And good luck at the *Brainiacs* audition! We're so excited for you!"

"Thanks," I said. "There are only fifteen places on the show so…" I let my voice trail off.

"But they all have the same chance as you, yes?" she said.

"I guess," I said. "So, pretty slim." I felt my cheeks go red as soon as I said "slim" but Niko didn't seem to notice.

"She's so going to get through," Miki said as he did up his seatbelt. "Jemima is such a geek, I mean, genius."

"Ha! I wish I could say the same for you!" Niko said.

I listened to Miki and his mum speaking to each other in Japanese on the way home. I had no idea what they were saying, but the words sounded kind of gentle and warm, like when it rains in the summer. It made me wonder how it would feel for my mum to pick me up and take me home. For her to ask about how my life is going. I shook the thought out of my mind and gazed up at the street lamps. The chances of that happening were even slimmer than my chances of appearing on *Brainiacs*. And suddenly, a question came into my mind so big that I didn't even dare consider the answer.

After Miki's mum dropped me off, I went upstairs, dumped my *Brainiacs* revision cards on my desk and knocked on Jasper's door. The door opened a tiny bit. I could just make out an eyeball through the crack. A fake one.

"What do you want?"

"I need to talk to you about something," I said.

"Okay, hurry up." Jasper opened the door and quickly closed it behind me.

I hadn't been in Jasper's room for ages. It still smelled weird. The poster of Grandad as the Amazing Apollo still covered the back wall. It said, *The Amazing Apollo's Magic and Wonder Show!* The corners were starting to curl and one of the sides had a rip in it. Jasper's room was usually eerily tidy; it was one of the ways he showed off to Dad. But tonight, boxes were scattered all over the carpet. He picked up one labelled DISAPPEARING TRICKS and took the lid off.

"It's such a mess! What are you doing?" I asked.

"Just looking for something," he said, spinning the fake eyeball on his palm.

"Gross. What have you lost?"

His real eyeballs shifted nervously towards his tarantula's tank. The empty tank.

"JASPER!"

"Shh! Dad will hear you!" He pulled a plastic tray out from under his bed where he kept all his magic stuff. It was organized into boxes and each one had been specially labelled. He printed them out last year from Dad's computer. He'd also printed out a label that said FAT and stuck it on my desk. It was one of the few times he's ever been in proper trouble.

Jasper lined up the boxes next to his bed. DEFYING GRAVITY, ILLUSIONS, LEVITATION, MIND POWER, SIXTH SENSE CUBE. It took me about five seconds to realize he was putting them in alphabetical order.

"This was the trick I was supposed to do with her the other day." He held up the DISAPPEARING TRICKS box. "Before Dad totally overreacted. I'm pretty sure I put her back in the tank."

"Wait a minute. Are you saying she's been missing since you did that ball of flames trick?"

Jasper gulped.

"Jasper! That was four days ago!"

"Shh! I've been looking for her! But she's gone." He opened and closed the DISAPPEARING TRICKS box a few times, like she might magically appear out of nowhere.

"I don't think she would hide in there, Jasper. She can't actually read."

He sat on the floor looking through the boxes. "I just don't get where she can be."

"She'd go somewhere dark. And warm." I opened his wardrobe doors. "Maybe she's escaped because she's sick of doing your boring magic."

But Jasper didn't say anything back, so then I felt bad. I peered inside his wardrobe. Maybe there was some kind of porthole in our house which family members disappeared through. Like the one that led to Narnia. It definitely wasn't inside Jasper's wardrobe though. That was just made of wood. I'd already checked years ago.

"She's got to be in here somewhere," Jasper said. He tapped the torch on his phone and crawled under his bed.

"I'm sure she'll come back when she's hungry." I typed

into Google. "Uh oh. It says here they can survive without food for *two years*."

Jasper wriggled out from under the bed. "Maybe I could tempt her out with crickets."

"Gross, Jasper. You have to tell Dad."

"No way! He's petrified of her. If he finds out she's missing he'll call pest control or something." He looked at me with eyes exactly the same silvery-blue as Luna's. "If you tell him, I'll kill you, Jemima."

"Hmm," I said. "I wonder what pest control would do. Probably some kind of thermal fogging."

"What's that?"

"Think *Ghostbusters*, but instead of the proton stream, it would be insecticide."

"That's horrible!"

"Yeah, well, death threats aren't exactly very nice either."

"Sorry," Jasper said, wincing like apologizing to me was physically painful.

"Have you checked everywhere?" I asked.

"Yeah. Apart from Dad's room. We're not allowed in there."

I sighed. "Jasper, I don't think Tornado's aware of that rule." I headed towards the door. "I'll keep Dad talking downstairs. You go and search it."

Jasper smiled at me. "Thanks. Hey, what did you want to talk to me about?"

"Oh, just…" I felt nervous for some reason. Probably because we hadn't talked about Mum for so long. We used to talk about her a lot when we were younger. What we'd do if she phoned, or sent us a card, or turned up one day. But when none of those things happened, talking about them seemed kind of irrelevant too. "I was thinking about Mum today. Like, say I did get through to be on *Brainiacs*, what if she watched it?"

Jasper's eyes moved around his room, looking everywhere except at mine. "I dunno." He went over to his desk. "Here. I found some old photos last night when I was looking for Tornado. This was under my desk." He handed me a photo of me and Mum splashing on the shore in Dolphin Bay. I only looked about two. Mum was holding both my hands so I didn't topple over.

"See that tattoo?" Jasper pointed to Mum's wrist. I looked closer and could just make out a black swirl. "It reminded me of this thing she told me. It's kind of stupid but…"

"What?" A lump came into my throat. I looked at Mum on the beach, gripping my hands tightly, my feet half-disappearing into the sand, wondering how it would feel to see her again.

"It's really stupid," Jasper said. "So you'll probably like it."

I fake-smiled.

"We'd stayed on the pier really late, and it was pitch black when we walked home. Mum pointed up at the sky and told me…" He stopped, cracked his knuckles and picked up a pack of cards from his desk. He shuffled them perfectly, in one hand, like Grandad used to do. "Forget it. It's really stupid."

"Please, Jasper. I won't think it's stupid."

"She said shooting stars are the universe telling us that magic exists. And she told me to never stop believing in magic." He blinked a few times. "See? I told you. It's like something Luna would say. I only remembered because that's her tattoo. A shooting star. And because that's the night she had that massive argument with Dad. Then she left."

I stood by the door for a minute. Neither of us said anything. I didn't tell him about the empty feeling I got in my heart whenever I thought about her. Because I knew he had it too. He'd told me that years ago.

"Anyway, forget it," Jasper said eventually. "Shooting stars don't even exist."

I nodded. Jasper was right. Shooting stars aren't real. They're not even real stars. They're meteors. Fragments of rock burning up in space. Not shooting anywhere, just incinerating into dust. But sometimes, your heart doesn't care about any of that. Because there were Mum's hands gripping mine. Stopping me from sinking. Protecting me from the waves. And I wanted that feeling back.

I went downstairs to keep Dad talking so Jasper could check his room, but he was already on the phone. He was laughing and looking at his iPad. He called that "double screen time" and moaned any time I did it. I raised my eyebrows at him and he walked to the other side of the kitchen so I couldn't hear what he was saying.

I sat halfway up the stairs, leaning against the banister with Hermione on my lap, thinking about Mum. And *Brainiacs*. Part of me wanted Mum to notice me. I didn't even care about impressing her. I just wanted to wave at her from across the universe so she might remember I exist.

That night, I stayed up really late revising for the Selection Day. Because I couldn't stop thinking that maybe Mum was out there. Waiting. With a gigantic hole in her heart like mine. If Mum believed in shooting stars and signs from the universe, maybe she'd been waiting for a message to come back. Seeing me on *Brainiacs* could be that message.

And I had exactly sixteen days to make it happen.

29

WEIRD SCIENCE

By the next night, I'd learned so many facts I felt like my brain might burst, so I dumped my revision stuff on the floor and picked up *Sweet* magazine. I tore open the plastic wrapping and the free gifts dropped onto my lap. A fluffy key ring, peach lip balm, cat nail stickers, and a mini set of Electric Energy Hair Chalks. I turned an illuminous pink pot over. *Washes out instantly.* I unscrewed the lid and pulled a strand from the back of my hair, underneath, where Dad wouldn't notice. I pulled it through the chalk a few times and smiled as my hair turned from sludgy sand to electric pink. I stuck a few cat faces on my fingernails and peeled them off again, then flicked through the magazine.

Every girl smiling out at me was thin. Even the ones

on the *Meet our Readers!* page. Maybe you were supposed to look like a model just to read this magazine. As I turned the pages, it was like watching a conveyor belt of perfection. Each body a million times better than my own. I wondered what I'd look like if I was model-thin. I didn't think about stuff like that when I was reading *Go Science!* magazine. When I was reading that all I thought about was how much trouble I'd get in for doing their "dastardly experiments" at home. Then I had an idea.

I rummaged through my desk for an old photo of me, cut out my face and stuck it on some paper. Then I scoured *Sweet* magazine for the best bits. I cut out the torso from a girl advertising perfume, arms from a girl band member, legs from a vlogger and feet from *This Week's Trend Crush*. It was like dissecting the anatomy of the perfect girl. A girl everyone would want to see on TV. I picked up my glue and started sticking.

I'd almost finished when I heard Dad's footsteps on the stairs. I quickly stuck down the left arm as Dad opened the door without even knocking. It's an invasion of privacy. Not illegal according to the United Nations, which just shows you how much they know.

"You're not still revising are you, Jem? I know it's important to you, but seriously! It's a school night. It's nearly ten o'clock!"

I rolled my eyes.

"What *are* you doing?"

"Nothing." I tried to hide my picture, but the glue hadn't dried and it got stuck to my forearm.

Dad peeled it off and looked at my creation. Me as the perfect girl. Only I didn't look very perfect. My arms were thin and misshapen because I'd used too much glue, and they jutted out at unnatural angles. My feet looked about twenty sizes too big for the skinny legs and one of the ankles looked fractured. It was terrifying. I looked worse than the people on *Plastic Surgery Disaster*s. The only normal part of it was my head. Although I looked bald because I hadn't stuck Ariana Grande's hair on yet.

"Is this…homework?" Dad asked. "Or a science experiment gone wrong? Because, I'm sorry, Jemima, but you look like Frankenstein's monster!"

He burst out laughing as we both took in the freakish mishmash of skinny limbs under my face. It did look like something Frankenstein would create. And I knew that ended badly. I'd read it at primary school.

Dad made the arms twitch, shouting, "SHE'S ALIVE! SHE'S ALIVE!"

In three seconds flat, Jasper burst into my room. "She's alive?"

"My mini-me," I said, holding it up. "Dad was pretending

213

to be Frankenstein. Although Frankenstein doesn't even say that in the book. His exact words are—"

"Yes, thank you, brainbox." Dad narrowed his eyes at Jasper. "Who did you think I meant was alive?"

Jasper squirmed. "No one! I was just checking Jemima was okay, you know. She did yoga yesterday." He fist-bumped my shoulder. "Always here for you, sis."

I pushed him off.

"Yoga?" Dad said. "That's great, Jemima! Now, get some sleep. Hopefully your creation won't give us all nightmares. Come on, Jasper, leave your sister to get ready for bed. Future Brainiacs need their beauty sleep. As do future YouTubers."

Jasper mouthed "Thanks" as he closed the door.

I looked down at the picture in my hand. In my head, she was the girl I wanted to look like. But in reality, she looked a million times worse than I did already.

The backs of my legs still ached from yoga yesterday as I stood up and walked over to the mirror. I looked at my body, supporting my head like it's supposed to. I was two weeks away from the *Brainiacs* Selection Day, and thousands of light years from looking anything like the girls in *Sweet* magazine. But looking down at my desk, filled with severed limbs and decapitated heads and half-screwed-up smiles, that wasn't necessarily a bad thing.

30

BRUISES

The next day, I got to school just as Lottie and Alina were walking through the gates. Jasper headed to his form class and I waited for Miki on one of the concrete benches, watching the wind blow leaves into little eddies. I noticed Lottie looking over. She said something to Alina, but I couldn't hear because of the wind.

"Jemima!" Lottie called, waving me over. "Come here!"

I slowly got up off the bench and walked over to where they were standing.

"What's that in your hair?" Lottie screwed up her nose.

At first, I thought she was attempting a joke. When we first started in Year Seven, she asked what was on my face, then said, "Oh, nothing! Sorry, you're just ugly." I didn't laugh so she said, "It was just a joke, Jemima!" If they asked Lottie for the definition of "joke" at the *Brainiacs* Selection Day, she'd be in serious trouble.

"There's something in your hair! Something pink. Look." Lottie pulled a strand of my hair from the back and I caught a glimpse of electric pink. The hair chalk. I'd forgotten to wash it out.

"Oh, it's hair chalk," I said. "I got it with a magazine."

"It's nice," Alina said, tugging on Lottie's arm. "Let's go."

But Lottie didn't move. "It is nice," she said. But this look flashed in her eyes. I'd seen it loads of times before. She grabbed my hair again. "When I first saw it, I thought you might be turning into a pig!" She snorted. "A. Big. Fat. Pig."

I pulled my hair out of her hand and stepped back. Then I noticed Brandon was walking right towards us.

"Don't worry, Jemima." Lottie laughed. "Looks aren't everything."

"L-Lottie…" Alina stuttered as Brandon's face appeared in between theirs. He coughed, and stood there for a moment, arms folded, staring at them. He'd had his hair shaved at the sides.

Lottie gulped. Everyone at school knew Brandon Taylor. He was someone you avoided. At all costs. He got suspended last year for sellotaping two Year Eights together.

"I don't like what I just saw," Brandon said to Lottie. "It didn't look very nice." He leaned his face towards hers. "You better leave my friend Jemima alone."

"S-sorry!" Lottie spluttered at approximately the speed of light. "Sorry, Jemima! I didn't mean it!" She grabbed Alina's arm and scuttled away like a dung beetle. Only with honey blonde hair. And not able to pull over a thousand times her body weight.

"Thanks, Brandon," I said.

Brandon shrugged. "Fat Club code, innit?" Then he disappeared into the crowd.

It took Lottie a few days to even look at me after that. She didn't say anything in form when Mr Nelson reminded us that the camping trip was in less than three weeks. Like anyone could forget that impending doom. But that wasn't the only thing that changed. On Friday, the day before we broke up for half-term, I passed Dylan Taylor in the corridor on the way to Gina's class. And it was the first time (since approximately Year Two) that he didn't say anything to me. Having Brandon as a friend was an unexpected perk of Fat Club. A bit like Percy Spencer developing radar transmitters during World War II and accidentally inventing the microwave.

On Friday, we were doing Gina's class in one of the cookery classrooms for a change and when I got there, Heidi, Harry, Nate and Maya were already waiting outside.

"I don't get how we're supposed to lose weight if she keeps feeding us," Maya said. Some boys walked past and she squeezed against the wall like she was trying to disappear into it. "Ms Newton said we're doing mixed sports after half-term." Maya rested her head on the wall. "Maybe I can get my mum to write a note."

"PE's the worst," Harry said. "Actually, getting changed for PE is the worst."

We all nodded. There were only two cubicles in the girls' changing rooms, so any time we had PE, I raced to get in the changing rooms first. The teachers stay in the office while you get changed, so anyone can say anything to you. But at least there were cubicles in the girls'. Miki said there were none in the boys'.

"They call me Tiny," Harry said, half-laughing. "As a joke."

"Yeah, but it's not funny, Harry!" Heidi said. "I keep telling him to go to Mrs Savage about it. Show them."

Harry shook his head.

"Just show them, Harry."

"It's not a big deal," Harry said. "Just banter."

Heidi stared at him.

He sighed and took off his blazer. "It looks worse than it is." He undid a few of his shirt buttons and pulled it down over his shoulder. The top part of his arm was covered in bruises.

"Oh my God!" I blurted out. "Sorry, Harry. It just looks...bad."

Some of the bruises were brand-new, but some were old and had gone kind of yellowy. It's called bilirubin. It's what's left over after your body has collected all the iron from the bruise. Who knows how many had disappeared completely.

"Woah, Roberts! Who hit you?" Brandon said, coming round the corner.

"It's nothing," Harry said. "Just this thing my mates do."

Brandon looked confused. "I'd crush them with one punch, mate!"

Nate said, "Yeah, mates don't do that, Harry."

"That's what I've been saying," Heidi said. "Friends don't give you bruises. You've got to tell Mrs Savage or Ms Fraser. We have to go camping with them after half-term!"

"It's not that bad, Heidi! They just do it as a joke." Harry lifted his arm and pulled the skin to get a better look.

"Harry, my friends would never do that," I said. "Miki sticks up for me." I didn't mention the fart machine. Mrs Savage could have installed listening devices around the school. She already had CCTV up in some places apparently. "And what is funny about punching someone?"

Harry's cheeks went red. "It doesn't hurt that much."

"Oh my goodness! Harry! What happened?" Gina put down some bags she was carrying and took Harry's arm. Harry quickly pulled his shirt back up. "Harry, what happened?" Gina asked again, looking around at us all.

We looked at each other. But no one said anything.

"This isn't a one-off. Who's been doing this to you?"

I guess Gina noticed the bilirubin too.

She unlocked the classroom door and said, "Come inside, Harry."

We waited in the corridor for about ten minutes while Gina and Harry sat talking in the classroom. Apart from Heidi, no one else really said anything.

"And they've been getting him to buy them stuff from the canteen at break. I'm so worried about the camping trip," Heidi said. "They'll probably set his tent on fire or something! As a joke." She moved over to the classroom door and looked through the window. "Poor Harry. What do you think Gina's saying?"

Brandon squashed his face up next to hers, pressing his

nose against the glass. "Probably offering to make him a cauliflower smoothie."

Gina looked over and Brandon gave her a thumbs up through the window. She tilted her head and pretended to be mad for about a quarter of a second, then turned her smile up to the maximum. I think it's physically impossible for Gina to be mad at anyone. Like, her body is so dense in nutrients she doesn't have the space for it.

"Sorry, everyone! Thank you for waiting so patiently! Come on in! Brandon, grab those shopping bags, would you?" We filed into the classroom; Heidi went straight over to Harry while Gina stood at the front saying, "So, today's class is all about superfoods! The superheroes of food!"

I tried not to groan too loud.

"You're going to be making some *super* simple, *super* delicious, *super* healthy recipes!" She clapped her hands each time she said "super". It kind of felt like brainwashing. "Get into pairs, and I'll bring you an iPad so you can watch your recipe on YouTube! And…we get to taste all of them at the end!"

I walked with Maya to a corner kitchen as Gina handed us an iPad and a box of ingredients. Inside was a recipe card saying *Courgette noodles with avocado pesto*.

"This is the fun bit!" Gina said and typed the recipe

into YouTube. A woman wearing thick, black eyeliner with perfect flicks was paused on the screen. "There!" Gina said. "You're ready to go!"

Maya tapped the iPad and the video came to life. The cook was American, and approximately three hundred per cent more enthusiastic than Gina, which I didn't think was physically possible. She said, "Mmmm!" and "Let's do this!" a lot. It's not what cooking's like in my family. Dad shouts up the stairs for us to come and help, then he spends ages saying the recipe makes no sense. Then burns himself, then yells, "Why hasn't anyone set the table?" and usually it ends with the smoke alarm going off. No one says "Mmmm!" at any point. Especially not when we're eating it.

Once everyone had finished cooking, we sat down at the big table in the centre of the classroom. There were napkins, a jug of water, some salad, sourdough bread Gina had made at home, apparently, although it looked professional to me so she could have been lying. She placed a vase of yellow roses in the middle and it was sort of really nice. For once, I didn't care about eating in front of people at school.

Brandon and Nate handed out their wholemeal flatbreads and pots of hummus while Gina talked enthusiastically about the incredible qualities of chickpeas like they were real superheroes. Heidi dished out the rice she and Harry had made out of a cauliflower, while Harry sat gazing out of the window. Gina said everything tasted amazing and told us about the nutritional content of courgettes. It wasn't as boring as it sounds, because they contain potassium, which is one of my favourite chemical elements. It's the one that burns with a lilac flame and makes a huge tower of foam if you mix it with hydrogen peroxide. Nana only let me do that experiment with her hair bleach once, but it was pretty good.

I listened to Gina talking about cauliflower and tried not to yawn. She knew so much about food she could probably audition for *Brainiacs* if she wasn't already too old. She looked about the same age as my dad, but maybe she wasn't that old. She could have aged prematurely because she smiled so much.

When the bell went, Gina said, "Jemima, would you mind staying behind for a sec?"

I thought I was in trouble to begin with, but she handed me a small parcel wrapped in green paper.

"I heard it's your birthday on Sunday, so here's a little gift from me."

"Erm, thanks. Who told you it's my birthday?"

Gina smiled practically one hundred per cent. "Oh, just a little birdie!"

I guessed she must have accessed my school record. I wasn't totally sure it was allowed.

"It's also to wish you luck at the *Brainiacs* Selection Day. What with half-term, I won't see you before then. I expect you're glad to be getting a break from my class! But listen" – she perched on the edge of the table – "there'll be a lot of other kids at the competition. Maybe you'll have some eyes on you. But remember, you've earned your place just like they have, maybe even with a higher score. So hold your head up, you hear me?"

"Thanks, Gina," I said, and I felt her words swelling up inside me, like my heart was listening.

On the way out I stopped and turned round. "I do like your classes, by the way." I felt kind of stupid, in case she thought I only said it because of the present. But I hoped she knew I wouldn't do that. And definitely not before I'd opened it.

"What did you get?" Lottie whispered to me that afternoon in maths as Mrs Lee handed out our test papers from last lesson. I could see ninety-six per cent written on Lottie's paper in green ink, and Mrs Lee's swirly writing saying, *Excellent!*

I wasn't afraid of Lottie. Not in the normal sense. I just

got this prickly feeling in my chest anytime she spoke to me. Like being stung by a jellyfish. They have these special cells in their tentacles containing venom that can go through your skin in a matter of milliseconds. Lottie seemed to have them on her tongue.

I covered my test paper with my elbow and said, "Ninety." I stupidly thought it might make her leave me alone.

Lottie smiled so hard her face almost cracked open. She picked up her test and fanned herself. "I got ninety-*six*! Maybe you should have revised instead of..." She waited until Mrs Lee was on the other side of the classroom. "Eating so much."

Lottie turned back to face the front. I moved my elbow off my test paper and looked again at what Mrs Lee had written. *100% See me for some higher papers!*

"Why didn't you tell her your real score?" Erin whispered. "She's so annoying!"

I shrugged and looked back at Lottie. She was smiling at herself in the mirror on her pencil case. Erin was right. Even the back of Lottie's head was annoying.

Mrs Lee tapped the screen and a series of equations with unknown quantities appeared.

"Now, before we start, I want to say a special well done to Erik and Jemima, both of whom scored one hundred per cent in the test!"

My cheeks flushed as everybody started clapping. Lottie whipped her head round and glared at me. I felt that stinging feeling in my chest, then noticed Afzal and Jaz smiling at me from the other side of the classroom.

Erin showed me the sixty-four per cent written on her paper and whispered, "I wish I was like you!"

And something happened in my stomach. Like someone had ignited a tiny flame. I leaned forward. "Don't worry, Lottie." I smiled. "Brains aren't everything." And I accidentally trod on her foot on the way up to solve the first equation.

31

MYSTIC AVANI

It was the first Saturday of half-term, the day before my birthday, and I'd spent the entire morning revising. The *Brainiacs* Selection Day was only nine days away and I still had advanced spelling, ancient history and world literature to cover. It was going to be a long week.

When I went downstairs, the front door was wide open and Dad was putting Luna's fold-up table into the boot of her car. I still had my nightie on, so I didn't go outside.

"My psychic energy feels so strong today!" Luna was saying. She immediately turned round, like she could sense me, and walked inside. "I'm doing a psychic fair in Saltford Village today! Want to come?"

Dad quickly followed behind her. "Jemima's probably

got homework to do. And studying for *Brainiacs*. Besides, I don't want her head filling with…"

Luna put her hands on her hips.

"Distractions."

"Oh, come on, Rion! It's her birthday tomorrow! And the first day of half-term! She's got all week to revise. It's only for a few hours." Luna looked at me. "Fancy it?"

"Well," Dad said, "would you like to go with Luna? I was hoping we'd go to Nana's this afternoon. There's a tea dance on."

I thought about it for approximately zero seconds.

"Great!" Luna said. "There'll be crystal healing, and reiki, and spiritual guides, aromatherapy, and Willow's bringing her vegan burger van!"

"Can Miki come?" I asked.

Luna said, "Sure!" just as the smoke alarm started going off.

Dad ran into the kitchen, shouting, "With all your psychic energy floating about, you'd think you'd notice the toast's burning!"

A few minutes later, at the kitchen table, Dad put a plate of half-burned toast and mashed avocado in front of me and sat down. "Listen, Jem…"

I didn't need to be psychic to know he was starting one of his lectures.

"I can't eat burned toast. It's bad for you," I said. "It's got acrylamide in it."

"No, avocado," Dad said, laughing. "Now, listen. Luna and her friends at these psychic fairs have lots of very *interesting* ideas about the world. Same as your nana. Anyway, as you know, I don't share their—"

"Gift?" I said.

Dad smiled. "Exactly. Their gift. And I don't really want you sharing it either. These fairs attract some right weirdos. Luna's under strict instructions not to let you speak to any spiritual guides or witches or ghosts or whatever."

"Don't worry, Dad. It's not Halloween yet."

"You know what I mean."

I took out my phone and tapped the screen. "Miki says he'll come."

"Good! I'm glad someone sensible's going along!" It was typical of my dad to call someone with a fart machine sensible.

I walked over to the bread bin to make some more toast and Dad gave me a strange look.

"Erm, Jemima! I know people at these fairs dress a little crazy. I mean, look at Luna. And I wouldn't normally tell you what to wear, you know. Wear whatever you want round the house! But…that dress you've got on. I mean, it's a nice dress! You do look nice. I just don't know if it's right for the fair."

"Dad, it's my nightie."

"Ha! Okay! Good! Right! Get dressed then." He couldn't get out of the kitchen fast enough.

I waited until Dad had driven off, then I went upstairs and sat in front of the mirror. I carefully applied Electric Energy Hair Chalk to each section of my hair until it resembled a rainbow. A rainbow plugged into fluorescent lighting. I stood up and twirled around 360 degrees. Maybe the chemicals in hair chalk did something strange to your eyes. Because I looked okay. Sort of better than okay.

I took a selfie and sent it to Miki saying: you ready???

He messaged back: omg!!!! 😵

I pulled on some leggings and a yellow dress with a triangle pattern that Luna had made me a while ago. I liked it because the fabric was stretchy, and it came down past my knees. Plus, the triangles were all equilateral. Which meant, if I got bored, I could practise geometry. I picked up my cardigan and went downstairs.

Luna's mouth dropped open. "Jemima! Your hair!"

"Does it look okay?" I fiddled with a bright orange strand next to my face.

Luna put her hands on my cheeks. "It looks amazing!

Like a rainbow! But…you know your dad is going to kill you, right?"

"I'll wash it out as soon as we get back, so he'll never know. Anyway, I'm thirteen tomorrow. I can dye my hair how I like when I'm thirteen."

Luna whisked me out of the front door, down the drive, through the gate and into her car in one graceful movement. That's the thing about Luna. She makes everything seem magical.

When we got to Miki's house, his mum said, "Wow, Jemima! I love your hair!"

"*Arigatou gozaimasu*," I said, scraping my hair to one side.

"Miki said your Auntie Luna does psychic readings. I have to get her number."

Miki came downstairs and stood in the doorway. His mum ruffled his hair.

"*Jemima wa kyou mo kawaii ne*, huh?"

Miki nodded as Niko walked over to Luna's car.

"She said you look pretty," Miki said. "Jem, your hair looks *phosphorescent*!"

"Er, thanks. Why are you speaking like that?"

"Thought you'd like it! Mum got me this app called Word Doctor. You type in a word and bigger words come up that mean the same thing. I'm going to use it all the time from now on!"

231

"I don't know, Miki," I said, walking back to the car. "You just told me my hair looks like it's been exposed to radiation."

Miki laughed. "Oh my God! This app is more awesome than I realized!"

"Have fun, you two!" Niko called as we drove off.

"Thanks, Mum!" Miki called out the window, tapping his phone. "Have a *humongous* day!"

We drove for about half an hour, and Luna stopped outside a village hall with a sign up saying: *The Eyes of the Universe Psychic Fair*. It didn't take long to help carry Luna's stuff inside because she doesn't have that much equipment. She says the only special equipment she needs are her tarot cards and The Gift which she inherited from Nana. The same as her folding table.

Miki wandered around, and stopped at a stall selling dreamcatchers while I wrote Luna's sign.

Luna Diamond
Tarot Readings * Aura Readings * Celestial Wisdom
Discover your Destiny!

CASH ONLY

In each corner I drew a shooting star. Luna opened her

mouth like she was going to say something, then changed her mind.

"Thank you so much for helping. Now, I need a moment of peace to channel my energy." She handed me some money. "Here. Enjoy yourself!"

I found Miki near a stall draped in purple fabric with a huge statue of Buddha in the centre. He elbowed me and pointed to an old lady sitting at a table opposite. Her sign said:

Mystic Avani
Palm Reader
Your fate is in your hands

I accidentally made eye contact and Mystic Avani leaned forward, like she was going to tell us all the secrets of the universe. I remembered what Dad said about not speaking to spiritual guides and tried to work out if palm readers came under that classification.

"Come on!" Miki said, tugging my arm. "I've never had my fortune told before!"

Before I had a chance to protest, Miki had sat down and the old lady was holding his left hand. I pulled a chair out and sat down next to him.

"Ah, a water hand!"

Miki looked at me. I shrugged.

"An artist!" Mystic Avani said and peered into Miki's palm like it was a deep well. "You have great gifts, my child. Tremendous gifts." She patted his hand with hers. "You're talented, kind, joyful! Cherish these gifts!" She carried on talking, moving her finger over his hand, talking about heart lines and head lines and what they signified.

I knew about the lines on your hand. I'd read about them in my human anatomy book. They're called palmer flexion creases. They're so you can stretch and scrunch up your hand. But I doubted Mystic Avani cared about what it said in human anatomy books.

"Be confident," she said to Miki. "Your destiny is on the stage." She bowed her head.

"Did you hear that?" Miki said. "The stage! That is so weird."

"Yeah, spooky." I didn't mention he was wearing a hoodie saying: *WARNING! I break out into show tunes.*

I was about to stand up when the old lady grabbed my hand and pulled it towards her. She held it firmly and examined it like a Petri dish.

"What is it?" I asked, but she slowly shook her head.

"Nothing, my child. End of reading." She bowed her head again and I noticed her earrings were shaped like

234

hands, with tiny eyeballs in the centre. Like my nana's tattoo.

"Did you see something in my hand?" I asked. "Is it bad?"

It had to be bad because she wouldn't tell me. I already knew from Luna that psychics don't give negative readings. I picked a card called Death once and Luna even managed to make that sound positive.

Mystic Avani leaned forward and looked at me for a long time. Like I was a puzzle she had to figure out. She took my hand again and I looked into her eyes. They were deep brown and full of energy, like stars exploding. It was as though the whole universe was looking back at me. Tiny specks of dust floated in the sunlight between us. She lifted my hand up, then closed it, like she was trying to catch the light.

"You'll find what you've been looking for, child." Then she let go.

Logic told me my hand couldn't reveal my future. But weirdly, when I looked down at my hand, it felt like those tiny lines etched into my skin were more precious than ever.

32

GRAVITATIONAL PULL

Outside the psychic fair, Miki and I sat by Willow's vegan burger van while Luna was telling her last fortune of the day inside. No one gave me a second glance. Maybe because my rainbow hair was kind of conservative compared to how some people looked. One man had tattoos covering every centimetre of his face. Dad would totally freak out if I did that.

"So, what do you think?" I asked Miki, still picturing Mystic Avani's eyes glittering behind specks of dust and the words: *You'll find what you've been looking for.*

"A bit weird," Miki said and took a huge gulp of Fanta. He put his hand to his chest, like he was waiting to see if a burp was coming. I'd known Miki long enough to know it probably was. "It sort of tastes like baked beans."

"I meant the palm reader, Miki, not the burger!"

He licked ketchup off his fingers and said, "Well, I think she's right. I definitely could be a famous actor one day."

"And what she said about my mum?"

"Erm, I dunno," Miki said. "She didn't actually say 'mum', did she? And you haven't been looking for her, so..."

I put my half-eaten burger down and stared at the floor.

"I mean, she probably meant your mum though! Like, whoever she meant, probably your mum, it's definitely good news." His phone beeped. "That'll be my mum. Oh no, what? It's Lottie." He held up his phone.

Lottie: Hey, downloaded this if you want to watch it one day next week?

She'd sent him a picture of the *Mary Poppins* film. Immediately I felt sick. Not because Lottie was generally bile-inducing. But because I knew what she was trying to do. The same thing she'd done with Alina. Just the thought of not having Miki as my friend any more felt like being in outer space when your oxygen tank's exploded.

I fiddled with the ring pull on my can. "What are you going to say?"

"Hmm! I don't know," Miki said. "Hanging out with Lottie would be bad. Let's see what the Word Doctor suggests!" He tapped his phone. "What about, *Sorry, Lottie, that would be distressing?*"

I laughed and shook my head.

"Too strong? Okay how about, *That would be execrable*? What does that even mean?"

"It means extremely bad. It comes from the Latin word *execrabilis*, which means deserving of curses! It's probably a bit harsh, even for Lottie Freeman." I took a bite of my burger and thought for a moment. "I know! Put soporific. That just means boring. Well, literally, it means sleep-inducing, because *sopor* means sleep in Latin, so…"

Miki put his phone down and stared at me.

"What? Have I got ketchup on my face?"

"Jemima Small, if you don't get through to *Brainiacs*, I'll eat a thousand vegan burgers."

When I got home, the first thing I noticed was Dad's face. It was like he'd seen a ghost. Only, what he'd actually seen was my phosphorescent hair.

"What on EARTH have you done to your hair?" he said, leaping off the sofa faster than I'd seen a mammal move in my entire life. "Jemima!"

Jasper shot out of his room and halfway down the stairs. "Uh oh! Jemima's gone rogue."

I shot him the death stare.

"What HAVE you done?" Dad said again, even louder.

He looked pretty angry, so I decided the best idea was to deny all knowledge. "My hair? What do you mean?" I said and walked to the mirror. "Oh my GOD! What's happened?" I felt quite pleased with how my acting was going. Maybe some of Miki's talent had rubbed off on me. "Dad, I honestly have no idea how this happened."

Dad shook his head at me. Not in a good way. "Luna? Can you explain this?"

Luna came in and put her bag down. "Yes, she's beautiful!"

Dad shook his head again, even harder. I warned him he could damage his brain doing that. He didn't appreciate my concern.

"Right, you'd better start explaining yourself, Jemima! I told you – no hair dye. And look at you!"

I swallowed. "There was this old lady at the fair."

Dad put his hand on his forehead and closed his eyes. "I don't think I want to hear this."

"She must have been a witch. She read my palm, and afterwards I felt kind of dizzy. Now I think about it, she did briefly touch my hair. You were right about the witches at those fairs, Dad."

"Hey!" Luna said, jabbing Dad in the ribs.

He side-stepped away from her. "A spell," he said. "On your hair."

"It does happen sometimes at the fairs, Dad. You said it yourself. They attract some right weirdos."

"Rion!" Luna said. "I can't believe you said that to Jemima about my friends!"

"I didn't say that. I said…'interesting characters'."

I caught his eye to let him know I knew he was lying.

"Anyway, Jemima, I've never heard such nonsense in all my life! And in this family, that is really saying something."

I turned back to face the mirror. "It's not my fault I had a spell put on me."

Luna stroked my hair and winked at me in the mirror. "You know, Rion, I have seen this sort of thing happen before."

Dad sighed.

"Luckily, this doesn't look like a permanent spell to me. This is the type that should just wash out." She kissed the top of my head.

"Let's hope so! Or you're not going to the restaurant tomorrow! Birthday or not!" Dad pointed to the stairs. "Off you go."

As I went upstairs, Jasper whispered, "Your head looks like an Easter egg."

I knocked my bag against him as I walked past and said, "Accident."

I went straight into the bathroom and turned the shower on, but I could hear them talking about me downstairs, so I crept onto the landing and listened.

"Rion, it's not a big deal," Luna was saying. "So she coloured her hair for one day! She's thirteen tomorrow. So what if she wants to dye her hair? I don't know why you're so annoyed about it."

I smiled. Luna always stuck up for me against Dad's oppression.

"You used to dye your fringe bright blue."

"I was in college when I did that!"

"That actually makes it worse!" Luna said laughing. "Jemima's not hurting anybody."

"She hurt my eyes," Jasper said. "I'll never unsee that."

Dad sighed so hard I could practically feel the floorboards vibrating. "Keep out of this, Jasper. It's just with all this...*weight* stuff." He said the word "weight" quietly, like it was a bad word. "I don't want her drawing unnecessary attention to herself, you know? I mean, it's already been in the paper! And dyeing her hair seven shades of ridiculous. I don't want people..."

I went into the bathroom and closed the door. I didn't want to hear anything else. I got undressed, stood in the shower and let the water dilute my tears. Neon colours swirled down the plughole like a rainbow melting away. Until all that was left were grey-blue bubbles from my shampoo.

Later, I knocked on Jasper's door and asked to borrow his portable CD player. He half opened the door and said, "Can't you just use the one downstairs?"

"No, Jasper! It's…a revision CD. I need it for studying."

"I don't know where it is."

"Fine. Guess I'll have to tell Dad Tornado's missing."

"Shh! Okay, okay!" He reached his arm behind the door then handed me his CD player. "Don't break it."

Back in my bedroom, I rummaged in Mum's box until I found it. There was a crack across the case, but the CD inside looked okay. I put my lamp on, lay on my bed, plugged in my headphones and pressed play. The songs had that grainy, old-fashioned kind of sound, like they should be played on a record player. The first song was about a moon made out of paper, which wouldn't be heavy enough to stay in a planet's gravitational pull. I was going to turn it off and watch a film, but then a song came on called "Dream a Little Dream of Me". It had lyrics about fading stars and sunbeams and feeling alone and missing someone, and they didn't seem so unrealistic.

I pressed pause. But I could still hear the song playing because I remembered Mum's voice singing it to me. I remembered the light I used to have by my bed, with little star shapes cut out of the lampshade that made my ceiling look like the Milky Way. The same ceiling I was looking at now. I remembered how it felt to have Mum's arms around me, and her soft French tones singing that song to me over and over again.

I pulled off my headphones and sat up. I stayed like that for ages, staring into space, thinking about the Earth. About how its surface area is almost two hundred million square miles. And how somewhere, right now, in one of those square miles, was my mum. I still felt her gravitational pull. That feeling of belonging with her that never really went away, even when she did.

And that's when I felt it.

It was an unmistakable feeling. One I'd felt before. One that sent goosebumps over my skin and a chill over my heart and made me think that Mystic Avani knew what she was talking about when she said I'd find something. Only she wasn't talking about my mum.

"JASPER!" I shouted as loudly as I could whilst keeping my head perfectly still. "JASPER!"

The floorboards creaked outside my room and the door opened. A beam of yellow light spilled onto my carpet.

"Jemima! I'm trying to practise a trick! You'd better not have broken my CD player. What is it?"

"Not *what* is it," I said. "*Who* is it?" I carefully pointed to my head and gave Jasper the strongest evils of my life.

Jasper moved closer and gasped as Tornado's hairy legs walked slowly down the side of my face. All eight of them.

"Jasper," I said, through my clenched jaw. "I am literally going to kill you."

33

FULL MOON

When I woke up the next day, I was exactly 4,748 days old. Or 156 months. Or thirteen years. I'd been on Earth long enough for it to revolve thirteen times around the sun. I was officially a teenager. And that felt like something to celebrate.

"Happy birthday, Jemstone!" Luna sang as she came into my room, opened the curtains and kissed me on the cheek. She always got up early on my birthday. "Your dad's just gone to get Nana. I hope you like it!" From nowhere, she held up a zaffre blue dress. It's a colour made from cobalt oxide. Hundreds of gold sequins sparkled in the sunlight. It was the kind of thing Emma Watson would probably wear on her birthday. Only my size. I got out of bed and gave Luna a hug.

"It's amazing, Luna! Thank you!" I said, as she helped me try it on.

She made a few adjustments and hung it on my wardrobe door ready for later, then painted my fingernails and covered my eyelids in glitter.

"Your eyes look brighter than the stars!" Luna said, kissing my forehead.

I looked in the mirror and blinked a few times. I couldn't see them sparkling, but I made a wish anyway.

Please let me not mess up Brainiacs.

Downstairs, Dad arrived back from getting Nana. He said, "Happy birthday, sweetheart," and gave me a hug. "I'm sorry about yesterday. I may have slightly overreacted to your hair."

"Slightly?" I muttered, helping Nana out of her chair and onto the sofa.

"It's nice to see you looking back to normal," Dad said. "Let's focus on having a nice day, shall we?"

We all sat in the living room eating slightly burned croissants for breakfast while I opened my presents. Dad handed me a huge box wrapped in silver paper. Inside was a bright pink neon light that said:

"I'll put it up in your bedroom later, if you like?"

"Thanks, Dad. I love it." I took a gulp of my fizzy apple juice because I could feel tears starting in my eyes. Which wasn't a good idea because then I got hiccups. I don't know why a Jemima light made me want to cry. It's a stupid thing to nearly cry about. It's not even sad. But seeing my name written in pink neon, from my dad, I felt like maybe Jemima was an okay person to be.

"Here," Jasper said, throwing a parcel at me. "It's a unicorn that poos paper clips." Jasper always tells you what's inside your present before you open it.

Nana gave me some book tokens, the same as she did every year, and Luna put a book-shaped parcel into my hands. "Is it called *How to Become a Brainiac in Nine Days*?" I asked.

Luna smiled. "No! But I know you'll like it."

Nana said, "You could always buy that one with my tokens, dear."

"Thanks, Nana." I pulled off the wrapping paper. *Star Atlas*, it said in gold writing: *Your guide to the night sky.* "Wow!" I said, flicking through the pages of sky maps. "This is brilliant."

"The perfect guide for a star-gazer." Luna looked at me for ages, like she knew exactly how many times I'd wished on stars.

I put my cards up on the mantelpiece, trying not to think about the one from Mum that wasn't there. Every year I told myself it was stupid to think she'd send something. But every time, that empty space in my heart filled up with the thought that maybe this year would be different. And then, when nothing arrived, I'd tell myself that maybe she hit her head and got amnesia. Or lived somewhere that didn't have a postal service, like the International Space Station. But I can't ever make myself believe it.

Dad put his arm around my shoulder and squeezed. "We'll have a great day, I promise. Hey, there's a present here you haven't opened." He picked up a green box from the side.

"Oh, that's from Gina," I said. "And yes, I know. It's weird."

"I don't think it's weird. It's really nice of Gina! Not quite the deranged fitness freak you make her out to be, hey?"

I gave him a blank stare. "We don't know what's in it yet. It's probably a packet of buckwheat seeds."

He shook it gently. "Hmm, not sure," he said handing it to me. "Feels more like tofu."

I opened the box and held up a silver key ring with a star dangling from it.

"Nice! Thanks, GGB!" I attached it to the zip of my

rucksack and that's when I noticed the writing engraved on the other side: *You are capable of amazing things.*

"Isn't that lovely!" Dad said, reading it over my shoulder. And I agreed with him. One hundred per cent.

I spent the rest of the day trying to beat my highest score in Scrabble, until I'd beaten Dad three times and he forced us to go for a walk along the seafront. Then I beat Jasper at Zombie Crush in the arcade. The whole way home he said he let me win because it was my birthday. Which isn't true. Even if I'd been dying of some terrible, mysterious illness and it was my last day on planet Earth, Jasper would still try to beat me at Zombie Crush.

Later, when I was getting ready, Dad yelled, "MIKI'S HERE!" Even on my birthday, Dad still yelled at me up the stairs.

Just then, Jasper came out of his room wearing Grandad's old cape and a pair of sunglasses saying, "Show starts in five."

"It's getting a bit dark, Jasper," Dad said as we came downstairs. "You still okay to do the show outside?"

"I'm always ready!" Jasper said, sliding down the banister. He clicked his fingers and a loud bang went off as tiny sparks flew out of his fingertips.

Nana almost fell out of her chair.

"JASPER!" Dad shouted, clutching his chest in shock. "I thought I told you not to do that!" He stood poised under the smoke alarm. When nothing happened he said, "Do I need to warn the neighbours, Jasper? Tell them to keep their pets inside or something?"

"It's fine, Dad. That was the only loud noise, I promise."

"Happy birthday," Miki said and handed me the most beautifully wrapped present I've ever seen. The paper was light yellow with tiny lilac flowers. "Mum might have helped me wrap that."

"It's amazing!" I said. I stood up and let the gold dreamcatcher dangle from my hand. Its long white feathers spun round and the tiny jewels sewn into the net caught the light. "I love it, Miki! Thank you."

"It's supposed to stop you having nightmares," Miki said.

"But will it stop her from being a nightmare?" Jasper muttered. Nana gave him The Look and Jasper quickly added, "I mean, great gift, Miki. Really thoughtful."

Outside, the sky was clear, so I pointed out the intricate patterns of the constellations to Miki – the Plough, Ursa Minor and the Great Square of Pegasus – under the light of the full moon and the hundreds of tealight candles in jars Luna had hung on the washing line.

"What's that flashing one?" Miki asked.

I smiled. "Miki, that's an aeroplane."

Dad did a drum roll on his thighs and pulled a piece of paper out of his back pocket. Jasper always printed out his own introduction. "Please, welcome to the stage…the astounding! The incredible! The enigmatic! The…wait a minute. What does that say?" He flashed the paper in front of me.

I rolled my eyes at Jasper's blatant overstatement. "Phantasmagorical."

"The phantasmagorical illusionist, Jasper Small!"

"Jasper *Diamond*!" Jasper shouted, then leaped out from behind the fir tree carrying an axe.

Miki squeezed my arm. I couldn't tell if he was excited about the magic or scared for his life.

Jasper's show music started and he tossed the axe high up into the air. Its silver blade glinted in the moonlight as it somersaulted three times, then transformed into a shower of shimmering crystals. We all clapped and cheered. Apart from Dad, who was nervously sweating.

Next, Jasper placed a silver box in front of him and danced around it. I had to bite my tongue to stop myself from laughing. Finally, he opened the box and his tarantula crept onto his hand. Miki edged closer to me. Jasper raised and twisted his arms as Tornado climbed across his chest then from fingertip to fingertip. Slowly, Jasper placed her inside a large glass jar. He screwed on the lid, then began to spin the jar in the palm of one hand as it filled with smoke. The jar went faster and faster and I seriously hoped Tornado had a stunt double.

Suddenly, the jar stopped spinning. Jasper took off the lid, and when the smoke escaped into the atmosphere, the jar was completely empty. Tornado had vanished.

"Bravo!" Nana cheered as Jasper retrieved Tornado from one of Luna's pot plants.

My teeth were chattering from the cold by the time Jasper performed his final trick: the Vortex Tube. I'd seen it loads of times before. He gets what looks like an empty tube, does his weird magical dancing as he fills it with coloured handkerchiefs, then he pulls them out and they are magically tied together. Only this time, each handkerchief had a letter sewn on it, so when he held them up, it spelled *HAPPY BIRTHDAY, JEMIMA*. I guessed Luna had helped him with it, but it was still a pretty good trick. Kind of phantasmagorical, actually.

Afterwards, we squashed into Luna's car and drove up past the seafront to Bonuccio's Pizzeria. The restaurant was warm, and lit with millions of candles. A waiter smiled and led us to a table by the window. He moved a chair so I could push Nana's wheelchair in.

"Oh, isn't this lovely!" Nana said. "Your grandad used to take me dancing down there." She pointed to the palladium and told us stories about all the stuff she did before she got so geriatric.

"I'm starving," Miki said, looking at the menu.

"Eat as much as you want, Miki. It's on my brother." Luna smiled at my dad.

The waiter took our order, and Jasper tried to show off by speaking some Italian. Which made him look like an idiot because the waiter said he was from Lyme Regis. While we were waiting for our food, Dad told jokes like: *What do you call someone who doesn't like pizza? A weirdough.* And I think the entire restaurant could hear Jasper's laughter.

Jasper had been referring to his magic show in the garden as "*Le Grand Illusion*" all the way here, and I knew I'd probably be hearing about it for the rest of my life.

"It was wonderful, Jasper!" Nana said. "Reminded me of your grandfather! He'd be so proud. He wouldn't have touched that tarantula, mind."

"It was awesome," Miki said. "You should ask Miss Nisha if you can do some tricks during the interval of *Mary Poppins!*"

But Jasper said, "My magic warrants an entire show of its own." He turned to me and said, "You know, Jemima, it's fine remembering facts and doing little *Brainiacs* quizzes and stuff. But magic is a form of *art*."

"You're right, Jasper," I said. "Your show was so incredible, even the English language doesn't have the right words to do it justice." I caught Miki's eye. "Miki taught me how to say this phrase in Japanese and it just seems like the perfect way to congratulate you." Then I told Jasper his show was a weasel's last fart in Japanese. Miki and I couldn't even look at each other without laughing until the pizzas arrived.

Dad was talking about the sign for the new hotel he was painting, and I was about halfway through eating my pizza when I heard it. Maybe I wasn't supposed to. But I did.

"Well, they shouldn't bring her here, should they?" It was a woman sitting a couple of tables away, talking to her husband. "No wonder she's that size if they let her eat pizza all the time!" And then the biggest tut I'd heard in my life.

Luna must have heard it too. Because her hand clasped mine. I tried to act like I didn't care. But you can't hide your pain from a psychic unfortunately. Even if it is totally invisible from the outside.

"Don't listen. I'm going to send her some seriously negative energy," Luna whispered. "You're amazing."

"She's lucky I'm in this wheelchair, I tell you," Nana said.

Miki asked what we were talking about, but I told him it didn't matter. The murmur of the restaurant came back, and Jasper started complimenting his own magic show again. Nana nudged my arm and told me to finish my pizza.

And I sat there, wondering how I could be made of two hundred and six bones, over six hundred muscles, a hundred thousand miles of blood vessels, billions of nerves, and trillions of cells, and have orbited the sun thirteen times, but still feel like nothing.

34

ORION

I spent the rest of half-term lying on my bedroom floor half-revising for the *Brainiacs* Selection Day. But after the woman had said that thing at the restaurant, my enthusiasm for being in a room with two hundred and fifty people I didn't know had kind of waned. Miki was staying at his dad's, so almost the whole week had passed and all I'd done was listen to rain pouring down my window and stare at pages of revision notes. But I had come to a decision. I wanted to get a high enough score to beat Lottie, but low enough not to make it onto the show. The only problem was, I had no idea how high Lottie would score. Miki had messaged me saying Lottie's parents had hired a private tutor for the week. The only thing my dad hired was a bowling lane.

I objected to it on moral grounds, based on the fact that I hated bowling and Jasper always made a stupid comment each time my ball went into the gutter and there were only three days until the competition. But Dad said I'd been studying all week and needed to get some fresh air. Which was his way of telling me we were walking.

The bowling alley was in the arcade opposite the pier. It smelled of chips and popcorn mixed together, and there were no windows. The whole place was lit with this strange green light which made me feel like we were in a submarine. A games machines called DELTA II flashed and played sound effects of bombs exploding and machine gun fire, which was literally ridiculous. Delta II was an American rocket launching system. It did not carry any weapons.

Once we'd changed our shoes and chosen a lane, Jasper entered our names into the computer. He always wrote annoying ones for himself, like MAGIC MASTER or THE ENIGMA. This time it was THE CONQUEROR. I went first and my ball immediately veered off into the gutter lane. A giant zero came up on the screen and Jasper said, "Pathetic." I changed his name to THE COCKROACH while he chose his ball.

Dad usually took us to the fast food place in the arcade after bowling, but he said there was a new health food deli up the road that he really wanted to try. I believed him for about three seconds. Then Jasper gave me this look and I realized it was because of me. And what that lady in the pizzeria had said about me. And I felt like that giant zero was flashing over my name again.

At the deli, I was taking a bite of spinach muffin when I spotted Gina walking through the door. I wasn't totally surprised. It was a health food deli after all. It was probably her spiritual home. She waved and made an immediate beeline for us.

"Hi, Jemima! Great to see you! And, oh my goodness! It's *Brainiacs* in what…?"

I was still chewing the muffin, so I couldn't say anything. It was kind of hard to swallow. Mainly because it was so disgusting.

Dad stood up so fast he almost knocked our plates. "It's on Monday. You must be Gina! Hi!"

I finally swallowed. "This is my dad," I said, "Orion."

Dad looked at me like he really wanted to tell me off for saying his full name, but didn't want Gina to think he was a tyrant dictator. I smiled my best smile at him.

"*Orion?*" Gina said, raising her eyebrows. Her smile was up to at least ninety per cent.

"Yeah," Jasper said. "After the Orion cinema in that retail park outside town."

"Don't be stupid, Jasper," I said. "Orion was a hunter in Greek mythology who was placed among the stars. It's the most prominent constellation on the celestial equator. There are a few legends about Orion's life, actually, that I've been reading about—"

"Yes, well, don't feel you have to tell us about them right now, Jemima." Dad smiled at Gina. "It's *Rion*. It's great to finally meet you."

"Likewise," Gina said, giving Dad a full one hundred per cent smile. "I'm glad you decided to check this place out!"

I should have known this deli idea came from Gina.

"I'll grab something to eat and join you, shall I?" Gina said.

It was kind of rude of her, considering we were having a family meal. But Dad didn't seem to mind. In fact, I'd never seen him agree to something so enthusiastically. He was probably bored of Jasper talking non-stop about his bowling achievements. I know I was. Dad was so keen to escape he went up to the counter with Gina while she ordered her food.

"So, are you all ready for the camping trip?" Gina said as they sat down. "It sounds like fun!"

"I'm still hoping Dad will see sense and not make me go," I said.

Gina laughed as Dad rolled his eyes.

"Jemima's got this aversion to camping," he explained. "It started in early childhood."

Gina laughed so hard she almost choked on her falafel. Maybe it was an age thing. Like, you can't get my dad's jokes unless you're almost geriatric.

"Remember what I said about the *Brainiacs* competition, Jemima," Gina said outside as we were leaving. "Keep that head of yours held high."

And then she chatted to my dad for ages even though it had started raining again.

I spent that weekend reading and revising, then on Sunday morning, I woke up to hear Dad singing loudly in the shower. It was weird. I pulled on my dressing gown, picked up my revision cards and went downstairs.

Jasper had his head in the fridge.

"Hey, test me on these," I said to him, sitting at the table.

He emerged with half a block of cheese in his mouth.

"You're eating cheese for breakfast?"

"Protein!" he said, spraying bits of cheese everywhere. He turned a chair round the wrong way, sat down and put on a pair of sunglasses.

I didn't tell him about the bits of cheese stuck in his fringe.

He cracked his knuckles, took my revision cards and started shuffling them. "Jemima, I know you think this *Brainiacs* thing is a big deal, but let me tell you, it isn't. Nothing you do at thirteen's a big deal. You'll realize that one day."

"Jasper, you're only *fourteen*."

He slid his sunglasses down to the end of his nose. "And seven months."

I sighed and grabbed some cereal. "Just test me, Jasper. The emissions from your ego are damaging my brain cells."

Jasper pulled out his phone. "Okay. Quick fire. Thirty questions. And if you lose, you're on washing-up duty for two weeks."

"How can I lose when I'm the only person playing?"

Jasper raised his eyebrows. "Your greatest enemy is yourself."

"Just ask me some questions, Jasper! It's the competition tomorrow!"

"Fine," he said, picking up the first card. "But I want a share in the prize money."

261

That afternoon, Dad told me I needed to rest my brain before the competition. He put my revision cards on top of the fridge, then headed upstairs. I sat down to watch *World's Deadliest Sharks* while I made some more revision cards for the journey tomorrow. A few minutes later, Dad came downstairs smelling like aftershave, even though he doesn't shave, and it looked like he'd ironed his shirt.

"So, I'm heading out for a bit."

Jasper and I looked at him.

"You're going *out*?" I said.

"Yeah, just for a couple of hours," he replied.

I exchanged looks with Jasper. "You're leaving us *alone*?" I said.

Dad laughed and messed up my hair. "Not alone! Luna's in the garden."

"Cool. I don't need a babysitter," Jasper said and went back to watching TV.

"But," I said, "where are you going? Can I come with you?"

"No. Just into town, Jemima! I won't be long. And, hey, I thought I said no revising tonight."

I put my cards on the coffee table. "But…you never go out."

"Exactly!" He went to open the front door.

"But," I said, "you can't just leave me here alone, Dad.

It's illegal!" I had this weird feeling in my stomach. Sort of like absolute terror. I wasn't exactly sure why. Maybe my psychic powers were awakening and I was having a premonition.

Dad took a deep breath. "It's not illegal, Jemima. You've got Jasper to look after you."

"Have you forgotten his ball of flames trick that almost burned the house down a couple of weeks ago?"

Jasper hit me with a cushion.

Dad sighed. "Fine. I'll ask Luna to sit with you, okay? Honestly, Jemima! It's just a couple of hours. I'll be back to help you do some last-minute cramming if you want, but honestly, I think it's better to relax tonight. Now, if you've finished your interrogation, I'll get Luna."

I knew in my head that Dad going out for a couple of hours was no big deal. That he wasn't leaving for ever. But the message hadn't quite made it to my heart. My heart was kind of stupid like that.

"Fine!" I said and turned back to the TV as a tiger shark devoured an albatross. When Dad had gone outside I said to Jasper, "Why is Dad acting so suspiciously?"

"I don't know," Jasper said. "Maybe he wants to get you a present for the *Brainiacs* thing tomorrow or something."

I felt an immediate relief, like at Miki's house once when the food was too spicy and his mum gave me a glass of milk. It has this protein in it called casein which takes the burn off your tongue.

"Oh yeah," I said. "That could be it. Dad is such a bad liar." I watched the screen as a great white shark tried to pound its way into a cage containing two divers. "Doesn't explain the overpowering aftershave though."

"Woah!" Jasper yelled, ignoring me. "I'm never swimming in the sea again!"

"Don't be stupid. They've probably baited it with something. It can detect blood in the water; that's why it's attacking them. The chances of being killed by a shark are about one in 250 million. It's actually far more likely for you to get hit by an asteroid while you're sitting right here on this sofa."

"Thanks," Jasper said, looking suspiciously at the ceiling.

I finished making my revision cards in my room, watching Tabitha Hendrix "Love Your Body" vlogs on YouTube. Then I practised timed multiplication, recited geographical facts and revised words from the phobias section of my *Champion's Guide to Spelling* book which Miss Reed had bought me ages ago when she forced me to do the Spelling Bee. Like pteromerhanophobia, which is the fear of flying. I worked out what that one meant without looking it up because it's got *ptero* at the beginning, which means wing in Greek. It was easier to understand than chionophobia, which is the fear of snow. I knew that *chion* meant snow; I just didn't understand how anyone could be frightened of something that could get you a day off school.

35

THE BOX JELLYFISH

The next morning, as everyone else was going back to school, I was travelling at approximately one hundred miles an hour towards London, reading the *World's Deadliest Animals* book I'd borrowed from Jasper. It was hard to concentrate on facts about giant hornets though, because it felt like I was hurtling towards something even more dangerous.

"Stop worrying!" Dad peered at me over his *Art + Design* magazine. "Everyone there will be nervous."

I nodded and looked out of the window. Lottie probably wouldn't be nervous. I hoped I didn't have to sit next to her. I wouldn't be able to concentrate with her sneering at me.

"Jemima, ever since you started school, all I've heard

from your teachers is how freakishly smart you are."

"Thanks," I said rolling my eyes.

"What I mean is, *Brainiacs* will be looking for someone exactly like you today."

I looked at the outline of my reflection in the train window, and tried my hardest, my absolute hardest, to believe him.

My phone beeped. It was a text from Miki telling me to *SLAY IT!* next to the Japanese character that means "courage".

I typed back:

Thanks 😊

But I knew I couldn't slay over two hundred and fifty people.

I turned the page of my book and read: *Did you know? An adult box jellyfish contains enough venom to kill over sixty humans.* Too bad I wasn't a box jellyfish.

We arrived at Paddington station, where a huge clock told us that we were running late in Roman numerals. Dad hurried down the steps, dodging tourists wheeling suitcases, just in time to drag me onto a giant escalator heading underground to catch our next train.

"Phew! Just made it!" Dad announced to the entire carriage as the doors slammed shut. "She's got an audition!"

My skin stung with embarrassment.

An old couple smiled warmly at me as I sat down near some empty seats, but two women sitting opposite looked at me, then smiled at each other. Maybe they couldn't figure out how "audition" and me went together. I closed my eyes and started silently counting the seventy-eight times tables, trying to drown out the voice in my head telling me I shouldn't be here. That voice needed to shut up. I had maths to do.

At the hotel, we followed the signs saying BRAINIACS COMPETITION – CHAPLIN SUITES.

"Look – that's Big Ben across the river!" Dad said, pointing out of a huge window.

I told him that technically it was the Elizabeth Tower, because Big Ben is the bell inside. He told me to save the "swot talk" for the competition.

The Chaplin Suites were three rectangular-shaped rooms joined together. Huge white wooden shutters had been pushed back, on some sort of pulley system, to create one enormous space. By the entrance, there were people milling about next to a table covered with name badges. I couldn't spot Lottie or Noah Chamberlain, but I noticed a parent giving me a second glance. I stayed in Dad's shadow as we walked over to the table.

A woman wearing a yellow *Braniacs* long-sleeved

T-shirt found my name badge and said, "Good luck, Jemima! May your brain be with you!" She handed me a schedule and a list of rules, then I had to stand in front of a huge yellow screen to get my photo taken.

A few people nearby watched me while that was happening. Which made it pretty hard to "Smile like a Brainiac!" like the photographer told me to do.

The flash was still in my eyes as Dad headed to a sofa opposite the registration desk, where he read out the rules for the day. There were millions. Don't take off your badge. Don't talk about the games you've completed with other competitors. Don't take your phone into the competition room. The adjudicators' decision was final. My brain ached and the competition hadn't even started yet. A klaxon sounded, and people started filing into the room.

Dad hugged me. "Good luck, sweetheart. Whatever happens, try to enjoy it!"

I nodded like that was even possible. As I handed him my phone a text flashed up from Luna:

Channel your inner goddess ⚡

I looked down at my schedule. Unless my inner goddess had been revising logic and strategy games, Luna's advice was kind of useless.

Inside the Chaplin Suites, a man was on a stage at the back.

"Welcome, Brainiacs!" he boomed into a microphone.

Everyone clapped and cheered. There were two hundred and fifty people there, but it felt like thousands. Some were wearing their school uniforms like me, some were in jeans, a few were wearing business suits. I scanned the room for Lottie, but I couldn't see her anywhere. I felt instantly bad for accidentally wishing she'd get the norovirus last night.

"I'm Damien Jones," the man onstage said. "I'm one of the producers of the show. Thank you all for coming here to compete for a place on Britain's toughest brain-busting competition...*Brainiaaaaaaaaacs*!"

Everyone cheered again. I could feel the sweat on my palms each time I clapped my hands together.

"As you can see, the room's been divided into four zones. Each of you will complete timed tests in each zone, and our adjudicators – they are the very friendly looking people in yellow tops – will record your scores."

A sea of yellow arms went up as the adjudicators waved. A boy standing near me waved back.

"Your families will be in the Garson Suite upstairs while the competition is taking place. If you need them urgently for any reason, please tell any member of our crew. Now, competitors!" The microphone squeaked. "I'm sure I don't need to remind you what's at stake!

The fifteen of you with the highest overall scores will go through to appear on our TV show for a chance to win the amazing *Brainiacs* trophy and five thousand pounds for your school! It only happens once a year, people! Make some noise!"

Everyone cheered even louder, one of the adjudicators drummed on a table and the boy near me wolf-whistled. I hoped I wouldn't get tinnitus after this.

"You've read the rules, but here's the most important one," Damien said. "DO. YOUR. BEST! Good luck and may your brains be with you!"

The klaxon sounded again so I headed towards a sign saying Logic and Strategy Zone. And that's when I spotted Lottie. My stomach lurched. She was wearing her school uniform, but she looked different. She was wringing her hands and glancing around the room like she didn't know where to go. I walked over.

"Hey, Lottie," I said. "Do you know which zone you're doing first?"

Her face changed and she said, "Yes, of course, *Jemima*. I've got the Languages Zone."

"I've got Logic and Strategy," I said, and she stared at me. I could tell she was nervous because the water in the bottle she was holding was sloshing around. "Well, good luck. May your brain be with you!" I said and regretted it instantly.

"Like I need you to tell me that," she replied. "Oh, no! Look – they got your name wrong."

I automatically looked down at the badge on my lapel.

"It should say *Jemima Big*."

She brushed past me and headed towards the World Languages and Spelling Zone. I knew it was only Lottie, but it felt like someone had thrown a bowling ball at my stomach. I glanced around to see if anyone else had heard. I didn't feel upset, just stupid. And feeling stupid was not a good way to start Britain's toughest brain-busting competition.

I watched the back of Lottie's head disappear into the crowd, then I surveyed the room. Two hundred and fifty people. Each one of them competing for a place on the show. Some of them probably wondering why I would want one. I turned and looked back at the double doors I'd just come through. A man in a yellow T-shirt with a Bluetooth device in his ear was about to close them. There was still time to turn back.

Or, I thought, turning around and lifting my head up, *maybe it's time to channel my inner box jellyfish.*

36

DNA

In the Logic and Strategy Zone, an adjudicator with curly red hair showed me to a booth which contained a yellow table and two chairs facing each other. And it was tiny. My cheeks flushed as I pushed the chair as far back against the wall as I could.

"I'm so sorry, Jemima," she said, pushing the divider back a bit so I could at least breathe. "Space is really tight in this zone. The others aren't so squashed." Which was nice of her and totally embarrassing at the same time.

She disappeared, then came back a minute later with a boy who looked a few years younger than me. He was wearing a suit with matching waistcoat and a yellow tie, and his hair was parted in the middle. He looked like he'd jumped straight out of a Charles Dickens novel, which was appropriate because his name badge said *Oliver*.

He shook my hand and said, "Hi, I'm Oli. And I'm going to completely annihilate you."

Before I could say anything, the adjudicator turned over a chart on the wall. On it were pictures of fruits, each with a number next to it. It took me about 0.5 seconds to figure out we would be doing algebraic equations. A tiny fizz of excitement (and maybe relief) shot through me as she explained the rules. I tried to steady my hands. It was only choosing the right fruits to solve the equations, I told myself. It was mental maths. I'd done this a million times with Mrs Lee, and this time, I didn't have Lottie blowing her cheeks out at me. I just had Oliver Twist glaring at me instead. I took a deep breath as the adjudicator placed a yellow buzzer on the table in between us.

"One hundred and forty-eight," she said and clicked a timer. I scanned the values on the chart, searching for a way to make 148. It took me almost ten seconds to work it out because I was so nervous. Luckily, Oli wasn't any quicker.

I pressed the buzzer. "Pineapple times apple squared minus grapes."

"Correct!"

I blew out a long breath as Oli gave me evils over the table.

After twenty questions, I'd beaten him 18–2.

I stood up, shook his hand and said, "It was good meeting you, Oli. I mean, *annihilating* you."

After that, I beat a girl called Sinead at brain-teasers, solved logic problems faster than Diego, cracked more codes than Madison and then messed up a chess game against Zane.

A klaxon sounded and Damien Jones bellowed down the microphone, "End of your first zone!"

There was a short break, so I filled up my bottle from the water station near the stage and sat down. The room felt really stuffy, but I didn't want to take off my blazer. I dabbed the sweat on my top lip with a tissue and wafted my schedule to get some air on my face. I kept forgetting I'd given my phone to Dad, and reached into my pocket a few times to get it. I had a cereal bar in there, but I hated eating in crowds, so I sat and watched the other people. Some competitors were standing in groups chatting, but a lot were like me, just sitting at the edge of the room. A boy nearby, whose name badge said *Andrew*, was reciting the two hundred and twenty-three times table. Some people were smiling; some looked defeated already. I guess I was in the middle. Like Jupiter. And approximately the same temperature as its core.

When the klaxon sounded, I double-checked my

schedule, then headed to the Memory Zone where I had ten minutes to memorize picture cards. One hundred of them. I spread them out on the table and took a few deep breaths through my nose. It's called belly breathing. It helps get more oxygen to your brain, according to the NHS website. (I did some strategy googling on the train.) Not that I really needed it. I'd been able to memorize a whole pack of cards since I was seven years old and I'd managed all seventy-eight of Luna's tarot cards last week. I cracked my knuckles, picked up the cards and shuffled them, just like Jasper.

When ten minutes was up, a man with a thin moustache came in with a clipboard and a timer. I had two minutes to recite as many objects as I could. I took a deep breath and closed my eyes.

I was on thirty-two – a pink octopus – when I made the mistake of opening my eyes. Lottie was standing opposite my booth. She was about five metres away, but I could still see her filling her cheeks with air. I don't know what happened to my brain after that. In fact, I do. There's this chemical called norepinephrine that makes your brain freeze up. After that, I could only remember a few cards before the time ran out. And you don't have to be a Brainiac to know that thirty-five out of a hundred was light years away from good enough.

In the next booth, I had to memorize a Metro map of Paris. It had approximately a million destinations and was approximately impossible to remember. My opponent was called Daniel. He'd drawn a smiley face with sunglasses on his badge underneath his name.

"Hello, Jemima! Or should I say *bonjour*!"

He over-pronounced *bonjour* exactly the way Jasper did; I knew I had to beat him.

The adjudicator clicked a timer, then read out impossible-sounding questions like, "Which station is five stops north-west from Concorde?" and "How many stations contain the letter T?"

Daniel kept over-pronouncing the French words, which was so annoying it seemed to supercharge the neurons in my brain. And in three minutes, I'd won 14–6.

In the next zone, I got full marks in the spelling test, anagrams and vocabulary match-up, but didn't do so well in the foreign words round. It started okay. I mean, when you live with Jasper, you can't not know that *araignée* means spider in French. And when Miki's your best friend, you know *sensei* is teacher in Japanese. Afzal had taught us some Arabic in form time last year, and I knew a few Polish words from Alina. But I had to guess the rest, which was annoying. They really ought to teach you Luxemburgish at school.

When the klaxon sounded it was time for my final zone: the Universe of Knowledge. I sat at a yellow table with a buzzer in front of me and the late morning sun blazing through the windows onto my face. Sweat was soaking through my shirt at the back. I had to take my blazer off. I peeled it down my arms and put it over the back of my chair, then tucked my chair right up against the table.

"Jemima! We meet again!" It was Zane, who'd beaten me at chess earlier. "Good luck!"

I wished him luck too. And silently wished for there not to be any sweat on the plastic chair when I stood up.

Our adjudicator told us, "This game's really straightforward. Quick-fire general knowledge. Buzz as soon as you know the answer. If you're wrong, you lose a point and your opponent gets a try. Good luck! May your brains be with you!" He raised the question cards and I placed my trembling hand on the buzzer.

"The first question is: the chemical symbol Au—"

Before I even had a chance to blink, Zane had hit his buzzer. "Gold!"

"I'm afraid I hadn't finished the question, Zane," the adjudicator said, adjusting his glasses. "You go on to minus one point and, Jemima, you now have a chance to answer. The chemical symbol Au has which atomic number?"

I smiled awkwardly at Zane. "Seventy-nine?"

"Correct!"

Time flew by faster than a cosmic ray, and after twenty questions, our scores were tied. Which could only mean one thing: a tiebreaker. Zane wished me luck and the adjudicator said, "Which constellation is home to the Ring Nebula?"

I hit the buzzer at approximately the speed of light. "The northern constellation of Lyra." It's the kind of thing you know when you gaze at the stars with your auntie a lot.

"Good match, Jemima Small!" Zane said, shaking my hand. "You've got a big brain in there!"

And my smile probably went as wide as the Ring Nebula. But it faded quickly. Because the next opponent walked in: Lottie Freeman.

I closed my eyes. I knew she'd be staring at me. I wished I hadn't taken my blazer off. I folded my arms tight across my tummy, and tried to ignore my heartbeat, which was increasing by the second. I took some deep breaths and focused on what I knew about the nervous system. It releases chemicals in your brain to help you respond to danger. It's probably what helped our early ancestors survive all those millions of years ago. Sometimes those chemicals give you brain-freeze, but sometimes they surge through your brain like a super power. I opened my eyes.

Predictably, Lottie was staring at me. "Thought you'd fallen asleep!" She tilted her head slightly. "This is probably quite exhausting for you."

Just then, an adjudicator with bright-blue hair walked into our booth. "Take a deep breath, girls! It will help your nerves." A titanium crystal was hanging from her neck, glowing electric blue in the light. Luna had one of those. She said they're so energizing, they awaken all of your seven chakras. Before that, I didn't even know I had one chakra.

"Good luck, Jemima!" Lottie said in her angelic voice.

"That's right, Lottie! It's not a battle! Just answer as many questions as you can in three minutes. May your brains be with you!" The lady smiled and held up the question cards. The *Brainiacs* lightning bolt logo glinted gold in the sunshine. My heart pounded in my chest as Gina's words came back to me: *Hold your head up.*

I sat up straight in my chair, put my hand on my buzzer and looked at Lottie with stone-cold eyes. Eyes like my great-great-aunties' in those old photographs. As though I could feel their blood pumping through my veins.

It is *a battle*, I thought. *But I have beard-growing-bare-knuckle-fighting-mind-reading women in my DNA. And I don't plan to lose.*

37

HORIZON

Lottie put her hand on the buzzer and inflated her cheeks. I took a deep breath, looking directly into her beady eyes. The rodent has a lot of predators. But none so deadly as the human.

"Kosciuszko is the highest mountain in which country?"

I slammed my hand down. "Australia," I said and Lottie flashed a sarcastic smile as the adjudicator said, "Correct!"

"Who was the third man to walk on the moon?"

I hesitated. I wasn't one hundred per cent sure, but as soon as I saw Lottie's hand flinch, I pressed mine down. It was worth risking a guess. "Charles Conrad Junior?"

The adjudicator smiled. "Correct."

The questions flew so fast it felt like I was dodging bullets. Lottie did well on sports, and geography and she answered one about a composer I'd never heard of. So when the adjudicator said we only had one more question, I didn't know if I'd done enough.

"Good luck, girls," she said. "Calculate the following…"

I could feel my hand shaking on the buzzer. But I closed my eyes and watched the numbers she read out form a sum in my mind. I don't know how long it took me to work it out. It felt like an eternity.

All I know is it wasn't as long as Lottie. "Eight hundred and seventy-nine."

"Correct, Jemima! The final scores are: Lottie six, Jemima nine."

The klaxon sounded three times.

Damien shouted, "That's it, Brainiacs! Game over! Well done!"

Everyone around me was cheering, but I didn't join in. I didn't feel excited or relieved or happy or victorious. If I could pick an adjective to describe how I felt right then, immediately after beating Lottie at the *Brainiacs* Selection Day, I'd pick *aliferous*. It means having wings. I felt as though I'd soared above the Chaplin Suites, high above the city, right up to the very edge of our atmosphere and touched the boundary between Earth and space.

Lottie's chair screeched against the wooden floor as she stood up. She muttered, "Well done," then left the booth without looking behind her. It had never felt so good to see the back of her head.

"Thank you, competitors! You've been fantastic! This year's show is going to be the best and the toughest EVER! I wish we could take all of you through, but we only have fifteen places. You'll find out very soon if you've done enough. Don't forget to collect your *Brainiacs* goody bag on your way out. Thank you!" Damien clapped his hands above his head and a huge cheer went through the room like a rip tide.

I stood up and joined in that time.

The *Brainiacs* people had put out a buffet for everyone, but Dad said we could eat somewhere else if I wanted. So I chose a Japanese restaurant near Paddington station where you pick your food from a conveyor belt going all the way round the room. We ate miso soup and cucumber rolls and aubergine nigari and I didn't notice anyone looking at me twice. Not even once. Maybe because we were in a big city. Or maybe because I'd mixed too much wasabi into my soy sauce and I felt like my nose was about to explode.

☆ ☆

Later, as our train approached Clifton Station, Dad put his arm around me.

"I'm so proud of you, Jem."

"We don't know if I've got through yet," I said.

"I'm proud of you regardless of that." He smiled at the other passengers waiting to get off. "My daughter's just auditioned for *Brainiacs*!" he said to literally the entire train.

I considered hitting the emergency stop button but it said there was a one-hundred-pound fine for improper use and I'd only just cleared my pocket money debt from the conical beakers I broke.

"Good luck!" a woman called as we got off the train. "I'll keep my fingers crossed for you, love!" And she smiled like she actually meant it.

I took out my phone and read the messages from Miki: yessss!!!!! omg!!! 🐀 ✸✸ lololololol!!!

Dad wrapped his coat around my shoulders as I read the one from Jasper: proud of you sister.

I'd read a lot of spelling and vocabulary books over the past few weeks, but I didn't know a word to describe that feeling you get when you know people are proud of you. It was like being filled with sunlight, the kind of sunlight that refracts across the horizon. And it made that hole inside my heart feel not so infinite.

The next morning, Dad said "*Brainiacs* Selection Day fatigue" wasn't an illness, so I had to go to school. As I packed the *Brainiacs* mini dictionary, pencils, banana-scented tissues and lightning-bolt geometry set I'd got in my goody bag into my rucksack, I thought at least Lottie would finally leave me alone. Now I'd beaten her at *Brainiacs*, she couldn't say anything to me. But my theory was proved wrong. Like, the-Earth-is-flat theory wrong. It made her worse.

It was pouring with rain, so of course in PE we were playing hockey. I had no choice but to run my fastest because our teacher, Ms Newton, is demented.

She shouted, "RUN, JEMIMA! RUN, GIRL! RUUUUN!" so loudly I could barely remember whose team I was on. If she didn't think someone was moving fast enough, she'd come right onto the pitch shouting, "GO GO GOOOOO!" It was definitely illegal.

After the game, I used the last few kilojoules of energy left in my legs to run back to the changing rooms so I could get a cubicle.

"Sweating much, Jemima?" Lottie said, then snort-laughed as I went past.

"It's all that extra weight," said Pippa Williams, the team captain.

They were each carrying an armful of hockey sticks and their mud-spattered legs still looked slim even with shin pads in their socks.

"Well, she is *officially* obese," Lottie replied.

"You're officially annoying," I called behind me and quickly opened the door.

I was about to walk into the changing room when I heard Alina say, "Leave her alone. It's not funny. And by the way, Lottie, you're sweating too."

I stopped and looked back down the corridor.

Lottie stared at Alina for a moment then said, "Fine. Get your best friend Big to help you with these." She dropped the hockey sticks she was carrying at Alina's feet. Pippa looked at Lottie, then she did the same and they both ran towards the changing rooms, their high-pitched laughter echoing down the corridor. Pippa told me to get out of the way as they barged past. Alina watched them, then looked down at the pile of hockey sticks in front of her. I let the changing room door swing shut behind me.

"Thanks," Alina said as I helped put the sticks away in the sports cupboard. "I'm sorry for what Lottie's been saying. She doesn't mean it."

I shrugged. I didn't believe that was true, but it was the first time I'd spoken to Alina in ages, so I didn't say anything.

"She thinks it's funny."

"Then she must be missing part of her right frontal lobe," I said.

Alina smiled. "Where the sense of humour is in your brain, right? I remember." She put the last hockey stick in the rack and closed the cupboard door. "Listen, Lottie said she's going to get back at you. For beating her yesterday. She said you've knocked her out of the competition. I told her it's stupid, but she doesn't listen to what I think. She said something about the camping trip next week, so…"

A wave of nausea went through my stomach.

"I just wanted to warn you. I better go and get changed," she said and jogged down the corridor.

"Thanks," I said, but it was too late for her to hear me.

38

TEAM SMALL

A couple of days later, when Jasper and I got back from school, Dad was in the living room holding a bright yellow box. He'd trimmed down his beard and it looked like he'd had a haircut for the first time in years.

"Who's that for?" Jasper asked, switching on the TV and plonking himself on the sofa.

"I got a very exciting call today!" Dad said. "Jasper, turn the TV off for a minute, would you?"

Jasper pressed the remote. "Is it Luna's birthday?"

"It's no one's birthday," Dad said. "I was just about to tell your sister about a phone call I got today."

"Who from?" Jasper asked.

Dad turned to me with the biggest smile in the history of humanity on his face and said, "It was from a certain producer of a certain TV show about a certain very clever young lady who has made the final fifteen!"

Oh my actual God.

My skin went ice cold. My chest felt tight. I felt like I might faint, right there on the living room carpet, while Dad smiled at me like he'd won the EuroMillions jackpot.

"Isn't it fantastic?" Dad hugged me, squashing me into the parcel he was holding. "Jemima! You did it! You're going to be on *Brainiacs*! Can you believe it, Jasper?"

"No," Jasper said. "I can't believe it."

I couldn't believe it either. I was probably going to die from shock before I even got there. Everything Dad and Jasper were saying went silent as three thoughts raced through my mind:

I'm going to be on Brainiacs.

I'm going to be on Brainiacs.

I'm going to be on Brainiacs.

"Here's a little present from me to say well done!" Dad put the yellow box in my hands. "Jem, are you all right?"

I nodded, but my hands were shaking as I opened it. A label on top said *Revise It Kit!* in Dad's handwriting. There were books, notepads, postcards, coloured stickers, highlighters, motivational quotes, a pencil case and sticky notes shaped like slices of watermelon.

"Thanks, Dad, this is—"

"EPIC!" Jasper said, peering in. "I need one for doing my GCSEs!"

"The show's being filmed on the twelfth of November, so…"

"Oh my God," I said. "That's in less than three weeks!"

"Listen." Dad put his hands on my shoulders. "You won't be studying for this on your own. Me and Jasper are here to help. And Luna will…erm, ask the universe for brainy energy or something. You've got us all behind you." He took a step back, flexed his arm muscles and said, "TEAM SMALL!"

I told Dad under no circumstances was he to do that on TV.

I heard the back door fly open and Luna rushed in holding several calendars. She threw her arms around me then cupped my face tightly in her hands. My cheeks squashed together making my lips protrude about twenty centimetres.

"I'm so proud of you, my angel!"

I did not look like an angel. An angel fish, maybe.

"What am I always telling you? The universe is always listening!"

"Thanks, Luna," I said, rubbing my cheeks. "But I hardly have any time to revise!"

Luna's face turned serious. "What date is the show?"

Dad told her and she quickly sat down and spread out her calendars on the coffee table. One said *Seasonal Energies* and another was called *The Flow of the Universe*. One just had pictures of cats on it.

Luna looked at them for a moment then sat up. "The First Quarter Moon," she said. "The Goddess Anunit."

"Okay," I said. "Is that…good?"

Luna's silvery eyes flashed. "The moon goddess of battle!"

"What does that mean?" I asked.

Dad started tidying up the calendars and said, "It means your auntie's going to help you with your studying, isn't that right, Luna?"

Luna stood up and gripped my shoulders. "Forget studying, Jemima! You need a crystal."

39

HUMAN BOWLING

The next morning was Friday and my arm was practically dead from the amount of times Miki had squeezed it on the way to form while shouting, "YOU'RE GOING TO BE ON TV!" Lottie didn't look up as I walked in, but Mr Nelson greeted us wearing a cagoule and wellies over his suit.

"Good morning, 8N! Here is your last visual reminder about some of the essentials you need to bring on the camping trip on Monday. There's always someone who forgets to bring their underpants!"

Everyone laughed.

"And I think we all know who that's likely to be..."

Everyone looked at Caleb, who looked confused.

I was officially dreading going camping. The only

good thing about being in the middle of nowhere was the sky. I'd be able to see planets, distant galaxies, nebula clouds. Probably even some meteors burning up that looked like shooting stars. Maybe it was worth stepping in a few cowpats for that. I looked over at Lottie. As long as I watched out for the biggest cowpat of all.

Mr Nelson handed out a camping-themed word search, and I was just highlighting *excitement* and telling Miki why that shouldn't be on a word search about camping, when Mrs Savage walked in.

"Good morning, Mr Nelson! Good morning, 8N! What a joy to see such a busy class!"

Mr Nelson made us all say good morning to her like we were in primary school. I noticed her eyes resting on me.

"I've popped in to say an enormous congratulations to Jemima – stand up! Come on! Don't be shy!"

I slowly pushed out my chair and pulled my blazer round my stomach. My cheeks felt hot as I stood in front of Mr Nelson's desk and Mrs Savage cleared her throat.

"8N, I am extremely delighted to tell you that Jemima has won a place representing Clifton Academy on *Brainiacs*!"

She started clapping and everyone in my class joined in. Mr Nelson gave me a double handshake and Miki whooped and Afzal cheered and Erin gave me a one-person standing ovation and Alina beamed at me.

Lottie clapped loudly and said, "Well done, Jemima! She only beat me by three points!" She had a smile the width of the equator plastered on her face.

I tried to smile back, but it was like my face was allergic to her. I looked behind me at the collage of camping pictures Mr Nelson had put on the screen and thought about what Alina had said after PE. Could Lottie really come up with something worse than Camp Go Wild! itself?

At lunchtime, grey cumulonimbus clouds were gathered in the sky pelting everyone with fat blobs of rain. I walked quickly to the sports hall, sheltering under my physics textbook. Inside, Gina was pumping up a giant beach ball.

"Jemima!" she said. "Oh my goodness! Congratulations on *Brainiacs*! I was thrilled when your dad told me the news!"

"Er, thanks," I said, wiping my dripping textbook with a tissue. "My dad didn't have to phone you about it."

"Don't be silly! I'm so excited for you!"

"No way!" Brandon shouted as he strode in. He patted the giant beach ball as if checking it was real. "We're zorbing!"

"Not zorbing, Brandon," Gina said, pushing in the stopper. She began spinning the ball round expertly with her hands. "But it will be fun!"

"Lame," Brandon said, then immediately apologized.

"Right. Find a space, everyone!" Gina ran over and handed each of us a blindfold. "I don't want to make it too easy for you!"

I looked at the giant orange ball rolling around on its axis. "We could be killed!" I said quietly to Heidi, but my voice echoed down the sports hall and Gina smiled at me.

"It's not going to kill you, Jemima! It only weighs a few kilos!"

Maybe Gina hadn't heard of Newton's laws of motion, or noticed Brandon warming himself up like he was about to enter a boxing ring. I put on my blindfold and surrendered myself to my fate. At least if I was seriously injured, I'd get out of the camping trip.

Brandon shouted, "Human bowling!"

I pulled my blindfold off. "See?"

"Yeah, tell him, miss," Maya added.

Gina laughed. "I'll keep an eye on Brandon, don't worry."

I sighed and fastened my blindfold back up while Gina explained the rules. It was basically a giant game of blind catch. If I ended up needing facial surgery, then I was definitely suing the school. And Brandon Taylor.

Gina shouted "Go!" and I heard the ball bouncing towards me, the squeak of my trainers on the floor, the thump of my heart. It totally felt like human bowling. I put my arms out and prayed.

"YES! You got it, Jemima!" Gina shouted. And I think I actually *heard* her smile.

The games Gina made us play that lunchtime were definitely illegal. But after twenty minutes, my stomach muscles were hurting from laughing so much. Afterwards, we sat in a circle and Gina pulled some ice lollies out of a cool box.

"A little treat for you all! Home-made ice lollies! Thought you might need cooling down!"

We all looked at each other. It wasn't telepathy, but I knew we were all thinking the same thing. The sports hall filled with our laughter.

"What?" Gina said. "What's so funny?"

"Don't tell me," Nate said. "Avocado flavour."

"No." Maya laughed. "Sweet potato!"

Gina put her hands on her hips. "Oh, I see. Very funny!"

"I know!" Brandon shouted. "Ming bean and wet grass!"

Gina laughed. "It's *mung* bean, Brandon, and *wheatgrass*. And no."

"Cashew nuts?" Heidi asked.

"Cauliflower!" Harry shouted.

Gina laughed and shook her head. "You are all very

funny! But I really don't think you'll guess this one! Jemima?"

I looked at the lollies slowly defrosting in her hands. "Dragon fruit?"

Gina's mouth dropped open. "She's right!" She pulled a dragon fruit out of her handbag. "They're dragon fruit and lime! I brought one in to show you! Amazing, Jemima! How did you know that?"

I shrugged. "You always put weird things in stuff."

Gina laughed and everyone stared at me like they thought I was a genius. Or a Brainiac. But it wasn't that. I'd seen the dragon fruit poking out of Gina's handbag when I walked in.

We ate the lollies while Gina told us about the nutritional value of dragon fruit and lime. She was a walking Wikipedia for fruit.

"Now, Harry, Heidi, Jemima, here's my exciting news! I've been asked to go on the Year Eight camping trip!" She smiled hard enough to emit a Wi-Fi signal. "Isn't that brilliant!"

"Great!" I said, and I hoped Gina couldn't tell I was lying. Gina Grantley-Bond at Camp Go Wild! was the last thing in the world I wanted.

Maybe you think I didn't like Gina. That I didn't want to see her gigantic seventy per cent smile while I was negotiating a field of guy ropes and cowpats. Or that I didn't want to hear about the nutritional value of a roasted marshmallow. But it wasn't that. At Camp Go Wild! I'd be doing abseiling, rock climbing, running and loads of other outdoor sports.

I just didn't want Gina to see me fail at everything.

That weekend, I barely took my head out of a book. I made revision cards and mind maps, wrote lists, and covered all the possible quiz topics given in my official *Brainiacs* invitation letter. Any time I took a study break, I spent it begging Dad not to make me go camping. But even qualifying for *Brainiacs* doesn't get you taken seriously in my family.

On Sunday night, Dad came into my room holding a brown rucksack. It had badges sewn on the pockets saying: *Camping is in-tents!* and *Life's short, camp naked!*

"I found this in one of the boxes we cleared out of the garage!" he said. "Perfect, or what?"

"If your definition of 'perfect' is me dying of humiliation, then yeah."

Dad actually laughed. Hermione jumped off my bed and started sniffing the rucksack. Even the cat could tell there was something wrong with it.

I pointed to the *camp nuked* badge. "You can't be serious."

"Oh, lighten up! It's only a joke! No one will even notice. I'm not buying a brand-new rucksack just for one camping trip." Dad unzipped it and I'm pretty sure a moth flew out. "They don't make rucksacks like this any more!"

"There's a good reason for that. I'm going to be the laughing stock of Year Eight. Where's the rucksack Jasper took when he went?"

"Ah, yes. Good question. In fact, it's probably still at Camp Go Wild! That Brandon Taylor threw it in the lake, apparently. Anyway, this one's far sturdier. I can't believe I almost dumped this at the tip!"

"That would have been a real tragedy." I looked through the camping stuff he was bringing in from the landing, wondering if my life could get any worse.

"Ah-ha! Here they are!" Dad held up two waterproof trouser legs, the colour of desert camouflage. "My old gaiters! These bad boys will keep your legs dry when you're wading through the river!"

"I won't be *wading*." I picked up the Camp Go Wild! brochure to double-check. "It doesn't say anything about wading. Or army-issue gaiters. The only thing we're doing on the river is kayaking. Which is the main reason I'm hoping to get abducted by aliens tonight."

"Jemima!" Dad said. "It won't be that bad! But, if it's anything like the camping trips I remember from school, you won't stay in the kayak very long. That's when these beauties will come in handy!"

I pictured trying to get in a kayak like the one in the Camp Go Wild! brochure. I imagined it wobbling and tipping over, and splashing into freezing cold water wearing my dad's gaiters, and probably catching Weil's disease, while my whole year laughed at me.

"Do I really have to go? Can't I stay here and revise for *Brainiacs* instead? That's more important than camping. The show's only two weeks away. I can't risk serious injury."

Dad smiled. "You'll have a good time once you're there. You don't want to be the only one in your whole year not going."

"I wouldn't be! Jennifer Simons in Miki's maths class isn't going."

Dad thought for a moment. "Isn't she the one who's just had her appendix out?"

I sighed. Why did I always tell Dad stuff like that?

"So, I'll leave you to pack. Oh, and don't forget your swimsuit."

"My swimsuit?" My skin went cold as though I'd been submerged in icy water.

"Yeah, for under your wetsuit. For the games in the lake."

"But it says on the website they don't do swimming in the lake in October."

"Only if the temperature's dropped, which it hasn't. Mr Nelson's email said that the first activity is water polo. I thought you knew."

"Oh my God." I could not imagine anything worse than wearing a wetsuit in front of my entire year. Even getting Weil's disease would be better than that. "Please don't make me go."

"Jemima," Dad said, kneeling next to me on the floor, "you've got to stop worrying about this weight thing. Heidi and Harry will be there, won't they? And Miki? And Gina?"

I nodded.

"I'm telling you – everyone will be so excited to be there, no one will give you a second glance."

Maybe I could take a T-shirt to wear over my wetsuit. And maybe Dad's gaiters to cover my legs. Hippocrates knew what he was talking about when he said desperate times call for desperate measures.

"It looks like a beautiful lake!" Dad said. "It will be wonderful! They do it in all the Scandinavian countries, and look how healthy they are! If I was going, I don't think I'd bother with any swimwear at all. There is nothing quite like swimming in the nude!"

"Dad!" I put my hands over my face.

Jasper shouted, "GROSS!" from across the landing.

Dad laughed. "You'll have so much fun, you'll come back wondering why you made such a fuss about it."

"*If* I come back," I said. "We're foraging for our own food. I might accidentally eat poisonous mushrooms."

"Jemima, don't eat poisonous mushrooms just to get out of swimming. You don't want to be in a tent with severe vomiting and diarrhoea, do you? How embarrassing would that be?"

Dad was right.

"I could fall down a ravine."

"Don't fall down a ravine. At least not without a rope attached."

"You wouldn't fit down a ravine!" Jasper shouted.

Dad paced across the landing and put his head into Jasper's bedroom. "Stop it, Jasper. Maybe I should tell her about how you were so scared of the dark you had to sleep in the teachers' lodge! Now, see if Luna needs some help with dinner, will you? She said something about nettle soup earlier. Check she wasn't serious."

"Dad, there are many health benefits to eating nettles," I said. "Including lowering stress levels."

"Is that right?"

"Yeah, so you should probably have seconds."

Dad tutted. "Ask Miki if he wants a lift in the morning," he said and went downstairs.

I put the gaiters over my leggings and looked in the mirror. They looked absurd. I took a photo and sent it to Miki.

He replied:

WHAT ARE THEY 😲

I replied:

I literally don't know

my dad's 😵

like massive waterproof socks!

want a lift to school tomo?

Miki replied:

ok. what time?

I picked up the camping letter then typed:

omg coach leaves at 6am!!!!!

Miki replied:

noooooooo 😲 😲 😲 😲

I tipped out the contents of the rucksack to see what else Dad had packed. There was a torch with spare batteries, knitted jumpers, and one of those silver blankets in case you get hypothermia, which sounded pretty likely. A small packet that said EMERGENCY PONCHO.

The rain would have to be at monsoon level for me to consider wearing that in front of people. Dad had thought of everything. A first-aid kit, bobble hat, baby wipes. A flare! We were camping in the middle of nowhere, I suppose. And it might be needed to scare away wild animals. I stuffed it back in the rucksack. There was Travel Scrabble, a pack of cards, energy bars. I pulled out a pink box. It looked brand new. Maybe Dad had bought me a special present for the trip!

I opened it. *SHECANWEE: the perfect device for urinating outdoors.*

I had one thought: *Just kill me now.*

40

CAMP GO WILD!

"**S**traight lines!" Mr Nelson yelled across the car park.

I moved forward, trying to suppress a yawn. Being at school before 6 a.m. should be illegal.

"I want a perfect metre between each form class!" Mr Nelson was in full Roman dictator mode. If Roman dictators wore high-visibility cagoules.

"Nice rucksack, Jemima!" Lottie said, cutting in front of us. "I hope you're not going to camp naked. I think I'd be sick."

I looked at Miki, but he had his headphones on and was singing "Let's Go Fly a Kite" to himself and our entire line.

"It's a joke, Lottie," I said. "Anyway, it's not mine. It's my dad's."

"Your dad camps naked? Ewww!" she squealed, and shouted down the line, "Jemima's dad's a NUDIST!"

Miki pulled his headphones off just as Mr Nelson walked past.

"Really, Lottie? That is fascinating! Jemima's dad's a nudist!" Mr Nelson smiled at me, then turned back to Lottie. "I must say, I never noticed at parents' evening last year!"

"He's not a nudist, Mr Nelson," I said. "He's a painter. It's just this joke on his rucksack."

"Lottie thinks she's funny," Miki said.

"I see!" Mr Nelson said, tucking his clipboard under his arm. "A comedian! Do you know – I love hearing jokes! Especially on long journeys. Congratulations, Lottie, you've just been upgraded to first class."

"W-what?" Lottie said.

Mr Nelson smiled. "Also known as the seat next to me on the coach. Hop in!"

I smiled and Miki gave me a high five.

"That will keep Rat Face quiet for a few hours," he said. "Hey, isn't that Gina?"

I turned round and saw Gina coming straight towards me.

"Maybe she wants to tell you the nutritional content of cowpat."

"Hi, Jemima!" Gina beamed at me. "Isn't this exciting?

I've just spoken to Heidi and Harry and I've asked Mr Nelson to put you three in my group so I can give you some extra support. But really it's so we can have some extra *fun*!" She lifted off the ground a little bit when she said that. "Apparently there's a mud challenge tomorrow!"

I was too tired to ask what a mud challenge was. The name suggested it wouldn't be the highlight of my camping experience.

"I thought we could do some extra swimming after the water polo, if you like? Instead of kayaking? As we'll already be in our wetsuits. I just love swimming outdoors! And there's a hike to an old fort we could do instead of the abseiling, if you'd prefer? Heidi said she doesn't like heights, and I thought you'd probably enjoy the history! Mr Nelson said it's fine."

I had to blink a few times to check I was definitely awake. Did Gina just get me out of abseiling and kayaking?

She held up her hands for a high ten and said, "*AWE*SOME!"

I clapped my hands against hers. Gina was way better than an Empress on a tarot card. She was a real-life sporty guardian angel.

I fell asleep against the coach window and woke up to

Miki jabbing my arm saying, "We're here!"

I rubbed my eyes. A sign saying CAMP GO WILD! stared out at me from a hedge.

"I lost my phone signal about half an hour ago," Miki said. "Check yours."

I pulled my phone out of my pocket. "No bars," I said. "But I packed Travel Scrabble!"

Miki chucked his travel pillow at me.

Our coach parked in a clearing next to a huge forest where Mr Nelson dropped the bombshell that we'd be walking to camp. *Two miles.*

"Don't disturb any of the wildlife!" he called after we'd all collected our bags. "Observe don't disturb! That's the countryside motto!"

"Two miles?" I said to Miki.

"Wildlife?" he replied. We stared at each other. "They'd better have Wi-Fi at this camp." He put his rucksack on both shoulders. "And waffles."

We'd been walking for about half an hour when we climbed over a stile straight into a field of cows.

"Forward!" Mr Nelson said.

A few people followed him, but the rest of us stayed in the corner by the fence.

"Come on! Observe don't disturb! Cows are completely harmless!"

"Cows kill five people a year," I said, leaning against the fence to get my breath back. "And probably injure hundreds more. They look slow-moving," I explained to a small crowd gathering, "but they are actually lethal predators. They can run at forty miles per hour."

Mr Nelson stopped. He surveyed the growing group of people assembling near me by the fence. "Are you going to believe me, a Duke of Edinburgh Award Leader and Head of History, or Year Eight student, Jemima Small?"

"But," Afzal said, "she is going on *Brainiacs*, sir."

A cow mooed loudly and a few people jumped.

Mr Nelson put his hands on his hips. "Right, well, if Jemima's correct about these cows being killing machines, you don't want to wait here like sitting ducks, do you? Onward!"

Slowly everyone started walking. I stayed towards the back, and Miki stuck close next to me. This walk was definitely against our human rights.

"Come on, you two!" Mr Nelson said. "Pick up the pace a bit!"

I looked at the empty signal bars on my phone. "Mr Nelson," I called, "if there's an emergency, how do we make a call when there's no signal?"

Mr Nelson laughed. "You shout 'HELP!' like we did in the olden days!"

I was so glad Dad had packed me that flare.

After a while, a blue triangular flag appeared in the distance.

"Nearly there!" Mr Nelson shouted. "Head for the flag!"

I could make out a line of people waving flags of different colours like they were trying to tell us something. Or maybe warn us. It's this thing from the olden days called semaphore, a bit like Morse code. The way you hold each flag signifies a letter of the alphabet. It was probably the way people had to communicate around here because of getting no phone signal.

Once we arrived in camp, we didn't even get a proper rest before we had to put up our tents. I dumped my rucksack in the grass, then Heidi, Jaz, Erin and I put up our tent. Other people were struggling with theirs, but it was simple logic really. Plus, we all got a set of instructions. Ms Fraser said ours was looking the best, so we were "rewarded" by being made to help everyone else.

"Great job, Jemima!" Gina said, holding a cup of something that smelled like hot chocolate, but probably had broccoli or something in it.

Miki almost tripped over our guy ropes on his way over. He was wearing luminous orange waterproof trousers.

"Don't say anything!" he said. "Mum was worried

about me getting lost on the orienteering."

"She'll probably be able to see you orienteering all the way from Clifton in those!" Gina said, laughing.

I smiled. "They're probably visible from space." I turned to Gina. "Which one's your tent, just in case there's an emergency?"

"Oh, I'm staying in the teachers' lodge over there." She pointed to a cosy-looking cottage at the edge of the field. It was so typical of our teachers to make us get hypothermia while they stayed in luxury accommodation. "The team leaders are camping out here with you."

I picked up my rucksack. "Oh no!"

It had been sitting in a giant cowpat.

"Gross!" I said, pulling out a packet of baby wipes.

"Oh, don't worry, Jemima!" Gina said. "It's only a bit of fertilizer! Won't do you any harm." She started walking towards the meeting point. "It's pure NPK!"

"What does that even mean?" Miki asked, taking a baby wipe and helping me clean off my bag.

"Thanks. Oh, nitrogen, phosphorus and potassium, probably. Notice she didn't mention the dangerous pathogens or high levels of ammonia! This whole camp is a deathtrap."

Miki smiled. "You literally know the nutritional value of a cowpat," he said, wiping his hands.

I went to the toilet block while the other girls got changed. I deliberately took ages, so they'd gone to the meeting point before I got back. I got undressed, put my swimsuit on, my clothes back on over the top, then pulled Dad's gaiters over my jogging bottoms. I was sweating by the time I'd finished. I couldn't believe I'd been worried about hypothermia. Our tent was like a sauna.

I unzipped the doors just as Mr Nelson's voice came booming through a loudhailer.

"Hurry up getting changed, all of you! It's not a fashion parade!"

Like I needed him to tell me that. I was wearing my dad's gaiters.

"Assemble at the meeting point! Last group here will be on lunchtime washing-up duty!"

It was exactly like camping with my dad.

In a few minutes, I had to put on a wetsuit in front of all the girls in my year. If they even had one that would fit me. I'd never wanted to stay inside a tent so badly in my entire life. Even one that stank of cowpat. I zipped the tent back up and slowly headed over to the meeting point, watching the Camp Go Wild! team leaders' flags whipping in the wind. And I wondered what the semaphore was for "help".

41

STAR DUST

I was sitting at the side of the lake at Camp Go Wild! with my towel wrapped around me, half-freezing. I'd told Frankie, our team leader, that I couldn't swim. She didn't believe me. She already had a list of non-confident swimmers, apparently. She'd told me I'd regret it later. That I wouldn't be cold in the water because the wetsuit's insulation would keep me warm. But I already knew that. Anyway, I'd been told when I was putting it on in the changing rooms that I didn't need one because my blubber would keep me warm.

I looked over at the lake. Everyone was playing water polo with a giant ball and hoola-hoops for goals. Whoops and cheers and screams and laughter carried over on the wind.

"You sure you don't want to join in?" Frankie shouted from the water. Her hand was over her eyes, shielding them from the sun. You could make out almost every muscle in her arm.

I shook my head. Nothing could convince me to let the whole of Year Eight see me in skintight neoprene.

I spotted Heidi's head in the water. I wished I hadn't been so slow getting my wetsuit on, then I could have gone in with her. I took my phone out of my bag. Still no signal. This whole campsite was from the Stone Age. I checked the grass for cowpats, then lay down and looked up at the thick clouds. I doubted I'd even be able to see any stars later. Borrowing Jasper's binoculars had been a waste of time. I wondered if he'd realized I'd taken them by now.

"Jemima!"

Gina. The last person I wanted to see. She probably looked like a goddess even in a wetsuit. She could never understand how I felt. I stayed lying down, looking up at the clouds.

"Why aren't you playing?"

I decided to keep it vague. "I don't feel very well."

"Oh," she said, and I heard her walk onto the wooden deck next to the lake. I didn't move, just watched the clouds forming different shapes in the sky.

"Not well, huh? I used to say that any time someone invited me to swim," she said.

I lifted my head, and propped myself up on my arms.

She was sitting on the edge of the deck with her feet dangling in the water. "Now, I couldn't care less if people stare. Or give me those second glances, or nudge their friend to point me out. Because I love swimming. If they don't like what they see, that's their problem."

I sat up, so I could see her properly. "Why would people do that to you? Your body's, like…perfect."

She turned round and smiled. "Thanks, Jemima! That's exactly how I feel about it too! But some people do like to stare at my leg." She swivelled her legs out of the water. She was wearing a thigh-length wetsuit and on her right leg, below her knee, there was a turquoise prosthetic. It was patterned, like the scales of a mermaid. I couldn't believe I hadn't noticed it before. Gina smiled like she was reading my mind. "My usual one is a bit more subtle. This is my aqua-limb! It's water-resistant." She stretched out her legs and turned her face to the sky. "It is a pretty cool prosthetic. Maybe that's why people stare."

I smiled. "Because of the mermaid scales?"

"Exactly!" Gina laughed. "They could be jealous. It is a lot more interesting to look at than boring old skin." She walked over and sat next to me on the grass. "You

315

know, Jemima, some people spend their entire lives not doing the things they want because they're worried about what people think. But, you know what really matters?"

"What people think?"

"No!" Gina tipped her head back and laughed. A laugh that came all the way from her belly. It was sort of infectious. "What matters the most is what *you* think. About *yourself*. Am I going to not wear a swimming costume or shorts in the summer because a few people might stare at my prosthetic? Am I going to believe I should hide myself away?"

I shrugged and looked out at the lake. "Maybe."

"No, Jemima," she said. "I'm not going to think like that. There are enough barriers in place for someone like me; I'm not going to add even more." She looked out at the waves splashing against the wooden deck. "I used to hate people staring, you know, when I was younger. But now, if people stare at me because my body doesn't look exactly like theirs, then good!"

"Good?" I said. "How can people staring be good?"

Gina fixed her eyes on me. "Because it reminds me that I'm no longer hiding away. I'm not avoiding doing the things I love – like swimming – just because of what my leg looks like. I don't put limits on what I can do because of what other people think of my body. Not any more. I focus on how my body feels. To me. So those looks I get sometimes? They remind me that I decided not to be invisible."

She stared at me for a moment. "Our bodies share the same elements as stars, Jemima. We're literally made of star dust! But you already knew that, right?" As she said that a huge cheer came from the lake. "Looks like they've scored!" She stood up and walked onto the deck. "I know you're smart, Jemima. You're a Brainiac now! So if you want to spend your life sitting on the sidelines, hiding your body in a Spider-Man towel, that's up to you. But from here, it looks like our team's losing." She tapped her finger on her lip. "If only we had someone on our team who could shoot."

It took me about ten seconds to make up my mind. I made a much bigger splash jumping into the lake than Gina. But then, my team were seven goals down, so they kind of needed someone to make a big splash. When Frankie blew the whistle for the end of the game, we were two goals up. Six of them scored by me. It's called deciding not to be invisible.

Later, in the changing rooms, drying myself on literally the most embarrassing towel Dad could have found in the airing cupboard, I thought about what Gina had said. And I thought about the stars. How they're held together by their own gravity. The biggest kind of star is a hypergiant. They're the rarest type of star too, and the brightest thing out of everything that exists in the universe. I looked at my body in the mirror. Maybe I just got a little bit of extra star dust.

42

TEAM GGB

It was pitch-black. I was lying in my sleeping bag with my head poking out of the tent and the door zipped up just above my face. My legs were aching from hiking about eight thousand miles up a hill to the ruins of an Iron-Age fort and I felt kind of sick after eating a bag of Gina's "delicious" home-made marshmallows. But the sky looked a thousand times more incredible than I'd imagined. It was such a good idea to bring Jasper's binoculars. I could see everything – star clusters, meteors, nebula clouds, the Andromeda Galaxy spiralling its way towards ours. It was kind of mind-blowing. All that energy – burning, exploding, colliding and fusing. Down here it was almost completely still and silent. Apart from Heidi's snoring.

"Jemima," Jaz whispered. "Close the zip. It's freezing."

I took one last look at the sky, then wriggled back into the tent. "Sorry," I whispered.

"I can't sleep," Jaz said. "I keep hearing wolves."

"They're owls, Jaz. There aren't any wolves."

"Harry said that wolves could live in the forest and no one would even know," she whispered.

"That's stupid. We don't have wolves in England."

Jaz shone her phone light on her face. "He said they could have escaped from a zoo!"

"He was just trying to scare you. Anyway, most species of wolves don't pose any risk to humans. The deadliest thing at Camp Go Wild! is probably that lake water we were swimming in earlier," I whispered back. "You can catch all kinds of things. And the catering equipment did not exactly look hygienic to me." I told Jaz about the different forms of bacteria that live in water, and the general breaches of health and safety and human rights I'd seen so far at Camp Go Wild! "Jaz?" I whispered. "Are you still awake? Jaz?" And that's how I discovered talking about bacteria and health and safety might be slightly soporific.

I wriggled as far into my sleeping bag as I could, hoping that the "payback" Lottie was planning wouldn't be any worse than the mud challenge Camp Go Wild! had in store for us tomorrow.

☆ ☆

The next morning, huge blobs of rain slid down my face as I tried to run through the forest. It was the mud challenge. Or, more accurately, the five-kilometre mud challenge uphill through a monsoon. And, contrary to Gina's prediction at the start line, I was not "smashing it". I was finally grateful for Dad's gaiters though. They were keeping my legs dry. It was just a shame about the rest of me. I could feel sweat collecting against the fabric of my cagoule. I'd slipped over approximately a trillion times. One thing was for sure – Camp Go Wild! was a lawsuit waiting to happen.

Miki was way ahead with his group and Lottie had gone past ages ago, telling me not to have a heart attack.

"Keep going!" Frankie, our team leader, shouted as she ran past in shorts and a vest.

I looked up and slipped over on a muddy tree root.

Frankie smiled. "It's all part of the fun!" She helped me up and told me, "Rest but don't quit!"

I really did not like her.

I found a tree stump that was half-sheltered from the rain and unzipped my cagoule. "I'll catch you up," I said to Heidi.

"Okay. I'll go slow."

I watched her half-jog, half-skid across the forest floor.

I stretched my aching legs out in front of me and wiped the sweat from my forehead. A five-kilometre mud challenge. In a deluge. It was basically physical torture.

"Jemima! There you are!" Gina's smile appeared through the rain. "Heidi said you needed a rest! Are you okay?"

"I'm not running," I said. "It's too dangerous."

"That's okay," she said. "We can walk. But you have to finish. Team GGB Code, remember?"

I sighed. "How far is it?"

"Not far!" she said. "The camp's about five hundred metres up that hill." She crouched next to me and pointed through the trees. "See the flag?"

I could just make out a tiny spot of blue in the distance.

"You can do it, Jemima!" she said, but I didn't move. "I'll tell you what, why don't I quiz you on the way? See how many questions you can get right before the end!"

I looked at her.

"Oh, come on! Don't tell me you haven't got some revision cards hidden in that cagoule."

I took a deep breath and pulled the revision cards out of my pocket. "Okay, but only because these are my laminated ones."

"*Awe*some!" Gina said, helping me up. Her hands were really soft; she must have used loads of moisturizer.

It probably came free in her luxury accommodation. "Hey! Look at us!" She pointed to our legs. She had virtually the exact same trousers on. "Team Gaiters!"

"They're my dad's."

"Well, your dad is seriously cool!"

"That's what he says."

I walked back to camp with Gina asking me questions all the way until finally, the meeting point came into sight. A crowd of people stood by the finish line.

"This is so embarrassing," I said, trying not to lose my breath. "Coming last."

"Oh, we're not last!" Gina said. "Ms Fraser's group went the wrong way apparently. They're miles behind! Anyway, who cares?" She dipped her fingers into a mound of mud and drew stripes across her cheeks. "Go Team GGB!"

And it was annoying because I couldn't stop laughing and it made it even harder to breathe.

About thirty metres away from the flagpole, I picked up my speed and tried to forget about what people might think. I focused on what my body was feeling instead. Which was mostly excruciating pain. Miki jumped up from the grass and shouted, "Go, Jemima!" as I crossed the finish line.

My trainers were covered in mud. My skin was covered in sweat. My hair was soaking wet and sticking to my face. And my cheeks felt like they'd been set on fire. But I didn't feel like that on the inside. On the inside I felt like one of Luna's tarot cards. The one with the woman riding on the back of a lion with her hair flowing out behind her, holding a heart of flames. The one that says *Strength* at the bottom. I felt exactly like that. And a bit worried about what Dad was going to say about my ruined trainers.

The showers at Camp Go Wild! were freezing, which had to be illegal. I was going to google it when I got a phone signal. I waited until the changing rooms were almost empty, then got dressed in the corner of the changing rooms, with goosebumps on my skin and aching legs. I pulled a plastic bag out of the back pocket of my rucksack and shoved my muddy trainers in it.

"Hey, you dropped something," Heidi said, pointing to something on the floor. "It fell out of your bag."

"Thanks." I picked it up. It was a brochure saying, *Bright Star Cruises: the luxury cruise ship that treats you like a star.*

We'd never been on a cruise. Definitely not a luxury one. Dad's idea of a luxury holiday was staying in Nana's old caravan in North Wales. There was no way Dad would pay for a cruise. He moaned about how much it cost to play crazy golf at Dolphin Bay. I wondered where it came from, but my hair was still wet and my hands were freezing, so I put it in my coat pocket, then sat under the hand dryer until I felt less like I might get hypothermia.

Miki was leaning against a tree outside the changing block. His hair was still slightly wet and flapping around in the wind. "Here." He handed me one of his mum's home-made cookies and I looked around for the coach. "We've got to walk, remember?" Miki said, munching on a biscuit. "Two miles!"

"Oh my God," I said. "I can't believe we had to pay for this experience."

Just then, Lottie ran past looking at me and laughing. And I got this cold kind of dread – probably how it feels to really get hypothermia – like she'd done something, and it was too late for me to do anything about it.

I guess that's what happens when you stay up half the night star-gazing and talking about wolves and bacteria. You forget to keep an eye out for the real predators.

43

EXPANDING UNIVERSE

I spotted Dad as soon as our coach pulled into the school car park. He was wearing his bright-yellow high-visibility jacket. In case my whole year might not notice how totally embarrassing he was.

"You survived!" he shouted at a hundred decibels as I got off the coach. "Incredible! No ingesting poisonous mushrooms, or being devoured by killer leeches or falling down ravines!" Then he laughed extremely loudly at his own joke.

"Yes, Dad," I said, climbing down the steps. "I survived all of that. Unfortunately, so did your gaiters. I'll just get my rucksack." I walked over to where the coach driver was putting everyone's bags. Dad waited with me for a minute, then started scanning the crowd.

"Is Gina here somewhere?" he said. "Thought I'd say a quick hello! I'll meet you back at the van." He spotted her and practically sprinted over. Gina's smile went as wide as ever. He was probably doing more of his jokes.

I waved goodbye to Miki, whose mum was waiting in the car like a normal parent (an alien concept to my dad). I waited by the van trying to telepathically tell Dad it was time to go. But it didn't work. Mr Nelson had joined the conversation. I could literally die of hypothermia in the school car park and no one would notice.

"Gina's so nice!" Dad said when he came back over. "She said you did great!"

"She's lying."

Dad laughed. "She said you scored six goals in water polo! And ran a 5K!"

"I came last. Apart from the group that got lost."

Dad started the engine. "That's not last then, is it? Mr Nelson said you didn't even complain, which I can barely believe!" Dad laughed again. "I thought I'd get a phone call from you in the middle of the night saying camping's against your human rights or something."

"I couldn't get a signal."

"Ha! Seriously, I'm proud of you. I didn't want to say before you left, but Jasper said that trip was a complete nightmare! You had fun though?"

"Well, let's see…I camped in the freezing cold, in the middle of nowhere, possibly with escaped zoo animals. I trekked halfway up a mountain, ran through a mud swamp and swam in an algae-ridden lake. And don't even get me started about the food."

"Exactly! Lots of fun! Oh, and by the way, Jasper's been looking for his binoculars."

"Yeah?"

"You don't know anything about where they might be, do you?"

"I might have borrowed them to look at the stars."

"Jemima! You can't just take things without asking!"

"I did ask!" I said, then turned to face the window and muttered, "It's just he said no."

As we pulled into our drive I said, "Dad, have you ever been on a cruise?"

He looked at me weirdly. "No, why?"

I took the Bright Star Cruises brochure out of my coat pocket and handed it to him.

"Where did you get this?" he asked sharply. "Did Luna give this to you?"

"No, it was in your rucksack."

The colour drained out of his face, like Jasper's did that time ages ago before he threw up all over the seat.

"Oh, it's nothing," he said. "I'll stick it in the recycling."

He got out of the van and stuffed the brochure in his back pocket. "Now, tell me all about this mud challenge!" he said, lifting my rucksack out of the back. "Gina said I was right to pack those gaiters!"

I followed him inside, but I didn't say anything about the mud challenge. I went straight upstairs and into my room. I leaned on the window sill, looking out at the expanding universe, wondering why an old cruise brochure could make Dad look like he was going to be sick.

I plugged in my phone. The screen glowed and it vibrated loads of times. I scrolled through the notifications. Then my heart stopped. As though I'd plunged into a freezing cold lake without wearing a wetsuit.

Lottie Freeman tagged you in a video.

I tapped the screen and there I was. Covered in mud. Sweating. With bright red cheeks. Hair stuck to my face. In my cagoule. And my dad's gaiters. Running towards the finish line. My heart thumped harder and harder as I read her post.

Wishing my friend jemima small good luck in #Brainiacs !!!! #uk #cliftononsea #cliftonacademy #goteam #mudgoals #genius #tv #lifegoals #jemimasmall #friends #lol

There just wasn't a hashtag for how much I hated Lottie right now.

44

OPTICAL ILLUSIONS

As soon as I woke up the next morning, I remembered the video and felt sick. I sat up in bed and pressed my phone.

Miki had messaged me saying:

Don't worry we'll tell mr nels he'll sort it out. ♥

But that feeling of nausea didn't disappear; it pumped around my veins like venom. I wondered how many people from school would have watched the video by now. I tapped on Lottie's profile and scrolled down the comments.

There were some nice ones from some people in my class.

Afzal had put: go jem!

Jaz had written: cant wait youre so brainy!!!!!

Erin said. mud challenge was so bad lol.

But there were some other comments too, from people I didn't know.

woah that is VILE keep runnin girl

That's not healthy

Whaaaaaat? Is this girl on TV in England? 😫

Lol gross

I hope that's a fitness camp!!!!

I could probably have dealt with those ones. They were bad. But if they were arrows, the shield I'd been building over the past few weeks was strong enough to withstand them. I think. But not the one I read next:

her mum should be ashamed

My imaginary shield could have been made of titanium and that arrow would have still got into my heart. And an arrow that sharp is kind of fatal. Because there's no way you can be on TV with your heart punctured like that.

"JEMIMA!" Dad shouted. "You're going to miss the BUS!"

I heard Jasper's voice outside my room shouting at me to hurry up. "DÉPÊCHE TOI, JEMIMA!"

But I stayed lying in bed. I couldn't face school today. Not now everyone on the planet had seen the video. And the comments. It would probably be on YouTube before lunchtime. I stared up at the ceiling, wishing it had an escape hatch to a different universe. I'd climb out and never come back. Because who'd want to stay on a planet where your body should make your mum ashamed of you?

I looked over at the revision kit Dad had made and felt myself take a giant breath. I squeezed my eyes shut, and pressed my hands on them, because I didn't want the pain of it all coming out.

But there was nowhere I could hide from the truth. I couldn't go on *Brainiacs* and have my mum feel ashamed of me. The empty space in my heart felt bigger than ever, like a galaxy stretching on for infinity, entirely devoid of stars.

Dad opened my door. "Jemima! You're going to be late! Why aren't you out of bed?"

"I don't feel very well," I said, turning to face the wall.

Dad pressed his hand against my forehead. "You're fine. You haven't got a temperature. You're probably just tired from the camping trip! Come on! You can have an early night tonight."

"Lottie's posted a video of me online," I said in short breaths. "A horrible one."

Dad did an extra-long sigh. "Well, she certainly shouldn't be doing that. But it's not a reason to miss school. Jemima, get up!"

I tried to hold the tears in, but I couldn't. And they came out in a kind of deluge. "I look so horrible, Dad! People commented. Really bad things. About me being fat and gross." I gulped deep breaths of air as huge tears soaked into my duvet.

Dad sat on the edge of my bed and rubbed my back. "Oh, Jem. That's awful," he said gently. "I'm so sorry. It's all right. We'll get it sorted out."

I heard Jasper creep in.

"What's happened?"

"Someone's posted a video of Jemima online," Dad said. "There's some…not very nice comments."

"Let's see, Jem."

I wiped my eyes and handed Jasper my phone. I watched its light reflecting in his eyes.

"Jeez, that's bad."

"Jasper!" Dad said. "You're supposed to make her feel better about it! Give me that." Dad took my phone and tapped the screen. "Wow! Is that the mud challenge? Look at you go! Jemima! I know you're upset, sweetheart, but I think that's a great video!"

"Are you actually joking? The whole reason Lottie's put it on there is because it's so bad. She wants people to laugh at me. She's even tagged *Brainiacs* in it! She's trying to ruin my life! Read the comments."

Dad scrolled down. He kept grimacing and looking away, like he did whenever we watched the *World's Deadliest Animals* documentaries. "Honestly! Do some people not have anything better to do?" He shook his head. "You poor thing. If there's anything that's vile around here it's those comments. Listen, those people are nasty. Don't listen to a word of it. Do you know how to delete it, Jasper?"

"He can't. It's on Lottie's profile," I said, wiping my eyes with the sleeve of my pyjamas.

"Take screenshots and tell Mr Nelson," Jasper said. "He'll get it taken down. That Lottie is a class A—"

"Thank you, Jasper!" Dad said. "For what it's worth, I think you look – what's that word you young people say? *Fierce*." Jasper snorted as Dad rubbed my shoulder.

I thought finally Dad was appalled enough to not send me to school. But he said, "Jemima, wash your face, get dressed, and you do what Gina says and hold your head up high. Don't let these people upset you. I'll take you to school in the van."

Miki was by the gates when I got to school.

"I *hate* Lottie!" he said. "I've messaged her so many times saying take it down. She's seen them but not replied."

My eyes felt swollen from crying, but I scrolled through the comments again to see if there were any more. Katie K had put: good luck jemima ♥. I think she was in Year Nine.

"Stop reading the comments!" Miki said, taking my phone and zipping it into my rucksack pocket. "I'll think of a way to get back at Lottie. I can't wait to see her face when you slay it on *Brainiacs*. That'll wipe the smile off her ratty face."

I stopped walking. "Miki, you don't seriously expect me to go on *Brainiacs* now?"

"WHAT?" Miki shouted. A few people by the science block looked over.

"I'm dropping out. It says in my letter they have reserves."

"What are you talking about?" I started walking again, but Miki grabbed my sleeve. "Jemima, what is going through your head right now? You can't drop out."

"I can't do *Brainiacs*. Think about what everyone's going to say about me!" I swallowed the enormous lump forming in my throat. "I can't believe I ever thought it would be okay. I was so stupid. If I go on the show, it would be exactly the same as those comments. But a million times worse."

Miki followed me up the stairs and along the history

335

corridor, past the display of posters we'd made last year about the Romans. I'd made a Roman Mythology Family Tree. Mr Nelson had written *Exceptional* at the bottom in green pen and given me a commendation. At the time I'd felt so pleased. Now, I couldn't believe I thought stuff like that actually mattered.

"Jemima!" Miki said. "It's less than two weeks until the competition! All the revising you've done! You can't miss out on *Brainiacs* just because of Lottie Fartman! I won't let you."

"It's too late, Miki. I've already decided. I'm not going on national TV so people can call me gross on YouTube for the rest of my life. I'm going to tell Mrs Savage at lunch." I stopped outside our form room and looked through the window. Lottie was staring at her phone and Caleb was next to her laughing. My stomach flipped over.

"Jemima, that's stupid. It's like me dropping out of *Mary Poppins* because Lottie's in it. I mean, I have to *hold her hand*!" He grinned. "I could catch Weil's disease!"

I laughed, but tears were in my eyes. "It's not the same, Miki. You'll be amazing in *Mary Poppins* and everyone will say you're a brilliant actor and the star of the show. Even if I won the *Brainiacs* trophy, all people would say is that I'm gross. And that my mum should be ashamed of me." I wiped a tear rolling down my face. I didn't even care about the people walking past. "Millions of people watch *Brainiacs*, Miki. Millions! And it will be on YouTube for ever. I'll be called Jemima Big for ever."

Miki hugged me, then got a pack of tissues out of the front pocket of my rucksack where I always kept them. They were the special *Brainiacs* ones I'd got in my goody bag that had lightning bolts on the packet and smelled of bananas. He handed one to me and I dabbed my eyes.

"Jem, *I* wouldn't say any of that. I wouldn't think that stuff. Neither would loads of people." He looked like he was telling the truth, but he had been acting a lot lately, so I couldn't be sure. "I'll be too busy getting my mind blown with all the weird facts you'll be saying! You'll be the best person on that show. And anyway, I think you rocked those gaiters."

Miki waited outside the toilets while I splashed my face with water. I still had red blotches around my eyes, but he linked my arm on the way into form and, as we sat down, he called Lottie a last weasel's fart in Japanese. And when the bell rang for the end of form, he waited with me while I showed Mr Nelson Lottie's video. It's called having the best friend in the whole entire universe.

"I see," Mr Nelson said, peering at my phone. "How long has she been doing this sort of thing to you, Jemima? This bullying?"

"Oh, it's not bullying," I said. "She just thinks it's funny to…" Then I stopped. Because it reminded me of when I saw the bruises on Harry's arm. And him dismissing it like it was nothing. Like his arm was nothing. I suddenly had no idea why I was defending Lottie Freeman. I took a deep breath and started again. "Since the start of Year Seven."

"She says stuff to Jemima all the time, sir," Miki said. "She blows her cheeks up like this. And calls her Jemima Big. She showed everyone in our class that article in the *Clifton Echo*. She calls her names…"

"Right." Mr Nelson clicked his mouse a few times. "It sounds like Lottie is behaving quite appallingly."

Finally! I thought, *Someone in my life is appalled!*

"I'll escort you to science and have a chat with Lottie. I think it's safe to say she'll be in Isolation today, and losing all her lunch breaks this week."

"But we've got rehearsals at lunchtime, sir," Miki said. "She's Mary Poppins."

"Oh dear! I suppose Lottie will have to learn that unless she starts behaving in a more Mary-Poppins-like fashion towards Jemima, the only place she'll be taking on a starring role this term will be Isolation. I'll make sure she takes the video down immediately, Jemima."

"Thank you, sir."

"Of course," he said, "in Roman times they'd pour molten lead down her throat!"

"That's a bit harsh, sir," I said. "You'd better not mention it to Mrs Savage."

And Mr Nelson's laughter echoed around the classroom.

At lunchtime, I walked with Miki to the drama studio. On the way there a few people had Halloween masks on, even though we'd been told in form time not to dress up.

"Run, Big, run!" someone wearing a *Scream* mask shouted.

"Please don't say anything," I said to Miki, so he twirled under my arm and started singing about flying a kite and sending it soaring up through the atmosphere. Probably because he knew I'd have to inform him that it's scientifically impossible to fly a kite up through the atmosphere, because for a start you'd need about eight million balls of string. I finished explaining when we reached the studio and we both smiled. It was the most I'd spoken all day.

Miss Nisha said I could come in and watch the rehearsal, but I said maybe tomorrow. I sat on the bench outside the drama block flicking through the screenshots

I'd taken of Lottie's post. It had disappeared from her profile, which meant the comments had gone too. Not completely though. They were still branded onto my memory, probably for ever. I was about to walk to Mrs Savage's office when I spotted Gina coming towards me.

"I've been looking for you everywhere!" she said. "Mrs Savage has asked me to do some brain-training with you!"

"Mrs Savage is trying to ruin my life."

Gina laughed like she thought I was joking.

"Brain-training for what?"

"For *Brainiacs*, silly! She wants me to teach you some competition strategies to give you the edge! Just between you and me, I think Mrs Savage might have a competitive streak! But, isn't it fantastic news! What's wrong?"

I really did not want to tell Gina. But my mouth opened involuntarily and I blurted it out.

I watched her study the screenshots on my phone.

"You want to know what I see when I look at this?" she said eventually. "I see a girl who didn't want to do the mud challenge. A girl who didn't think she could do it, so she sat on a tree stump and gave up. But this girl got back on her feet, ran up that hill and crossed the finish line with her head held high. I look at this, and I see a girl who is strong, determined and clever. A girl with a warrior inside her heart. I know that warrior is in there, Jemima,

340

because I've seen her for myself. I see a girl who is pretty exceptional, actually. And, you know what else? If your mum watches *Brainiacs*, I think that's what she'll see too."

I took back my phone and looked at the screenshots again. Gina told me it was like one of those optical illusions, where people looked at the same picture, but they saw different things. She said maybe my life would always be like that. Some people seeing Jemima Big, some seeing Jemima Small. She said the thing that mattered most was what *I* saw. My heart thumped, like there was a warrior in there trying to get out.

"Now," Gina said. "Are you ready to do some brain-training? Because that *Brainiacs* trophy isn't going to win itself."

45

PEGASUS

It was exactly a week before I was due to film *Brainiacs* and I was standing next to Mrs Savage, feeling like every litre of blood in my body had collected in my cheeks. I hoped I wouldn't pass out because it would be totally embarrassing.

"Good morning, Clifton Academy!" Mrs Savage bellowed. "I am *very* pleased to formally announce that this extremely bright Year Eight student will be representing our school on *Brainiacs*!" The hall filled with applause. "This time next week, Jemima will be heading to a television studio in London to take part in this very exciting competition! It won't be on your screens until Boxing Day, but Jemima, I want to say, on behalf of everyone here at Clifton Academy, good luck! And may your brain be with you!"

Everyone clapped and I heard Brandon's voice booming out, "GO, SMALL!" as I shook Mrs Savage's hand. She presented me with a special brain-shaped pin to wear on my blazer and squeezed my shoulder as the photographer pointed his camera at us.

"We are all so proud of you," she said as the camera flashed.

I stood there, in front of the whole school, on wobbly legs, with calves that probably looked too convex, an asymmetrical face, a round tummy, and definitely bright-red cheeks. And I smiled. It was the same smile I'd practised in the mirror all weekend, but this one felt real. I looked out at the mass of green blazers in front of me, most of them smaller than mine. I wondered how many people were seeing Jemima Small. Because I definitely felt like her.

The rest of the week went by so fast it felt like I was on the Vomit Comet. Mrs Savage let me miss afternoon lessons to brain-train with Gina. I revised in the library every lunchtime; Mr Nelson made his history club help me study and calculate and memorize everything I could. The librarian made a special sign saying *Quiet: Brainiac in Training!* And she let me have a comfy chair from the office. And the whole time, Lottie went out of her way to be nice to me. She offered to carry my books to the bus, lent me felt tips for my question cards, saved me the best keyboard in music, and actually properly apologized to me in maths. She must have really, really liked being Mary Poppins.

And every night, before I went to bed, I wished on all 250 billion stars in our galaxy that I wouldn't look totally stupid on TV. I hoped at least one of them was listening.

I blinked and it was Sunday, the day before I'd be filming *Brainiacs*. I stretched and looked up at the dreamcatcher hanging against my window. According to legend, dreams are sent down to you from the universe every night. Good dreams pass through the dreamcatcher, but bad dreams get caught in its web, then disintegrate in the morning sunlight. They just disappear into nothing, like magic.

I got dressed, tidied up my revision notes from the last few nights and opened my desk drawer to stuff them in. And that's when I saw it. The Bright Star Cruises brochure that fell out of my rucksack on the camping trip and that I'd taken out of Dad's hiding place after he'd gone to bed. When I couldn't find it in the recycling, I knew it would be in the ceramic jar on top of the fridge. He always hid things in exactly the same place. I'd forgotten about it with all the *Brainiacs* stuff, which didn't bode well for the memory round.

I opened the brochure and looked at a picture of people sunbathing on the deck of a gigantic cruise liner. I sat down and typed the website into my phone. The words *The luxury cruise ship that treats you like a star* popped up. I tapped on the links across the top. Their ships visited almost every country in the world! Why had Dad acted so weird about it? I swiped through photos of polar bears and glaciers, Egyptian temples and camels trekking across the desert, swimming pools and restaurants with giant light bulbs, and hot tubs, and pods of dolphins. It looked amazing! Then I stopped dead.

I zoomed in on one photo until the face was so big it filled my phone screen. So big it couldn't be a mistake. Or a lie. So big it was like I was standing there on that cruise ship, in the restaurant illuminated by giant light bulbs, staring into his eyes for real.

It was my Uncle Alfie.

The great illusionist, Alfie Diamond. Who broke Luna's heart irreparably. And emptied all of the money out of her bank account. And stole my grandad's old magic-show equipment from his garage. Uncle Alfie, who vanished into nowhere.

Only he didn't vanish into nowhere, because there he was. On a Bright Star cruise ship. And their brochure had been in Dad's rucksack.

I heard footsteps outside my door and Jasper walked in holding Tornado's tank.

"I'll pay you a pound to clean out Tornado's tank. Okay, two pounds. Hey, what's up?"

He put Tornado's tank on the floor and I handed him my phone. The horrible empty feeling in my heart slowly started spreading its way around my whole body, like an oil spill.

"That's Uncle Alfie! You've found him?"

"I found this in Dad's rucksack when I was camping." I handed him the brochure. "He works on one of their ships. Only he's called Alfie Stone now."

"But…I don't understand. I thought no one knew where he was." Jasper plonked down on my bed and I sat next to him. He zoomed out of the photo and started reading. "'Alfie Stone, our resident illusionist, performs his dazzling show to an enchanted audience on *Pegasus*, our scenic Mediterranean cruise liner.' That's so weird. You think Dad's known where he is this whole time? I wonder why he didn't say."

"Maybe he didn't want to upset Luna?"

"Yeah," Jasper said. "Maybe. It's weird though because he stole all Grandad's stuff. Does Dad know you've got this?"

I looked at him.

"Stupid question." He turned the brochure over. "Hey! There's a phone number written on here. It must be Uncle Alfie's!"

We looked at each other. The exact same thought made its way across the neural networks in our brains.

I carefully tapped the number into my phone. "We'll just see if it's him, then hang up straight away, yeah?"

Jasper nodded. I took a deep breath, then pressed *Call*.

It rang three times, then: "Hello? Hello? Is someone there? Can you hear me? Hello?"

I froze. Jasper grabbed my phone and pressed *End Call*. And we sat there for a moment, not speaking, me staring at Jasper, Jasper staring at the carpet. I wasn't totally sure what had happened, but I felt that warrior beating her drum in my heart.

Because that wasn't Uncle Alfie. It was a woman. With a half-French twang in her voice.

Jasper finally looked at me. His eyes glistened, and I knew he had the exact same feeling in his heart as me. Half black hole. Half shooting star. Then he said it. And it was like getting swept away by the ocean.

"That sounded like Mum."

46

CHAOS

Dad was drilling in the garage, but I hardly noticed the noise. All I could hear over and over again was the "Hello? Hello?" from my mum. As we got to the bottom of the stairs, Jasper stopped.

"You sure we should say something?" he said. "We can leave it for a bit. Like after *Brainiacs*? Or when Dad's not holding any power tools?"

But it was too late. Luna had already walked in and read our minds. Or our faces. "What's happened?" Her hair was wrapped in a huge bun right on the top of her head, like how Nana wore hers. "What's happened?" She took Jasper's hand and led us to the sofa. "Tell me."

"We've found Uncle Alfie," I said quickly, before I could chicken out.

Jasper squeezed my hand like I'd done the right thing. It felt nice. But slightly sweaty.

"I'm sorry, what?" Luna's eye's darted from my face to Jasper's. I had this feeling like I'd opened Pandora's box and let out something terrible.

"We think we've found Uncle Alfie," Jasper said.

Luna got up and opened the front door, as though she psychically knew where Uncle Alfie was and she was going to run all the way there. But she blew out three short breaths and then took a really deep one. Maybe that's what you do when your heart's repairing itself. But she looked like she was going to throw up.

"And Mum," I said. "We've found a number for Mum."

"ORION!" Luna shouted. "ORION! It's an emergency!"

"Luna?" My hands started to shake and my blood got that icy feeling. Like you're suddenly aware of the planet spinning. And you remember that everything in the universe, even the ground beneath your feet, is unstable, that things are shrinking and expanding and exploding and collapsing in a billion different galaxies all around you. And you can never be certain of any of it.

Dad stepped inside. His hair was covered in dust and he had a red bandana tied around his face so I could only see his eyes. Which is why I noticed them looking at

Luna, not at us. Something telepathic must have passed between their brains. Because Dad pulled his bandana down and ran into the living room with his dusty boots and put his arms around me and Jasper like he'd not done for half of for ever. Not caring he was getting dirt all over the carpet.

"Hey, it's all right," he whispered.

"Tell them, Rion, please. About Joanie." Huge tears fell down Luna's cheeks.

I blinked and they fell down mine too.

"I can't bear lying to them any more."

Dad took the Bright Star Cruises brochure out of my hand and stared at it. I wondered for a minute if this was all a big joke. Like Jasper would suddenly spring up with his vortex tube and pull out a row of handkerchiefs tied together saying, *IT'S ALL JUST A BIG TRICK!* And my heart would go back to normal.

But Dad said, "Your mum. I do know where she is. I'm sorry." He wiped his eyes. "She's living on that cruise ship with Alfie."

47

BREAKING POINT

That afternoon, I was sitting exactly eighty-three metres above sea level. I know because it's the highest place in Clifton-on-Sea. It's called Cowrie Point. It's named after this famous pirate whose ship was wrecked here ages ago. Not many people come up because the steps on the side of the cliff are rickety. And because people say its haunted. There's this howling noise, but it's not a ghost. It's just the sound the wind makes through the gaps in the rocks.

I slammed the front door really hard when I left the house earlier, after Dad admitted he'd known where Mum was this whole time. I'd usually get in trouble for doing that. But today I didn't care. You can't get in trouble if you're not even speaking to your dad. Anyway, what Dad did was worse than slamming doors or borrowing binoculars or even smashing glass beakers. He smashed our hearts to pieces. And it's not like they have spare hearts in the science technicians' cupboard. They do keep dead frogs in a jar though.

Jasper was phoning me, but I didn't want to speak to him either. He was still speaking to Dad, like the lie about Mum was a brilliant opportunity to suck up to him and make me look bad. I didn't care what Jasper thought. At least I knew exactly where Mum was now. Living on a stupid luxury cruise ship watching Uncle Alfie's stolen magic show instead of being our mum. Dad said she'd left him, not us. But that wasn't true. He'd just said it to make us feel better. But I still felt bad so it didn't even work.

The empty feeling in my heart hadn't gone away, like I thought it would if I found her. It had been there since this morning and right now, my heart felt so empty the wind could howl through it. Luna had held my hand for ages before I stormed out. She said she was sorry, and kissed me on the head. I didn't say anything back because I wasn't speaking to her either. It was hard though, because I wanted to. Dad had made her promise not tell us about Mum and Alfie. It was more evidence of him being a tyrant dictator. That was a proven fact.

I heard stones falling beneath me. I peered over and saw the top of Jasper's bobble hat.

"Hey," he shouted into the wind. "Dad's been out looking for you!"

"I'm surprised he didn't just forget about me!" I shouted. "And put my phone number in the back pocket of his rucksack! That's what he normally does."

Jasper made it to the top of the steps, sat down and looked out to sea. "He's sorry, Jemima. He did it to protect us."

"Protect us from what? Having a mum?"

"He didn't want to hurt us."

The wind was making my tears run sideways. I tried to speak, but my chest was shuddering, like my body was breaking from the inside out. If I died, it would totally be Dad's fault.

"It doesn't change anything, Jem. Mum's known where we are this whole time. We've not had birthday cards, or a phone call. Nothing."

"Maybe cruise ships don't have a postal service," I said.

Jasper moved closer and leaned his body against mine. "Maybe."

It was only a word, but it meant everything. Like for once, Jasper just let me be wrong. I watched him text Dad:

Found her 👍 at Cowrie Point. On our way back.

"I'm not going home," I said.

"You have to, Jemima." Jasper stood up and held his hand out to me. "Otherwise you'll get hypothermia for real."

"I'm going to phone Mum. Ask her if I can stay on the cruise ship with her." But even as I said it, I knew I wouldn't. She already had too many missed calls from me today and the last time I'd tried it went straight to voicemail. I looked up at Jasper and his eyes said the same thing my heart was telling me. If Mum had wanted us on that cruise ship she would have taken us with her in the first place.

"You've got to come home, Jem," Jasper said. "It's *Brainiacs* tomorrow! And I've bet Max Armstrong in my class ten pounds that you'll win."

I sniffed and rubbed my face, wiping off the salty trails where my tears had run. I took a deep breath of cold air and said, "I guess I can't stay up here for ever," as the wind howled through the gaps in the rocks.

"Not unless you like pirate ghosts." Jasper smiled. "And not when I've got my pocket money riding on you."

I took a last look out to sea. Dad used to say we were lucky to live here because you can see right to the edge of the world. When I was younger, it used to feel like I was looking into infinity. I took another deep breath and followed Jasper down the steps.

Jasper gave me a half-hug in the porch before we went in. It was only with one arm. But a half-hug from Jasper counted as progress in my family.

Dad leaped up from the kitchen table as soon as we walked in. His dusty footprints were still on the carpet from earlier. "Jemima! I've been worried sick!" He looked like he was telling the truth, but with his track record I couldn't be sure. "You must be freezing! Jasper, make her a hot chocolate, yeah?"

I sniffed and nodded. It wasn't exactly speaking to him, but it wasn't exactly not.

Luna came over and hugged me. "I knew Jasper would find you!" she said. "He has The Gift!"

"He has binoculars," I said.

Luna squashed my face with her hands and kissed my forehead. "That's more like it."

Dad sat on the sofa and apologized for the millionth time. "I didn't know where your mum had gone at first," he said. "I knew she'd gone with Alfie, but I didn't know where they were. I emailed for a while with photos and stuff, but I never got a reply. Then, about five years ago, she sent that brochure saying they were leaving for good. I didn't want you to have to deal with it. I planned on telling you if she ever got back in touch or when you were old enough to understand. Only, that came sooner than I realized. I'm sorry."

"It's okay, Dad," Jasper said. "It doesn't matter."

It did matter to me, but Dad was wiping tears from his eyes and right then that mattered more. Seeing your dad upset feels like there's something wrong with the universe, like it's turned inside out. And you'll say anything to make it right again. Plus, he'd apologized a million plus one times now and that was enough for one day.

"It's okay, Dad," I said. "I get why you did it. I'm not mad at you." Because, if you're not mad at the person who left you, what's the point in being mad at the person who didn't?

"Thanks, you two," Dad said. The skin around his eyes looked blotchy and he rubbed his beard as he let out a few long breaths. "Now, I've got something to show you. It's not quite finished! But it feels like a good time for you to take a look."

Outside, Dad flung open the garage doors and said, "Ta dah!"

The first thing I noticed was a TV on the wall. Then a sofa, a table made out of wooden crates, bookshelves made from old ladders and seats made out of giant tyres. There was an old arcade game in the corner and bean bags, some paintings waiting to be hung up, and fairy lights hung across the ceiling like stars.

"I got a load of stuff from the junkyard outside town!" Dad said. "It's amazing what people throw away. Those seats are old tractor tyres! I think I can get this arcade machine working once I've got the right parts."

"Dad, this is…*fantastique*!" Jasper said. "I can do my filming in here!"

Dad laughed. "I was hoping you might say that. And, I thought we might hold a little party in here. When it's finished."

"A party?" Jasper and I said at exactly the same time.

"Yes! I'll have you know I did quite a lot of partying before you two came along! I thought we could have a special TV screening, say on Boxing Day? I don't know if there's anything on that evening you'd like to watch?"

"Jemima completely humiliating herself on TV!" Jasper said.

I grabbed a cushion from the nearest tractor-tyre chair and threw it at his head. I didn't miss because it's quite a big target.

"Not that that will happen," Jasper said. "Right, Dad? Not with…" They both flexed their arm muscles and said, "Team Small!"

I closed my eyes. As tight as they would go. I wasn't

cringing at how completely embarrassing they were. I wasn't wishing for anything either. I just wanted to make sure my brain fully remembered this moment. Because I felt like I was in one of those families you get on TV. A family that believes you can do stuff even if you're not really sure yourself. I wanted this moment to be branded on my brain. Fused to my DNA. For ever.

Later on that afternoon, Luna took me to Good Vibes, her friend Jupiter's crystal shop on the seafront. I examined an orangey-red crystal from a cabinet by the door. It looked like solid fire.

"That one's for tranquillity and healing," Jupiter said. "It's called jasper."

I immediately put it down. It was so typical of Jasper to be named after a crystal.

"Is there one to help me win a quiz show?" I asked. "I need to be extremely brainy tomorrow."

Jupiter's eyes lit up. "Sure thing, sister! You need the tiger's eye."

He brought a tray of crystals over and placed each one gently on a silk cloth. I held a bluey-pink stone up to the light and smiled. It shone like a supernova.

"That's it," Jupiter said. "Your crystal's found you.

That's fluorite. It'll help your concentration and self-confidence." Jupiter fixed the crystal onto a long chain and put it over my head. "She's got some strong energy, hey?"

Luna smiled. "Yeah. She gets that from me."

I held the crystal tight in my hand as we left the shop and walked along the promenade, trying to absorb its energy. We were climbing the concrete steps by the beach when I saw them. A man and a woman on their way down. Both giving me second glances. But I didn't look away. Or try to shrink into the shadows. I fixed my eyes on them and smiled my best smile as they walked past.

I knew that almost three thousand people from fifty different schools took the same *Brainiacs* qualifying test as me that day in the hall. And to get through to the Selection Day, I had to score in the top ten per cent. And to be chosen out of all the other competitors at the Selection Day, I had to beat almost all of them. Because there are only fifteen podiums on the famous *Brainiacs* stage and one of them already had my name on it. And when you know that, maybe you don't want to be invisible.

48

BRAIN FREEZE

The TV studio had revolving glass doors leading to a reception where one wall was entirely covered by TV screens, each playing a different channel. The receptionist printed out a badge and attached it to a yellow lanyard that said:

BRAINIACS
JEMIMA SMALL
CONTESTANT

Nana said I looked like a celebrity. I knew she was lying. Celebrities don't have to wear ID badges. We went up in the lift to the second floor and a man called Alex, who I recognized from the Selection Day, greeted us.

"Hello, everyone! Welcome to *Brainiacs* HQ!" His thin moustache twirled up at each end and wiggled when he spoke. "I'll take you to our family green room where you can relax, meet the other contestants and get ready for the show!"

We followed him down a wide corridor as he explained filming would start in a couple of hours.

The green room had sofas, tables and chairs, a huge stack of board games in the corner, old-fashioned chalkboards on the walls and a massive TV screen playing *Brainiacs* clips with subtitles. Everything was yellow, not green. I guess green wouldn't match their branding. Some contestants were writing out equations on a chalkboard at the back; another was writing out pi; someone else was listing dates that must have been the Russian royal dynasty; someone else was reciting the periodic table to their mum. I recognized Zane from the Selection Day. He waved then went back to playing himself at chess.

"Welcome to Planet Geek!" Jasper whispered.

Dad laughed then gave him a gentle jab in the ribs.

"You're going to do great!" Luna said as she pushed Nana to the nearest table. "You've got your crystal, right?"

I nodded and pulled it out from inside my shirt.

"Phew!"

"Right!" Dad said, surveying the room. "Want to recite the entire works of Shakespeare or go over Einstein's theorem or something?"

I picked up a board game called Brainbox from the shelf in the corner. "How about a game of this?"

Dad laughed. "I'm so relieved you said that!"

After our second game of Brainbox, a lady called Maggie came in and called, "Families! It's time to say your final words of encouragement! I'm taking you through to join the audience."

Dad hugged me and wished me luck; Luna kissed my head; Nana said she was proud of me and slipped a packet of soft mints into my pocket. Jasper said something annoying in French. Then I watched them leave.

I was given a huge pair of noise-cancelling headphones and a pack of one hundred cards to memorize. Each one had a random picture and number on it, like *Santa 34* and *steam train 7* and *teapot 15*. A timer on the screen counted down thirty minutes. I put on my headphones and tried to ignore the boy next to me memorizing the cards whilst skipping. I was amazed Gina hadn't taught me that technique during brain-training.

When the thirty minutes was up, I followed the other contestants up the steps and into the studio. A thousand spotlights beamed so brightly I had to squint. Huge cheers erupted from the audience as we walked in, but I couldn't make out any faces. There were TV cameras everywhere, even attached to the ceiling, pointing at me like snipers. And suddenly, I felt heavier than ever, as though my bones were made of plutonium. But that wasn't the major problem.

It was my head. It felt as though my brain had floated out of my skull and off into the universe. And your brain suddenly figuring out astral projection is just about the worst thing that can happen to you on a TV quiz show. I tried to picture the cards I'd been memorizing, the periodic table, the dates of the monarchs of England, calculate some sums in my head. But nothing. Just a big, blank space where the answers were supposed to be.

"Jemima!" Maggie called. "You're over there, number thirteen. Hope it's not unlucky for you."

I walked to the podium that said 13 on the back and JEMIMA, CLIFTON ACADEMY on the front. I touched the brain pin badge on my blazer and felt sick. My hands were shaking and the room kept spinning and the only thought echoing around my head was how stupid I was going to look in front of millions of people. And, more specifically, one person, probably sitting on the deck of a 188-metre cruise ship.

"Good luck, Jemima!" the girl next to me said. Her

podium said ANANYA, GREYS HIGH SCHOOL. "I'm terrified! My brain has gone to mush!" She held out her hands. They were shaking worse than mine.

I tried to think of something to say, anything, but the only thing I could think about was the vast emptiness of my head. And the spotlights probably doing permanent damage to my retinas. I was suffering from the worst case of brain freeze ever documented. I was going to let everyone down. And it was going to be broadcast on TV.

"I like your crystal!" Ananya said.

"Thanks. Here" – I took it off and handed it to her – "hold it if you like. It's supposed to help with concentration and self-confidence. Although, I think it might be broken."

"Wow!" Ananya said as she watched it sparkle in the studio lights. She cupped her hands around it. "I think it's working!"

Zane gave me a thumbs up just as the presenter, Dexter Riley, jogged up the steps to the stage. The audience cheered again.

"Hello, Brainiacs!" His black hair was styled in a huge quiff, like a wave on the front of his head.

I felt so dizzy, I could barely concentrate on what he was saying.

"Congratulations on getting this far! Filming will start

in a moment. Stay calm. Speak clearly. And try to have fun! Buzz as quickly as you can because look at these faces!" He pointed down the line at us and smiled to reveal perfectly white teeth. "You've got some fierce competition! The quick-fire round is up first and the topic is nature! Good luck!"

A woman with a make-up trolley dabbed his face with tissue as he started talking to Yolanda and some other people wearing headsets.

Ananya handed me back the crystal and I put it around my neck, feeling stupid for even half-believing a chunk of polished calcium fluoride (CaF_2) in the shape of an octahedron (a solid composed of eight equilateral triangles, four of which meet at each vertex) might help my brain's ability to function.

Then, very slowly, as slow as the world's slowest mammal (the three-toed sloth, top speed of 0.24 kilometres per hour), it felt like something was happening in my head. As though the smallest butterfly in the world (the western pygmy blue, wingspan of fifteen millimetres) was waking up.

Wait a minute, I thought, as a menagerie of animal facts began creeping into my mind. *My brain is coming back.*

49

FINGERS ON BUZZERS

"Welcome to *Brainiaaaaaaaaacs*!" Dexter Riley said as he spun a perfect 360 degrees on his heels to face the camera again. He must have practised that loads at home. "These fifteen bright young boffins are about to pit their wits against each other for the chance to win the world-famous *Brainiacs* trophy! Let's give them a cheer!"

The audience was a sea of faces, but I spotted the silhouette of Nana's huge bun against the glare of the spotlights, then my eyes scanned to Luna, Dad and Jasper. I could see Miki holding up a banner, and the outline of Mrs Savage's head behind him. The number thirteen glowed yellow on the back of my podium. Thirteen is a prime number, forwards and back. It's called an emirp. And it definitely didn't feel unlucky.

"Fasten your seat belts! It's our quick-fire round on…
nature! Fingers on buzzers, Brainiacs! May your brains be
with you!"

I put my hand on the buzzer and wished as hard as I
could.

Please do not let me look stupid on TV.

I didn't care about winning. I just didn't want anyone
to feel ashamed of me.

Dexter Riley lifted the question cards. "What is a
cassowary?"

And that's the thing about wishes. Sometimes they
never come true and sometimes they come true in
approximately 1.25 seconds.

"A cassowary is a large flightless bird native to New
Guinea and they have been known to attack and kill
humans."

I heard a burst of laughter from the audience. It was
probably Jasper.

"That's a bit more than we needed, Jemima!" Dexter
said. "But, a flightless bird is CORRECT!" The zero on
my podium changed to five and, without meaning it to,
a smile spread across my face.

When the klaxon sounded for the end of the nature
round, my podium said thirty-five. I blew out a long
breath and looked at the scores on the others' podiums.

Mine was the third highest. I wasn't getting eliminated.

"It's the infamously tough *Brainiacs* MEMORY ROUND!" Dexter bellowed at the camera. "We'll be losing another three contestants at the end of this round, Brainiacs, so keep those cards in your head!"

I blinked a few times as the lights dazzled my eyes. Then I spotted her in the audience. Sitting next to my dad, surrounded by a yellow glow like an aura. Gina. Her mega-watt smile was turned up to approximately one hundred per cent of her face.

Tiny beads of sweat ran from Dexter's temple as he spoke to the camera. My mouth felt dry, and I could feel sweat soaking into the back of my shirt. I wasn't sure if I could remember a single card. Until I heard the first question.

"What is the total value of the teapot, the goldfish and the rose?"

My hand pressed down and my podium lit up. "One hundred and forty-eight?"

"Correct!"

"What is the value of the spoon minus the apple multiplied by the flute?"

"Two hundred and sixteen?"

"Correct, Jemima! Which colour background was on the sun card?"

My buzzer again. And again. And again.

The klaxon sounded and Dexter shouted, "What an incredible round!" over the applause. "And what an incredible memory one of our young Brainiacs has! Jemima, that was truly extraordinary!"

But Dexter Riley wasn't exactly right. The Memory Round only tests your working memory. It's the part of your brain that stores information for a short amount of time for processing. I'd forget all the cards by tomorrow. Your proper memories are stored in your cerebral cortex. They're the ones that pop into your head when you hear a song or see an old photograph. The three-dimensional ones that play in your head like a film.

Like painting a wooden cabin with your dad in the summer; holding his hand when you're rock-pooling because he doesn't want you to slip; him rushing you to hospital because you think you've broken your ankle playing basketball, and smiling with relief when it's only sprained, even though you had to wait there for hours; him sitting with you in the garden when it's freezing cold, really late at night, because it was the only chance in your entire lifetime to see Comet ISON before it went extinct. And driving all the way to North Wales in the pouring rain to stay in Nana's caravan, because he wants you to have a proper holiday, like he had with his parents when he was younger. So your brains will have some of the exact same memories stored up. And him sitting in the audience, looking like he's proud of you. They're the memories that are truly extraordinary.

50

SUDDEN DEATH

The studio lights dimmed, and a spotlight fell on me. It was the maths round. Two minutes to answer as many questions as you can. I dabbed my forehead with my blazer sleeve. I don't know why, but dimming the lights seemed to make it hotter.

I'd watched people answer too quickly, forget part of the sums, take ages thinking so their time ran out. It's the sort of thing that happens when you haven't been brain-trained by an ex-coach of the British Paralympic team. I glanced around the podiums. Zane had forty; Sophie, ten; Alejandro's said twenty-five. There were nine of us left. Four of us with the lowest scores would be eliminated. I did a quick calculation in my head. I needed at least thirty points to stay in. That was six correct answers. In two minutes. It didn't feel totally impossible.

I did what Gina told me to do in brain-training. I shook out my legs and arms, and moved my head from side to side. She said it helps disperse the adrenaline in your body so your mind can focus. It made me look like I thought I was about to do a hundred-metre sprint, not a maths round, but when you have to answer six questions correctly in two minutes, you'll try anything.

"Jemima, your time starts now. Minus five, zero, nine, twenty-two. What comes next?"

I felt the tiniest smile creep onto my face. Because it was a quadratic sequence. I must have done a million of them in Miss Reed's class at primary school. Occasionally as a punishment. "Thirty-nine."

"Correct. Minus four, twelve, thirty-eight, seventy-four. What comes next?"

"One hundred and twenty."

"Correct."

I didn't look at the timer, or pay attention to Dexter's quiff, which was starting to flop over slightly, or count the number of times he said "Correct". But when the klaxon sounded for the end of my time, I saw a Miki-shaped silhouette jump in the air.

"Well done, Jemima! Fifty-five points!"

Over the clapping I heard a loud, "*Allez allez*, Jemima!"

I looked over to where Jasper was sitting. The only person in the world who would cheer me on in French. Well, maybe not the only person. If they had TVs on cruise liners. I didn't mean to smile at Jasper, but I did.

When the studio lights came back on, Maggie told us to relax for a few minutes while she took the eliminated contestants to sit in the audience. A woman in a *Brainiacs* T-shirt brought us all some squash and banana-flavoured biscuits.

When the lights dimmed again, Dexter stared into the camera lens. "Welcome back. Our five remaining contestants are about to be tested on some of the most difficult words in the English language. That's right. It's Spelling Sudden Death!"

Ananya went up on her toes, Alejandro fiddled with the buttons on his blazer, Zane took a deep breath, Victoria looked up at the ceiling and prayed. I'm not sure what I looked like. Maybe surprised. Because it felt like there was an avalanche in my brain. The words from the *Spell Like A Superstar: Advanced Edition* book that Dad had bought me were falling through my mind all at once. I hoped I could think straight enough to catch them.

Dexter's teeth practically glowed in the spotlights. He could definitely get a job advertising toothpaste if he ever got sacked from *Brainiacs*. "This is our penultimate round, Brainiacs! And, remember, it's sudden death. Spell a word incorrectly and you could be eliminated. Jemima, we're starting with you. The word is: thalassophobia."

A heartbeat sounded loudly in my ears. At first I thought it was a sound effect playing in the studio. But it wasn't. It was my heart. That warrior in there was reminding me of home. Because *thalassa* is Greek for sea. Thalassa was a goddess who had horns made out of crab claws and wore robes made of seaweed. Pretty unforgettable really. Like a lot of the goddesses I knew about. I closed my eyes and spelled.

"Correct!" Dexter cried. "Ananya, your word is: phytoplankton."

Ananya went up on her toes like a ballerina and spelled the word without hesitating. I smiled at her as Dexter said, "Correct!"

After the first set of words, Zane had spelled appoggiatura wrong and been eliminated. He got a huge round of applause and mouthed, "Good luck," to me as he left the stage. Four of us were still in. Only three of us could go through to the final round. It all rested on my next word.

"Jemima, your word is: archaeopteryx."

There was a gasp from the audience. Maybe they hadn't watched *Brainiacs* before. The spellings always got harder as the round goes on. Maybe they didn't know much about dinosaurs either. Because the archaeopteryx was kind of important. It's not even that hard to spell. Not when your spelling book from Miss Reed had a dinosaur section. I closed my eyes and recited it, just like I had at home.

Dexter shouted, "Correct!" Only he said "Correct" three times after that too, which meant we all had to spell again.

I looked nervously out to the audience.

"Good luck, everyone. Jemima, your word is: staphylococcus."

There was another gasp from the audience.

"You have two minutes."

But I didn't need two minutes. Not when I'd already spent the whole of one break time staring at Mr Shaw's Bacterium and Viruses poster while he was lecturing me about breaking conical beakers. Staphylococcus are this type of bacteria that cluster together. I remembered because they looked like microscopic bunches of grapes.

"Correct! Aren't this year's contestants something else?" Dexter joined in with the applause, and then the studio fell into silence.

I closed my eyes. I didn't open them again until I heard the adjudicators ring the bell. They ring it when someone gets a spelling wrong. Which is how I knew Victoria had spelled rhinencephalon wrong. Which meant I didn't need to spell any more words because there were three of us left. No one else would be eliminated. I'd made it through to the final round of *Brainiacs*.

And that's called definitely not looking stupid on TV.

51

BIG DEAL

I'm going to tell you something that I never thought would happen in a million revolutions of the sun: me winning *Brainiacs*.

I was right. I didn't win. Ananya won. I came second. Luna said it was because I let her hold my fluorite crystal. But I don't believe that. It was because she knew that Plovdiv is in Bulgaria, and a Mississippi saxophone is a harmonica.

If Dexter had asked me about Pandora or Helene or Phoebe or any of the other moons in our solar system instead, then maybe I'd have won the trophy. But probably not. Because Ananya got all the other questions right too. She must be the only person in the world who knows more about the nutritional content of an avocado than me.

But coming second isn't bad. Coming second out of fifteen people is actually pretty good. You still count as a winner if you come second. According to *Brainiacs* you do anyway. Because they gave me a silver medal saying:

JEMIMA SMALL
Brainiacs
Second Place Winner

Jasper says second place is the first loser. But Jasper doesn't know anything. The best thing he's ever won is the Clifton Academy French Prize. He doesn't know that sometimes second place can feel like the biggest thing ever.

I'm standing at the end of the Plank – the little wooden platform in Dolphin Bay that points out to the ocean. It's wet from the sea crashing against the rocks. The wind is blowing my hair all over the place, and my fingernails are turning blue from the cold. I haven't been up here in a long time. Since I was seven years old actually. When someone says you look grotesque in your new swimsuit, you don't exactly feel like repeating the experience. So I didn't. Until today.

I look up the coast towards the harbour. The paddle steamboat is there, anchored, waiting for the new season next summer. Dad, Luna, Nana and Jasper are at home getting everything ready. Gina's probably there too. Because that's something else I found out after I filmed *Brainiacs*. My dad has been secretly dating Gina. I guess the only two people in the universe who think gaiters look cool are probably a match made in heaven. Besides, Dad said he's not keeping any more secrets.

Wherever the Bright Star cruise liner called *Pegasus* is right now, I hope it has a big TV. I hope every TV on the whole ship plays *Brainiacs* tonight. So my mum definitely sees me. Jemima Small. Not looking stupid. Still being her daughter and her still being my mum. Even though she's not here.

My human anatomy book says the heart has four chambers. But I think it has an invisible one too. A part they don't label on diagrams. Where the people you've loved live. When someone's been inside your heart they stay in that chamber permanently. There's no escape hatch. No emergency exit. Nowhere to disappear to. It's how I know me and Jasper are still in there. Frozen in time and space, like a photograph. Because someone who sings you to sleep and stops you from sinking and points at the stars and tells you to believe in magic, must have a secret chamber in their heart. Maybe it's so big she's afraid to open it. Like Pandora's box.

I watch a squabble of seagulls circle an anchored cabin cruiser. Collective nouns like a "squabble" are the type of thing you learn when you're friends with the current *Brainiacs* champion. I look past the boat and I wonder where the *Pegasus* cruise ship is right now.

Probably somewhere near the coordinates:

37° 09' 37.13" N

012° 18' 16.87" W

Which is near Gibraltar the last time I checked. You can download a live tracking app from the Bright Star Cruises website. It's the kind of thing you know if you're a *Brainiacs* finalist.

Gibraltar is exactly 1359.83 miles away from Clifton-on-Sea. But it feels a lot closer than that. It's closer than nowhere, anyway, which is kind of where Mum was before.

I look out to the horizon, where the sea touches the sky and I hope. I hope really, really hard. That she'll watch. And call. Or write. Say she's sorry for the light years of empty space. And change her mind about us. Hope isn't the same as wishes. Hope is more real. With hope, it feels like there's a bigger chance it can come true.

I wrap my arms around myself as tight as they'll go.

My body feels warm and soft against the cold air. It's actually okay living here. And going to my school. It's sort of better than okay now I'm officially a Brainiac. Now it's Boxing Day. And I'm about to be on TV. Nine Year Sevens asked for my autograph before school broke up for Christmas and the show hasn't even been on TV yet. They asked for Miki's autograph too. But that's what happens when you outshine Mary Poppins in the Christmas production. I'm going to be on the front page of the *Clifton Echo* next week. The journalist said the headline will be: *CLIFTON'S JEMIMA SMALL WINS BIG*. Mrs Savage will probably put it up on the wall in reception. The second place winner got five hundred pounds worth of books for their school. I'm kind of popular in the library now.

I take a step forward and peer over the edge of the Plank. Icy waves splash over the rocks underneath and I can feel the toe ring I borrowed from Luna digging in.

"Come on, Jemima!" Miki shouts.

I turn around. He's wearing the beanie I got him for helping me with *Brainiacs*. It uses the chemical elements boron and fluorine to spell out BFF. He says it's the geekiest thing he owns, but he's barely taken it off since I gave it to him. He's got my dad's emergency blanket under his arm and he's holding my phone ready to take the

381

photo. Me jumping off the Plank in my swimsuit. It's for my new profile: jemimasmall_bigdeal.

There are a few people on the beach standing watching me. I don't know if they're gawping because my body doesn't look exactly the same as theirs. Or because I am about to jump into the sea in December. But I don't really care that much if people are staring. I'm not going to spend my whole life being invisible. I'm not a quantum particle.

I take a deep breath and my lungs fill up with icy air. It's the way to get more oxygen to your heart. Your heart is the thing that matters the most. And I think mine's pretty big. It has to be. Because I can feel a whole warrior in there.

"Hurry up, Jemima! *Jump!*" Miki shouts. "We haven't got all day!"

He's right. Because we've got a party to get ready for. I can't miss my own TV debut. Plus, it is really freezing. I lift my head up high and look out into the distance. Right up to where the sea meets the sky. You can see all the way to the edge of the world from here.

TEAM GGB'S PAGE OF AWESOME

Sometimes it can be easy to forget how incredible you are – but if you ever do, try following Gina's tips:

- If you hear mean comments about yourself, remember that they don't represent the truth about you. Visualize the words disappearing into the sky and let go of the shame attached to them as they fly away.

- Make a list of things you like about yourself below.
  Reasons I am Awesome:

  _____

  _____

  _____

  _____

  _____

  _____

- Any time you're feeling down you can look back on this page and remind yourself why you're so awesome. Say them out loud. Say them a lot. Believe them.

- Don't forget: You are made of star dust.

GINA'S DOS AND DON'TS ☆

Don't create barriers for yourself

Do break through them

Don't decide to be invisible

Do take up space

Don't shy away from success

Do give yourself credit for being awesome

Don't worry about what other people think

Do focus on positive thoughts about yourself

Don't be afraid of making mistakes

Do try something new

Don't avoid doing the things you love

Do listen to your body and make a splash!

AND ALWAYS, ALWAYS REMEMBER...
YOU ARE CAPABLE OF AMAZING THINGS

TAMSIN WINTER
TACKLES THE UNIVERSE AND OTHER BIG QUESTIONS

What inspired you to write Jemima's story?

I had read a newspaper article about an eleven-year-old girl who received a letter from her school telling her she was overweight and I couldn't get it out of my mind. Almost the entire article centred around the mother's perspective – how she felt and what she thought about it. I looked at the photograph of that girl and wondered what she was feeling. I thought about how receiving a letter like that would have affected me at her age, when I was already self-conscious and insecure and my body was changing in so many ways. Jemima's story came from that.

What is the message you wanted to send and why?

I hope Jemima's story shows how important it is to respect every body, including our own. We spend so much time and energy worrying about what we look like, trying to hide or disguise our bodies, thinking and speaking negatively about them. On social media, we are bombarded with messages telling us how our bodies could be improved, yet our lives would be improved dramatically if we weren't judged for the way we look! In a recent Girls Attitude Survey, 52% of girls aged 11-21 said they sometimes feel ashamed about the way they look. Ashamed. It's an incredibly sad statistic but one that's not surprising. We are rarely encouraged to think about how incredible our bodies are, or the amazing things we can achieve just the way we are. Like Gina says, we are literally made of star dust. I hope Jemima's story helps readers to look in the mirror and appreciate all the qualities they share with the stars.

Did you draw on any personal experiences or those of people you know?

I can remember vividly the first time someone commented on my body. I was sitting on my nana's sofa and someone grabbed my leg and held it up for everyone to see, saying, "Look at the size of her legs!" I can remember feeling confused, embarrassed, uncertain about what was wrong with the size of my legs. Then later, I decided they must be too big. I was about eight years old when it happened, over thirty years ago, but I still hear that voice sometimes when I look in the mirror.

Of course, there was nothing wrong with my eight-year-old legs. They were legs that had won medals for ballet, legs that had earned swimming badges, legs that could run, tap-dance, roller-skate. But from then on, I forgot about all of that. I had the slow realization that what I could do mattered a lot less than how I looked. And all I saw when I looked in the mirror was everything wrong with me.

What followed was a period of disordered eating that lasted well into my twenties. I guess part of me wanted to write the story I needed when I was younger.

Did you ever find it hard putting yourself in Jemima's shoes?

Yes, mainly because she is a lot brainier than I am! The best part of writing for me is getting inside the character's head. It can be heartbreaking sometimes, but it's essential to make them real. Writing the scenes where Jemima tells her dad about the video posted online and decides to quit *Brainiacs* were the hardest to write, I think. I suppose Gina's pep talks were what I would tell the younger me if I had the chance. I didn't have the same experiences as Jemima growing up, but that feeling of wanting to be somebody else, or wanting to astrally project myself out of my body, is a familiar one to me. It took me a long time to feel comfortable in my own skin, to feel happy being myself. It was awesome to get Jemima there a lot sooner.

Did you do any research? How did you come up with all Jemima's interesting facts?

I had to do so much research! I read books, blogs, articles, watched YouTube a lot, talked to young people, teachers and parents about body image, self-esteem and body-shaming. Plus, I know so much about space now I could probably get a job at NASA. During my research, I read so many nasty body-shaming and fat-phobic comments, but I also learned fascinating and beautiful things about our bodies. We have approximately 100,000 miles of blood vessels just in our brains. 100,000 miles! I wish people would remember how incredible human bodies are before they comment on them.

Both Jemima Small Versus the Universe *and your previous book* Being Miss Nobody *deal with the subject of bullying – was this intentional or is it a theme that creeps into your writing?*

After *Being Miss Nobody*'s release I was contacted by lots of readers young and old who have been victims of bullying. Sadly, it is still a part of too many people's lives. From everything I found out during my research for *Jemima Small Versus the Universe*, I don't think I could have written the book authentically without touching on the bullying that many people face in and out of school for their size. Bullying often happens in hidden spaces, or comes from places we maybe wouldn't expect, like Harry's "friends". The scene where Harry reveals his bruises is based on something a young person told me during my research. The comments posted on Jemima's video are based on real comments I read online. Lottie's bullying is truly vicious, yet Jemima still wants to be liked by her. That aspect of bullying – feeling like you somehow deserve it, or it's not a big deal, or it's happening because of some flaw you have, rather than the bully being at fault – is something I wanted to explore in the book. I also wanted to show the importance of friendship. Miki's love and loyalty towards Jemima combats Lottie's spitefulness and ultimately helps her to speak out. After everything Jemima goes through, the final scenes felt wonderful to write.

How do the characters appear in your head? Is Gina based on anyone in particular?

Developing characters is my favourite part of the writing process. I knew from the very beginning that Jemima would be super-smart and have something of an attitude. Gina's massive smile, her enthusiasm and general health-freakness are maybe based a tiny bit on my sister. Jasper's character was so much fun to write. I always pictured him dressed in a cape, performing magic tricks, so researching and writing those scenes was a lot of fun. The sibling dynamic is something I love to write, probably because I am a middle child! Jasper is deeply annoying and his relentless boasting in front of their dad cracks me up, but he's lovable too, and he's there for Jemima when it really counts. Dad's exasperation with Jemima at times is maybe slightly reminiscent of my own teenage years. But really, the characters take on a life of their own. They sort of appear in my head, then never seem to leave.

Do you have an Auntie Luna?

Sadly, I don't have an auntie quite like Luna, but I'm an auntie myself and Luna definitely represents #auntiegoals for me. Her belief about all of us being intricately connected to each other and to the universe is something I definitely share. I promise I haven't done any naked moon-bathing, but I do believe the universe gives us little signs to guide us towards our destiny. I think we could all benefit from a deeper connection to the natural world, like Luna has. Don't we all feel the magic of infinite possibilities when we're looking up at the stars? Although maybe I'd draw the line at nettle soup.

Tamsin Winter grew up in a tiny village in Northamptonshire where there was nothing to do. She spent her childhood reading books and writing stories, mostly about cats (she loves cats so much that they still always appear in her books). She has a degree in English literature and creative writing, and has been teaching, travelling the world and daydreaming for most of her adult life, and now lives in Leicestershire with her son. She is passionate about writing stories that she hopes can make a difference to readers' lives.

"More than anything, I hope my stories teach young people to believe in themselves. Because that's what makes magical things happen."

 tamsinwinterauthor

 @MsWinterTweets

 @tamsinwinterauthor

#JemimaSmall

ACKNOWLEDGEMENTS

Firstly, a universe-sized thank you to Luigi and Alison Bonomi at LBA. You loved Jemima's story from the very beginning, and you have encouraged me every step of the way. Thank you multiplied by infinity for getting me here.

A Banan-ometer-busting thank you to my incredible editors Rebecca Hill and Sarah Stewart at Usborne for the universe-sized love you put into this book, for your Brainiacs-level advice, for believing Jemima's story was an important one to tell, and for the giant LOLs and love hearts on my manuscript just when I needed them.

An astronomical thank you to the amazing Usborne Publishing team for making me feel like part of the family, albeit one who leaves with lots of your books in her handbag. There are approximately 130 million books in the world. Thank you for making it 130 million + 1. A hypergiant shout-out to the amazing people at Usborne Books at Home for your phenomenal support of *Being Miss Nobody*. I'm keeping my fingers crossed you love this one just as much.

A gigantic luminous-pink neon thank you to Will Steele and Katharine Millichope for Jemima Small's beautiful cover design, and to Hannah Featherstone for your genius copyedits.

A gargantuan thank you to Martin Day, police officer and general superstar. Jemima's story has changed dramatically since we met, but thank you for answering approximately a million questions and helping out an author in need. I may need you again for my next book!

I'm sending a super-colossal thank you across the world to Donican Lam for your assistance with all things Japanese. And an infinity of thank yous to Louisa Broad, my lovely friend and general Brainiac, for helping me out when I had a major case of brain freeze. A hypergiant shout-out to Bettina Haddon for your endless support, love and social media big-ups. You rock.

A supernova thank you to Rose and Dr Vilanova for your kindness and support, and for reminding me how far across the universe I've travelled to get here.

YouTuber Tabitha Hendrix is a fictional character, but she owes a big thank you to all the bloggers, vloggers and influencers out there encouraging us to feel happy about our bodies, whatever shape they are. You are beautiful. You are amazing. You are changing the world. I wish I had you in my childhood.

A supergiant thank you to all the authors, librarians, teachers, booksellers, journalists, bloggers and vloggers who shout about books every day, and are relentless in your pursuit of getting books into the hearts of young people. Thank you for also shouting about mine.

To my electrocardiogram BFFs Laura, Brajit and Lauren: thank you for your infinity-sized love and support (and massive cups of tea/wine). I could not find better friends in a million galaxies.

A galaxy-supercluster-sized thank you to my parents for supporting me in a million different ways, mostly with babysitting and forcing complete strangers to buy my books. I'm so lucky to have you. A super-colossal thank you to my sister, Kirsty, for your relentless belief, support, excitement and for your intricate understanding of the periodic table. Andrew, thank you for being an amazing brother with brilliant advice, first-aid skills and an extremely helpful design studio. You're awesome siblings. Thank you for being my best friends too. I also want to take this opportunity to remind you that *Jemima Small Versus the Universe* is a work of fiction and any resemblance to actual family members is purely coincidental.

To my gravity-defying Felix – thank you for the love, craziness, wonder, joy, laughter and magic you bring to my life. Thank you for reminding me every day that I'm bigger than I sometimes feel. You're my proof the universe is always listening.

And finally, a big-bang-sized thank you to my readers – for your beautiful words (and art!) about *Being Miss Nobody* and for choosing to read Jemima's story out of the millions of other books in the universe. I hope it reminds you how amazing you are.

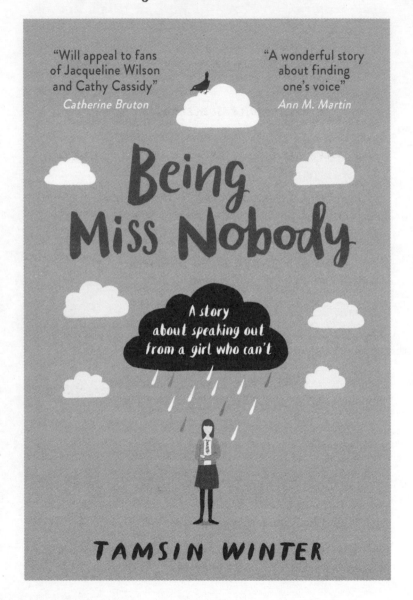

I have not been a very nice person

I have done some bad things

I have lied to a lot of people I know

*All these things I have done
pretty much deliberately*

I am Miss Nobody

Rosalind hates her new secondary school. She's the weird girl who doesn't talk. The Mute-ant. And it's easy to pick on someone who can't fight back. So Rosalind starts a blog – Miss Nobody; a place to speak up, a place where she has a voice. But there's a problem...

Is Miss Nobody becoming a bully herself?

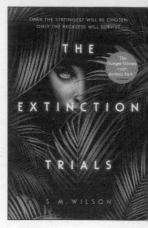